Praise for *An Unusual Boy*

'*An Unusual Boy* is the gripping tale of an exceptional, misunderstood child. It highlights the dark underworld of the internet and the way our systems are set up to serve our least vulnerable members, rather than our most. I found myself glued to this book from start to finish. While reading it, you can't help but become Jackson's mother, and the mother of every child who is misunderstood in our society. This book will get people talking for sure.'

Sally Hepworth, author of *The Mother in Law*

'*An Unusual Boy* is a beautifully-written book about a loving mother doing her best to protect her 'unusual' neurodiverse child in the most challenging of circumstances. The story is a page-turner, but it's the powerful descriptions of family relationships and friendship, both toxic and supportive, that will stay with me. Ultimately uplifting and hugely emotional, this is a wonderful and unusual book.'

Louise Douglas, author of *The House by the Sea*

'A tender-hearted story of loving patience triumphing in the face of impossible odds. Original, engaging and beautifully written.'

Amanda Brookfield, author of *The Other Woman*

'*An Unusual Boy* is the unforgettable story of an exceptional child and his flawed but loving family told with Fiona Higgin's characteristic intelligence, deep empathy and insight.'

Virginia Lloyd, author of *Girls at the Piano*

'Absorbing, intelligent, moving and real, *An Unusual Boy* is a novel with both heart and brains... a story tailor-made for our times.'

Kylie Ladd, author of *The Way Back*

'Oh, how I fell in love with this charming book! Fiona Higgins manages to strike the perfect balance of humour and poignancy to create a heart-warming and insightful novel that oozes humanity. I defy any reader not to fall in love with young Jackson and his idiosyncratic 'super powers'.'

Joanna Nell, author of *The Single Ladies of the Jacaranda Retirement Village*

'*An Unusual Boy* is not only a compelling read, it's an important one. This tale of an ordinary family dealing with the complexities of raising an extraordinary child had me gripped from the very first page. Intelligently written, this moving story will have book clubs talking long into the night. Fiona Higgins at her finest!'

Lisa Ireland, author of *The Secret Life of Shirley Sullivan*

AN UNUSUAL BOY

FIONA HIGGINS

First published in Great Britain in 2020 by Boldwood Books Ltd.

Cover Design by Becky Glibbery

Cover Photography: Shutterstock

'Hope There's Someone'

Music: Antony and the Johnsons

©2005 Secretly Canadian

Reproduced with the permission of Anohni

A CIP catalogue record for this book is available from the British Library.

Paperback ISBN 978-1-80048-301-9   Ebook ISBN 978-1-80048-295-1

Large Print ISBN 978-1-80048-297-5   Kindle ISBN 978-1-80048-296-8

Audio CD ISBN 978-1-80048-302-6

MP3 CD ISBN 978-1-80048-299-9

Digital audio download ISBN 978-1-80048-294-4

Boldwood Books Ltd, 23 Bowerdean Street, London SW6 3TN
www.boldwoodbooks.com

For Michael, who left too early.

1

'Shhh! You'll wake her up!'

Stifled laughter, the tinkling of a tea bell and the pungent smell of burnt toast drift beneath the bedroom door. Our three children are whispering outside, impatient to sneak in and surprise me. My hand slides across the mattress, reaching for Andy's, before the crushing realisation swamps me.

He's not here. Again.

A cold, hard nub of loneliness lodges in my chest. Andy's overseas trips are an unavoidable by-product of his smashing career success; New York this quarter, London next, Tokyo in the spring. I should be used to it by now, but the thought of spending Mother's Day solo makes me want to curl up under the covers and refuse to come out. For the sake of the children, however, I can't. It's *my* job to create magic on Mother's Day now.

I stare at the paint flaking off the ceiling above our bed. Recalling the early, easy years with Andy, before there were any Mothers' Days at all. All that spare time spent sleeping and strolling and staring into each other's eyes. Two languid years of mutual adoration, before my body endured three pregnancies, two breastfed babies and the singular exertions of gravity itself. Back when Andy and I still *saw* each other, somehow.

Something clatters to the floor beyond the door.

'Hold the tray steady!' Milla hisses at her younger siblings. 'Careful of that teapot, Ruby!'

'Shut up, Bossy Pants!' Ruby objects, with the trademark confidence of a third child.

Jackson remains quiet, presumably observing his sisters wage battle, before pointing out in his quiet drawl, 'She's woken up for sure.'

I make an exaggerated yawning sound, a sort of sigh and groan combined, then lie perfectly still. The ruse works: the tea bell rings sharply, the door nudges open and Ruby's stubby fingers curl around its edge.

I hear Jackson counting to three in Mandarin.

'Yaaah!' Ruby bursts forth in all her nine-year-old glory, zigzagging across the room in pink sequined pyjamas and purple fluffy slippers.

'Happy Mother's Day!' She launches herself onto my lap and gazes at me with earnest blue eyes. 'I think I've got nits. My head's itchy.'

'It's probably just your eczema, Rubes,' I say, smoothing down her frizzy mass of golden curls. 'But I'll check later, okay?'

It's only been three weeks since a lice contagion swept through Grade Three. Surely it's too soon for another?

Milla enters the room, bearing a wooden tray laden with Pamela's heirloom tea set, a stack of singed pancakes, several bowls of condiments, and a single pink rose in a blue Wedgewood vase. Milla's blonde mane is always plaited in two long, perfect braids, a carryover from her netball days, while I struggle to manage a blunt-cut bob.

'Morning, Mum.' She sets down the tray. 'Ruby burnt the croissants, sorry.'

'They're just well done,' objects Ruby, crawling off me to admire herself in the full-length mirror.

'I hope pancakes are okay?' Milla murmurs.

'Of course they are.' I reach out and squeeze her hand. 'You're doing a great job, Millsy.'

She smiles. 'Thanks, Mum.'

I'm gratified to see this compliment still means something to Milla, given most fourteen-year-olds seem far more interested in peers than parents.

Jackson files into the room now, carrying a towering pile of presents, his gangly limbs sprouting from too-small pyjamas. Unlike Ruby and Milla, whose flaxen hair, blue eyes and freckled cheeks resemble my complexion, Jackson's brown hair, buttery skin and startling green eyes reflect Andy's genetics.

Jackson whistles through a prominent gap in his front teeth, his head nodding erratically to some internal tune. Setting down the gifts at the foot of the bed, he drops to the floor and rolls into a headstand.

'Careful, yogi master,' I warn, watching his neck wobble beneath the weight.

Although Jackson is capable of holding this position much longer than most other eleven-year-olds – until he starts seeing stars – I can't help but feel concerned. The family therapist we've been seeing for almost two years, Dr Louisa Kelleher, points out that 'children with a low instinct for self-preservation' tend to cause greater anxiety in their mothers than their fathers. If Andy were here, he'd simply tell me to relax. 'Mothers minimise hazards and fathers maximise fun,' he'd remind me. 'Just let Jackson do his thing, Jules.'

Milla moves to the bedside table and begins pouring out a

cup of tea, assuring me that she's 'warmed the pot first'. Ruby arranges the stack of gifts from smallest to largest, while Jackson flops out of the headstand and smiles at me from beneath a zany fringe.

'Hungry, Mum?' Ruby seizes a singed pancake and thrusts it under my nose.

'Oh yes,' I say, visualising a warm croissant. 'With butter and jam, please.'

Ruby slathers the pancake, passes it to me, then starts on another.

'Whoa, sweetie. I can't eat more than one.'

'But you ate heaps last year!' Ruby looks crestfallen.

'That was Dad,' intones Jackson. 'He had three pancakes, two fried eggs, a slice of bacon and an apricot pastry.'

'Really?' I can't recall any such detail. 'That sounds like an awful lot for one father to eat.' Jackson is presumably exercising creative licence again.

'You only had one croissant,' says Jackson, lying down on the carpet. 'Dad ate everything else.'

'I miss Dad,' says Ruby, sniffing. 'Why does he have to go away for weeks?' The bereft look on her face tells me exactly how much she wishes her father was here right now.

'Oh, darling,' I say, kissing the crown of her head. 'We all miss Dad.'

'I miss our old house,' Milla says quietly. 'I liked Erskineville more, Mum.'

The mere *mention* of Erskineville – our family's home of fourteen years and maternal nest for our three precious babes – makes tears well up in my eyes.

It's been five months since we swapped our spacious inner-city terrace for this tiny red-bricker in one of Sydney's most sought-after suburbs. 'Our coastal cottage,' Andy likes to call it.

His mother spotted it for sale first, encouraging us to move to Queenscliff for the 'ready-made babysitting' and the 'healthy outdoor lifestyle'.

'But this place has so much potential,' I say, attempting to reassure myself as much as Milla. 'And the renovation we're planning will be...'

'Colossal,' says Milla. 'That's what Dad says.'

As will our debt levels, I reflect.

'How about I open some of these Mother's Day gifts?' I ask, diverting the conversation.

'Yesss!' Ruby squeals with excitement. 'Open this one, Mummy! Mine first!'

She pushes a small parcel in my direction.

I shake it theatrically. 'What could it be?'

'Look inside!' Ruby claps her hands.

I peel open the wrapping paper to reveal a beaded necklace, decorated with faux gems. 'Wow! Look at these amazing colours and patterns. Did you make this all yourself, darling?'

Ruby nods, her cheeks puffing up with pleasure. 'In my accessories' workshop.'

'Fit for a Kardashian,' says Milla, winking at me.

Ruby takes this as a compliment.

'Thank you, Rubes,' I say, looping the beads around my neck. 'They're really beautiful.'

It's yet another crafty creation that will join the collection beneath our bed, in a storage box filled with hand-made gifts too voluminous to keep, yet too precious to throw away.

'And *you're* really beautiful, Mummy,' Ruby says fervently. 'Take a selfie and send it to Daddy in New York!'

I laugh and pass my phone to Milla, who slides in next to me and extends her arm. Ruby leans against my shoulder, tilts her head to one side and pouts.

'Join the photo for Dad?' I ask Jackson.

From his position on the floor, Jackson shakes his head. Fingering the edge of his nostril, his eyes glazed over with concentration or bliss or who-knows-what-exactly.

Over the years, I've come to accept that Jackson's inner life is largely impenetrable to me. It's a common reality, I'm told, for parents living with 'neurodiversity' – a catch-all term used to describe children who don't conform to convenient diagnostic categories. In the absence of a definitive diagnosis, Dr Kelleher keeps urging us to focus on the one thing we *can* control: our *responses* to Jackson's behaviours.

Milla takes a barrage of selfies at multiple angles.

Jackson stands up from the floor and pushes a huge flamingo-pink parcel in my direction.

'That's a whopper,' I say. 'How exciting.'

Tearing off the wrapping, I read aloud the words printed on the side of the box: 'Combining the functions of twelve appliances in one compact unit.'

'A Thermowhizz!' I enthuse, praying my expression doesn't betray me.

Jackson grins. 'April Kennedy said every mum wants one. But it cost too much new, so Dad bought a second-hand one on eBay. It's only been used three times, Mum.'

While I'm thrilled that my son has a new school friend called April Kennedy whom he's consulting about Mother's Day gifts, I'm wondering why my husband could think of no better way of saying 'thank you for being a wonderful mother' than a machine that weighs, cooks, chops, emulsifies, whips and steams.

'Cool!' Milla enthuses. 'Maria's mum's got a Thermowhizz. They use it to make gelato and sourdough and puddings and...'

I've heard it all before, on the soccer sidelines of a Saturday morning. Perfect for Bolognese sauce, melt-in-your-mouth soufflés, hummus dip to die for. Wonderful in so many ways, but not *my* ideal Mother's Day gift – and a petulant part of me thinks that Andy should have *known* that, after fifteen years of marriage.

'Where will we put it, Mum?' Ruby asks.

'I'm not sure,' I say. 'The kitchen's a bit squeezy at the moment. Maybe after the renovation...'

'You don't like it,' Jackson announces. 'Do you?'

'Not true,' I say, attempting to salvage the situation. 'I'm sure I'll love it once I use it.'

Jackson looks unconvinced.

'There's one more thing.' Milla passes me a pink envelope. 'It's not much, sorry.'

Inside is a crisp square of white cardboard, with a haiku poem penned in Milla's neat hand:

> *MOTHER'S DAY*
> *Her arms always there*
> *Smiling warm, strong and mighty*
> *Keeps giving her love*

'Oh, Milla.' I pull her into a hug, blinking back tears. 'That's... your best yet.'

Poetry-writing has become one of Milla's primary pastimes since moving to Queenscliff.

Ruby looks concerned. 'Are you sad, Mummy?'

'Glad-sad,' I say. 'Sometimes I'm so happy I cry a bit. Is that the poem you're entering into the competition, Millsy?'

Milla shakes her head. 'I'm working on a different one for that.'

'More pancakes, Mummy?' Ruby motions at the remaining pile.

'I'm too full,' I reply, patting my stomach. 'I can't, darling, sorry.'

'But I can,' says Jackson suddenly, seizing a doughy round from the tray and biting into it with gusto. 'Yumbo!' he declares, washing it down with a sip of lukewarm tea from my cup, before starting on another.

I giggle, watching Jackson persist through every rubbery mouthful – swallow and sip, swallow and sip – until three pancakes have been wholly consumed and Ruby hurrahs with delight.

'What do you want to do today, Mum?' Milla stretches out her long limbs across the bed. She's growing womanlier by the week, and I've seen men starting to notice her. 'Something special for Mother's Day?'

'I have to go into work,' I remind her. 'I'm singing in the Mother's Day Concert at Care Cottage. And you girls have your gymnastics gala this afternoon, remember?'

'We know,' says Ruby, in a bored tone. 'But can't we do something special just for this morning?'

A few uninterrupted hours on the couch with a novel I've been aiming to read for about three years would be special enough.

'What about going for coffee?' asks Milla. 'We could walk down to Queenies or Beanster.'

'Perfect,' I say.

'Can we ask Nanna Pam, too?' Ruby asks. 'For Mother's Day?'

'That's a lovely idea,' I say. 'Shall we send her a message?'

I'd have suggested it myself, had Andy been here. But without him, I doubt that Pamela would actively *choose* to spend much time with me. Despite being married to her son, I've always felt thoroughly inferior in Pamela's presence. She's clever, multi-lingual and so well put together, while most days I'm a dishevelled wreck.

'I'll message her,' says Milla, reaching for my phone.

Watching Milla compose the message, I marvel at her double-thumbed agility. 'Make sure you remind Nanna Pam that Dad is overseas, okay?'

Milla nods. I hear the swishing sound of a sent message.

'Let's get ready,' I say. 'It might take Nanna a while to get back to us.'

Milla and Ruby climb off the bed, while Jackson wanders over to the window.

'Can we build our street library later today, Mum?' asks Milla. 'We've been postponing it forever.'

'Better to wait until Dad's back,' I say. 'I'm a singer, not a builder.'

Milla looks crestfallen.

Back in January, Andy agreed to build a street library – a small wooden box designed for neighbourhood book-swapping – in the front yard of our home. But the hardware has been sitting untouched in the shed for months now, awaiting that unlikely moment when Andy isn't jetlagged or deadline-driven or both.

'Okay, Millsy,' I relent. 'It's been way too long in the planning. Maybe not today, but definitely this week. We'll build it before Dad comes home from New York. Let's give him a surprise.'

Milla grins. 'Thanks, Mum.'

'Go get ready, kids.'

As the girls bolt away, Jackson stands transfixed at the window.

'Want to get ready too, hon?'

Jackson doesn't budge.

He wants to say something, I can see, but it's not coming out. The expression is one I've come to recognise since his toddler years.

'Are you missing Dad?' I move to his side.

Jackson says nothing.

'Thanks for eating Ruby's pancakes.' I put an arm around his shoulders. 'That was kind of you. I couldn't have eaten them all on my own. Not with them so "well done", anyway.'

Jackson doesn't smile at the joke.

'How about we FaceTime Dad a little later? I can message him right now to see if he's still up?'

Jackson beams, and my heart sinks. So he *is* missing his father, on the opposite side of the world. It's a feeling not easily remedied by videocalls and Andy may have turned in for the night already.

I pick up my phone.

'Look!' Jubilantly, I wave the message at Jackson. 'Nanna Pam says she can meet us at Beanster at nine o'clock, so you'd better get dressed. We'll call Dad as we walk.'

Jackson races out of the room.

I tap out a message to Andy.

You still up? Jackson would love to talk xx

Changing out of my pyjamas, I opt for my usual weekend garb of faded jeans, a plain white t-shirt and a comfortable navy hoodie. Along the hall, I hear drawers sliding, doors slamming and Ruby and Milla singing to the music of some precocious teen popster they both idolise.

'Ready, Mummy!' Ruby hollers from the hallway.

Standing in front of the mirror, I ignore the fact that my jeans are snugger than they used to be. But as I lean in to inspect my face, I can't help but sigh; that expensive age-defying serum isn't exactly delivering on its promises. I brush my hair, now a much darker blonde than it used to be, before tying it back into a no-nonsense ponytail. I pop a breath mint, slap deodorant under my arms, and dab some tinted moisturiser onto my face. Once upon a time there was proper makeup, in my cabaret days.

'Muuummmy!' Ruby yells impatiently. 'Reaaady!'

I hurry out of the bedroom to find the children already waiting for me at the front door.

'No lipstick, Mum?' asks Ruby. She pulls a tube of pink gloss from the pocket of her yellow polka-dotted dress. 'This could make you look a bit more...?'

Critiqued by the family fashionista, yet again.

'Thanks, Rubes.' I take the tube and smear it across my lips. The look of disdain on Ruby's face suggests an imperfect application on my part.

We close the front door behind us, navigate the missing timber planks in the veranda, then walk down the three rickety steps leading into the front yard.

Beyond the carport, Ruby turns and inspects the length of the driveway.

'Now that's what I call a cricket driveway,' she says, parroting her father. 'Want to practise bowling later, Jackson?'

Jackson shrugs, nonplussed. Despite Andy's best efforts to encourage him to play cricket, Jackson's never been passionate about the sport.

Milla scoops up a stray tennis ball on the lawn and tosses it in Ruby's direction. 'Since when have you been so into cricket, Rubes?'

'Since Dad taught me how to bat and bowl,' Ruby replies with a smile. 'Can I join a girls' cricket team next summer, Mum?'

'Absolutely, Rubes,' I say. 'Girls can do anything.'

'You'll hate the cricket uniforms,' warns Milla. 'No sequins or feathers. Not glam enough for you, girlfriend.'

'Shuddup.' Ruby waves her hands overhead, gesturing for the ball. 'Let's play!'

Milla pegs it at her, hard and fast. Ruby stretches out a hand and dives, catching it low to the ground.

'Nice one,' I call.

Ruby executes a triumphant little pirouette, then bows.

'Race you to Beanster!' she yells at Milla.

The girls bolt ahead in the direction of the café, but Jackson dawdles at my side.

'Girls can do anything,' he mutters.

I glance at him, then reach for his hand.

'Boys can too, Jackson,' I say, squeezing his palm. 'Boys, too.'

2

Amid the noisy hubbub of the café, I spot Pamela sitting at a low aluminium table in the very centre of the room, the weekend newspaper spread out in front of her.

'Hellooo!' she calls, smiling at the children over her half-moon spectacles.

The three of them mob her with hugs.

'Hello, Julia.' She greets me with a perfunctory wave.

'Happy Mother's Day, Pamela.' I kiss the polished cheek she offers me. 'That's a lovely shirt you're wearing.'

She has a closet full of them. Various colours, identical style.

Her gaze alights on my ancient jeans. 'Surely you haven't been... gardening this morning, Julia?'

She's had underlings all her life, I remind myself. *Ambassadorial minions.*

'Always,' I say. 'We have a problem with palm berries. It's practically a full-time job clearing them out of the back yard.'

Pamela appears decidedly uninterested.

'Ooh, that's nice, Nanna Pam.' Milla slides onto a stool next to her grandmother and motions at an iPad protruding from Pamela's handbag. 'It's new, right?'

Ruby and Jackson crowd around Pamela to see, while I take a seat on the opposite side of the table.

'I'm finally emerging from the Jurassic age.' Pamela looks pleased with herself. 'Your father had it delivered to me yesterday, then he video-called this morning to wish me a happy Mother's Day. It was almost like being in the same room!'

I try not to feel wounded by the fact that Andy purchased such a thoughtful gift for Pamela, but not for me. She *is* his mother, I remind myself.

'Milla, could you help me set up email and Facebook?' Pamela asks. 'You'll be so much cleverer at it, being a digital natural and all.'

'Digital native, Nanna.' Milla suppresses a smile.

Pamela passes menus around the table. 'What do we feel like this morning, children?'

As the three begin debating the virtues of smoothies versus milkshakes versus frappes between themselves, she turns to me. 'Breakfast, Julia? It's on me.'

I shake my head. 'Just a coffee, thanks.'

'Why don't we lash out and order a champagne and orange juice, for Mother's Day?'

'I have to go to work, sorry.'

I'm not quite in the mood for celebrating anyway, with Andy away.

'Of course.' Pamela glances down at her newspaper, then points to an advertisement for discount Venetian blinds. 'Look, Prestige Drapes is having a clearance. I assume Andy didn't fix your bedroom blinds before he left? It was such a shame Jackson pulled them down...'

I pretend to study the advertisement, replaying in my mind the incident.

I'd been sitting on the end of my bed with Jackson one Sunday afternoon last month, counting out cards for our umpteenth round of Snap, when Andy bustled in with his toolbox.

'Just the boy I wanted to see,' he said, gesturing at the damaged bracket above the bedroom window. 'Help me fix these Venetians, Jackson?'

One of Andy's fondest memories as a child was the do-it-yourself time he spent with his own father. Together, they'd magicked up handy aids for 'gracious living', as they jokingly called it, wherever Pamela's consular postings delivered them around the globe. Making or fixing things was how Andy had connected with his father.

'Which screws do you reckon fit these blinds, mate?' Andy squatted down and began riffling through his toolbox.

Jackson lay down his cards and moved off the bed, standing rather awkwardly at his father's side.

'The big screws, or the little ones?'

When Jackson didn't answer, Andy looked up. 'You need a haircut, mate. Looks like you've been electrocuted.'

Had Andy levelled such a comment at Ruby, she wouldn't have stood for it. But Jackson simply shrugged.

'Hey, can you use those muscles of yours and pull up the blinds for me?'

Jackson dutifully moved to the window, took hold of the cord and tugged. The slats flew upward, smacked the apex with an almighty crack, then tumbled out of the frame.

Sunlight slapped the walls of our bedroom as slats scattered across the floor.

Andy leapt to his feet. 'Why'd you pull so hard, mate?'

'They're really old blinds...' I started.

Andy held up a hand of warning. 'Jackson, I'm talking to *you*.'

Our son stared at the disarray on the floor, fingering the edge of his nostrils.

The silence infuriated Andy further; three audiology tests in the same number of years have proven there's nothing wrong with Jackson's hearing.

Andy seized Jackson by the shoulders. 'Think first before you act, mate. It's family rule number five. Now go to your room.'

Breaking free of Andy's grasp, Jackson scuttled towards me.

'Oh, no you don't,' said Andy, shunting Jackson out of the room and marching him up to the attic.

When Andy returned, I couldn't contain my indignation. No matter how many times I've told Andy that our son doesn't mean to cause trouble, he always seems to interpret Jackson's actions, or his inactions, as personal insults.

'That was unfair on Jackson,' I snapped. 'You asked him to use his muscles to pull the blinds up, and that's exactly what he did.'

'Oh, come on,' said Andy. 'He did it on purpose. He knew he was pulling too hard.'

It's been like this for more than eight years, ever since our challenges with Jackson started. With me defending Jackson from Andy's claims that he's being 'deliberately provocative', or deflecting his unfavourable comparisons between our son and our daughters.

'It's just the way Jackson's brain works,' I countered. 'When will you actually understand that?'

Andy glowered at me. 'And when will *you* understand that

I'm a different parent to you, Jules? A father is very different to a mother, you know.'

I glance up at Pamela from behind my menu, wondering exactly how Andy relayed the Venetian blinds incident to her.

'Well, Jackson didn't "pull down" the blinds as such...' I begin, just as a waitress materialises at our table.

'May I take your order?' she enquires in a lilting accent.

'Where are you from, dear?' asks Pamela.

'Argentina,' the waitress replies.

Immediately Pamela launches into fluent Spanish, her face animated as she describes her stint as Head of Mission in Buenos Aires. It's mostly unintelligible to me, but I hear her mention Edward, her late husband. Peter, too, Andy's younger brother, now living in London.

As their exchange concludes, the waitress glances around the table. 'So... that's one champagne and orange, three mango milkshakes and...' the waitress turns to me, 'a soy latte for you?'

'An almond latte,' I correct.

'Oh, I knew it was one of those strange ones.' Pamela leans towards the waitress. 'I prefer my milk the old-fashioned way, straight from a cow.'

You're the cow, I want to say.

'Muchas gracias,' Pamela calls out, as the waitress retreats.

'Mum, look!' Ruby points at Pamela's iPad. 'Our waitress looks just like Selena Gomez!'

Jackson leans over to scrutinise Ruby's claim, lowering his face until it almost touches the screen.

Why did Pamela bring the iPad to the café at all, when she's aware of the family therapist's advice about minimising screen time for Jackson?

I crane my neck to view the clip. An attractive Latinolooking brunette in tiny denim shorts is gyrating suggestively against a brick wall.

'That doesn't look very appropriate to me.'

The children ignore me.

'Excuse me, you three. Did you hear me?'

Jackson's gaze moves lazily from the screen, across the table, then back to the screen.

'Please shut it down,' I say.

'Can't they have a bit of screen time, just for today?' Pamela asks. 'On a special occasion?'

'The content seems... a little mature,' I say, my frustration building. 'Please kids, turn it off.'

Ruby yanks the tablet away from Jackson and passes it back to Pamela.

Robbed of the screen, Jackson shoves back his chair, drops to the floor and pushes himself into a headstand.

Pamela's eyes widen.

'Not in here, Jackson,' I mutter.

Ruby giggles and leans towards Pamela. 'Café yoga.'

The waitress returns and sets down Pamela's drink and my latte, eyeing Jackson nervously.

Jackson rolls out of the headstand and smiles, at no one in particular. He stays crouched on the floor, inspecting the sole of his shoe.

'So... how are the children doing at Queenscliff Public?' Pamela sips at her champagne flute, still watching Jackson. 'It must be hard to gauge, in those big primary schools. You do have their names down at Clontarf Grammar for secondary, don't you?'

I gulp a mouthful of coffee, unsure how to respond. It's another source of tension between Andy and me; while he was schooled in the exclusive British International system in far-flung locales, I attended a local public school near Kaminski's Dry Cleaners in Sydney's greater west. And we both turned out all right, as far as I'm concerned.

'I love Peninsula Secondary,' says Milla, relieving me of the need to respond. 'We do Pilates for sport.'

Pamela looks slightly perturbed.

'Mum!' Ruby claws at her scalp. 'I'm itchy again.'

'Oh dear,' I say, willing her not to mention the word 'nits'. 'A milkshake will make it all better. Look, here they come now!'

The waitress returns with three mango milkshakes, setting them down in front of the children.

'Stay a moment, dear,' says Pamela, as the waitress turns to retreat.

As my mother-in-law launches into Spanish again, I feel utterly superfluous. Clearly, Pamela would rather chat to a waitress she met five minutes ago than her daughter-in-law of fifteen years.

'Can I get this almond latte to go, please?' I ask the waitress. 'And my son's milkshake?'

The waitress looks momentarily confused, then bustles away.

'I'm sorry, Pamela, but... er... I have to get ready for work and... I need to buy Jackson some new soccer boots this morning. He's growing so quickly. Can I leave the girls with you for a little while?'

Milla's trying to catch my eye while I'm deliberately avoiding hers.

'Now?' asks Pamela. 'You need to go and buy soccer boots now?'

'I'm afraid so. Jackson's got soccer training later this afternoon, you see. Then he's going over to his friend Digby's place...'

I'm waffling.

'Soccer training on a Sunday afternoon?' Pamela frowns. 'On Mother's Day?'

'The coach is very committed. Training every Sunday, no exceptions. Monday afternoons too, he works the boys very hard. He's a diehard football nut.'

'Oh dear.' Pamela tut-tuts into her glass. 'And your boots are too small for you already, Jackson?'

Jackson leans his head against his grandmother's shoulder. It's a tender gesture that makes Pamela's face soften.

The waitress returns with our drinks in a takeaway tray.

'Why can't you just... get the boots for Jackson tomorrow, Mummy?' presses Ruby.

'It won't take long. Jackson's restless anyway. I'm sure Nanna Pam doesn't want to see any more... café yoga. Enjoy your Mother's Day morning, Pamela.'

I push back the stool and stand up.

'You too,' she replies. 'I'll drop the girls back in about an hour. Do you still need me to come over this afternoon while you're at Care Cottage?'

'Yes, please,' I say, feeling suddenly churlish. 'Thanks a lot, Pamela. Have fun at gymnastics today, girls.'

'Bye!' they call, before turning back to Pamela's iPad.

On the way home, we stop at Captain's Corner to buy flowers – a mixed bouquet of hardy natives – to cheer me up. Their fresh bushland scent buoys my spirits.

As we wander back along Seaview Street, Jackson turns to me. 'Are we really buying soccer boots, Mum?'

'Let's just see how training goes today,' I reply. 'If Coach Steve says you need them, we can go shopping tomorrow after school.'

Jackson seems relieved about this. He's never enjoyed shopping trips.

'So why did you tell Nanna Pam that we were?'

I feel my face flush.

'I just really needed some air, Jackson. I didn't want to be in that café any more, but I didn't want to... hurt Nanna Pam's feelings, either.'

Jackson nods slowly. 'You remembered your manners,' he says, referencing our fourth family rule.

I smile. 'I guess I did.'

We traverse the length of Seaview Street, past sprawling Hamptons-style mansions, angular villas of polished concrete, and a dwindling number of post-war red-brick cottages.

'Is Queenscliff growing on you?' I ask Jackson after a while. 'It's not quite hipster Erskineville, is it?'

Jackson links his fingers through mine. 'What's hipster?'

'Oh, let's see... Trendy, I suppose. A bit alternative. Lots of skinny guys with big bushy beards.'

My phone chimes. Reading the message, I can't conceal my disappointment.

'Dad's going to... call us tonight.' I watch Jackson's face fall. 'It's getting late in New York now. He's had a very busy day.'

We all have, I think.

Jackson's lips begin to tremble.

'Let's go breathe in the sea air,' I say, sounding more upbeat than I feel.

At the very end of the road, we climb the grassy hillock overlooking the beach and stand together, watching the waves roll into Queenscliff. The vast green expanse beckons, whitecaps glinting under a cerulean sky. A lonely gull hovers over the dunes, riding invisible eddies above us.

The beach is almost empty, bar a cluster of surfers bobbing

near the break. They sit motionless on their boards, contemplating the horizon, before leaping to their feet and carving elegant trails across the waves.

Growing up in the land-locked western suburbs, I never imagined a distant adulthood in which I'd have such ready access to the ocean. Yet since moving to Queenscliff, I've barely even taken a casual dip.

Filled with a sense of yearning, I turn to Jackson. 'Want to learn to surf with me next summer? I've always wanted to stand up on a board.'

Surfing has always seemed a rare and exotic skill reserved for cooler, sportier women. It's thrilling even to entertain the idea.

Jackson sniffs. 'Dad took me surfing last Christmas holidays. It didn't work out.'

'That's right.' I'd forgotten Andy's efforts to teach Jackson to surf last summer. Their second attempt at Coogee Beach had ended abruptly with Jackson's incapacity – or refusal, Andy deemed it – to take instruction.

'Dad hated surfing with me.'

'No, he didn't.' I wrap an arm around Jackson's shoulders. 'He was probably just... frustrated.'

'Dad hates me.'

'No, he doesn't. Dad loves you. It's just that sometimes, he... runs out of patience. We all do. We're human, right?'

Jackson shrugs.

I scout for something else to console him.

'You know, learning to surf might feel different if... Dad isn't involved. I mean, it's probably a bit like learning to drive a car. That usually works out much better when parents don't do the instructing. Maybe we should find someone closer to your age to help you learn?'

Jackson considers this for a full minute, then his mouth curves upwards.

'Maybe Riley could teach me?' he suggests. 'He's really good at surfing. His dad used to be a pro-surfer. Riley might say yes, because I'm Milla's brother...'

I'm trying to piece all this information together, but I'm stymied.

'Who's Riley?'

'Oh, Milla's new friend,' he explains. 'They hang out at the bus stop before school. He's super cool.'

'Milla's new friend?' I'm wondering how it is that *Jackson* knows more about Milla's burgeoning social life than I do.

'Riley might teach me to surf!' Jackson begins bouncing up and down on his toes, the words flowing with uncharacteristic fluidity. 'Maybe he could teach you too, Mum?'

'I don't see why not,' I say, delighted by his enthusiasm. 'If Riley's a friend of Milla's, then he's a friend of ours.'

Humming a Beach Boys tune, I launch myself into an awkward sideways surfing pose. 'Ready for some barrels next summer?'

It's not the most convincing surfer impersonation, but Jackson laughs all the same.

'Epic, Mum.' He grins. 'I can't wait to learn with you.'

These words deliver me the sweetest Mother's Day gift of all.

3

I'm sitting with Digby in Coach's black BMW with its smooth leather seats and open-shut sunroof and a talking computer that makes cool stuff happen. We're super sweaty from soccer training but Coach says it's best to keep the sunroof shut because he doesn't like the creepy-crawlies flying into his car.

Coach's car is way nicer than our van, which is a bit banged up now because Mum keeps bumping it into street signs and boom gates and sometimes even parked cars she's forgotten are there. Mum's so forgetful she has to carry heaps of lists around in her handbag to help her remember stuff, but I never forget anything.

It's almost sunset and I'm going to Digby's house to *hang out* anyway. I'm really excited because even though I've been at Queenscliff Public for five months, no one's *ever* invited me back to their place. Coach is dropping us there because Digby's parents work so hard they can't collect him from the oval, even on a Sunday and even when it's almost dark. My mum's busy too, she had to go sing to the patients at Care Cottage for the Mother's Day concert, which means I get to hang out at Digby's for a whole hour before Nanna Pam picks me up.

My stomach feels weird, maybe because it's almost dinner time, and suddenly I feel a bum-blurter coming and it's going to be hard to stop.

'Did you do a fart?' Digby asks, and we both fall about laughing because the stink is rancid. Mum calls them *pop-offs* and Ruby calls them *fluffs*, but Nanna Pam just pretends they're not really there, even though the smell is *really* real.

'Here we are,' says Coach, pulling into Digby's driveway already. 'Good effort at training.' He turns and grins at me. 'Lay off those curries, Jackson. And don't go spending too much time on that device of yours, Digby. Soccer's way better than any virtual game, boys.'

He leans over into the back seat and gives us both a high-five, then we hop out of the car.

Digby's driveway is a silvery grey colour, with pebbles that glitter under the street lights, and his house has massive windows all lit up like shiny yellow eyes. Suddenly the front door swings open and this really tall dad steps out of it.

'Thanks for bringing Digby home, Steve!' he calls out to Coach, who toots the horn in a friendly sort of way, not like the way Mum beeps when she's driving.

'You must be Jackson.' Tall Dad looks down from miles above me. 'I just got home myself.'

He pats me on the shoulder. 'What do you think of Queenscliff? Much nicer by the sea than in Erskineville, I imagine?'

It depends on what you call *nice*, but I nod anyway because I want to *Be Polite*. That's one of our family rules.

Erskineville was nice with old Mrs Walker who lived next door with her five cats, because she always let me lick the bowl whenever she made chocolate brownies. It was nice for its big bookstore and the skinny man who stood outside it playing a golden French horn. He sometimes let me have a turn, as long as I never touched the valves. Erskineville was nice for its big grassy park at the end of our street and our old house and my old room that smelled just right. My bedroom in Queenscliff smells like mouldy old barnacles and it's not even a real room. It's part of the roof – *an attic*, Mum calls it – with these narrow spiral stairs leading up to a little door.

'Come in,' says Digby's dad, waving us into his palace, which is even bigger than Nanna Pam's old sandstone house in Balgowlah Heights. 'The others aren't home yet. Rory's still at basketball training.'

'Good,' says Digby, because he doesn't like his brother much.

'How many houses is this?' I ask, and Digby's dad laughs as if I've just cracked the funniest joke.

'We've got four laptops and two desktops, three tablets, an X-Box X-Treme, a PSii, NextGen Netflix and semi-automatic Nerf guns,' explains Digby. 'We've got a robot vacuum and a Shopbot called Shoshanna and you can say, "Okay Shoshanna, order me the ingredients for macaroni cheese" and she'll do it for you. And we've got HAIR tech, I'll show you that later.'

'Whoooa,' I say, wondering if Shoshanna will ever move into *our* house after the renovation. Mum and Dad didn't have Shopbots when they were kids in the pre-internet era, which wasn't long after the dinosaurs. Back in the old days phones were still connected to cables so you were tied to the wall whenever you wanted to talk to someone. And if you wanted to play music, you had to use these silver circles called *compact discs* and before that, these big black plates called *records*. Mum still has an ancient record player and clunky brown speakers to play songs by her favourite singers like Eartha Kitt and Liza Minelli and Mabel Mercer.

Mum's a singer too, she studied music at a big old university a long time ago and became a cabaret lady who wore pretty dresses and feathery scarves on stage. Once she even had a show at the Opera House with four other cabaret ladies and a handsome man in a top hat, but when Milla started growing inside Mum's tummy, she had to stop. There were too many early practices and late nights when Mum was *sleep-deprived*, which was all the time because Baby Milla didn't like sleeping much at all.

So now Mum sings almost every day at Care Cottage for the Special Ps – that's short for 'Special People' – which is what Mum calls the patients at Care Cottage. I used to think a hospice was a retirement village, but what Mum does inside is called music therapy, and the scientists have figured out that it helps make sick people feel better even when they're dying. Mum's voice sort of wraps up all the Special Ps in an invisible velvet blankie and helps them think nice thoughts while they're waiting for the Otherworld.

'Are you hungry?' asks Digby's dad, pointing at a plate of yummy-looking muffins sitting on the kitchen bench. 'It's almost dinner time, but shall we break the rules?'

I look around to see which family rule we'll be breaking if we eat a muffin before dinner, but I can't see Digby's family rules anywhere. At our house, they're written on a big piece of cardboard stuck against the kitchen wall:

Be Polite
Be Considerate
Gentle Voices
Remember Your Manners

Think First

We made those rules when I was six years old, after I fell out of the gum tree in the back yard in Erskineville for the fourth time and Mum found me all woozy near the trunk. Mum shouted a bit and told me to 'think first' before climbing so high, then she noticed heaps of blood just bucketing out of the back of my head, so she rushed me to the hospital where this really nice doctor gave me a lollipop and thirteen stitches.

When we got back, Dad called a family meeting and talked to us about 'setting some ground rules for greater harmony at home'. I was a bit confused at first, because harmony is something Mum usually makes with her voice and her guitar. But this type of harmony gave us five family rules instead.

'Would you like a muffin, Jackson?' Digby's dad pushes the plate towards me. 'Miranda baked them before she took Rory to training.'

I smile to *Be Polite*, even though I'm wondering who Miranda is. There's no one else around, so maybe she's another Shopbot like Shoshanna? But how could a robot take Digby's little brother to basketball training?

'Have you made lots of friends at school?' Digby's dad asks me.

I'm not sure what to say because most of the boys at Queenscliff Public play rugby, which I hate because your head gets smacked in, and most of the girls just sit around swapping Collect-a-Petz Cards or chattering about girls' stuff. So every lunchtime in my first week, I just walked around the school library building six times one way and six times the other, until the bell rang. And because there are hundreds of kids at Queenscliff Public, nobody noticed me doing that, except for

Miss Marion the dance teacher. She noticed straight away, because she notices everything.

'You like walking in circles, Jackson?' Miss Marion popped out from behind a tree and gave me a big surprise. She didn't really look like a teacher, with her colourful spiky hair and crazy socks.

'Yes,' I replied.

'Do you like dancing in circles too?'

'Yes,' I said, even though I wasn't so sure.

'Why don't you try Senior Dance?' Miss Marion said. 'You'll be amazed what your body can do. It's a lot more than circles, honeybun!'

I liked how Miss Marion smiled and called me 'honeybun' and made Senior Dance sound like heaps of fun, so I just said yes, again.

From that week on, I went to dance every Wednesday and Thursday during lunchtime. After about three weeks, Miss Marion came and found me again one Monday recess when I was circling the library.

'You've got real talent, Jackson,' she said, walking next to me. 'Your high leaps and jumps are sensational. You're a fast learner.' After another lap of the library, she asked if I'd like to dance in a special role at the eisteddfod, which is a weird Welsh word for sitting, even though this eisteddfod was about dancing.

At first I thought she was joking, but then Miss Marion started explaining about how I'd have to learn 'aerial silks' on Monday and Friday lunchtimes if I actually wanted the special role. I'd never even heard of aerial silks.

'It's like flying to music,' she told me.

That sounded awesome, so I said yes to that too.

Then I did a pretty bad thing. We went to the staff room and

Miss Marion gave me a Parental Permission Note about risks and waivers and liability and duty of care and Working with Children Checks and how many weekend practices I'd have to do for my special role. But instead of taking the note home, I just signed it myself and gave it back to Miss Marion the next day. I didn't think Dad would let me do it if I asked, I've never seen him dance once.

So for three months now I've been dancing every lunchtime except Tuesdays. I'm the only boy there, all the other dancers are in Grade Six or Five and one of them is April Kennedy. She's in 5T like me and she's a bit shy, but really kind.

I start telling Digby's dad that April Kennedy is a special friend, but suddenly there's this loud chime like a gong and he looks down at his mobile phone and groans.

'This is urgent, sorry boys,' he says, then he heads into his swanky home office and before he shuts the door, I see a big desk and two gigantic screens inside.

'It's probably Chicago calling,' says Digby. 'My dad gets calls from all over the world, all the time.'

'My dad's in New York now,' I say.

'What's your dad do?'

'He runs an advertising agency.'

'Oh yeah?' Digby sniffs. 'My dad probably *owns* your dad's advertising agency.'

I'm not sure what he means by that, but I follow Digby to the kitchen bench. He's much taller than me because our school principal Mrs Daisy Bennett made him repeat Grade Three for 'extra learning support', so next year he'll be the only teenager in Grade Six. Digby's the oldest boy in our soccer team, too. His dad had to get special permission for him to stay with his friends in the Queenscliff Under-Eleven Dragons, all because of Mrs Bennett. Everyone calls her Crazy Daisy at school, because she's always screeching and blowing her whistle and doling out detentions.

Digby grabs a banana from the fruit bowl on the bench. 'Want one?'

He starts waving the banana around in front of his soccer shorts, which looks pretty funny, but I say, 'No, thanks.'

Digby peels the banana and bites the end off. 'Ouch, you're hurting me! You're hurting me!' His voice is high-pitched, like maybe it's the banana talking.

That makes me laugh, which makes Digby laugh too. Soon we're having a full-blown cack-attack, we both can't stop laughing. Digby's face goes all red like he might be choking, but then he spits the banana into the sink, so I know he's okay.

'Damn, that was funny,' he says, clapping me on the back.

He pours himself a glass of water, then pours one for me too.

Even though Digby's heaps bigger and older than me, he was the first person to talk to me at Queenscliff Public. He doesn't say much, though, which I don't really mind because when people talk a lot, my brain gets glued up. And sometimes when it gets really clogged, I start seeing things in black and white.

An optha-whatsit doctor checked my eyes once and told Mum that maybe I had something called 'achromatopsia in an atypical form'. Turns out I didn't, but lots of doctors and non-doctors have called me *atypical*. Nanna Pam likes to use other words, like *one-of-a-kind*, *unique*, *special*. *Atypical* sounds a lot like *A-type*, which is what Mum calls Dad when he works too much.

Digby points at the plate of blueberry muffins now, but I say, 'No, thanks' again. He shrugs and walks into another room and I try to follow him, but he slams the door in my face. The

sound gives me such a shock I cry out, and just as I'm
wondering if he did that on purpose, Digby calls through the
door, 'Hey dude, I'm taking a piss!' That makes me feel like a
total idiot because no one should ever follow anyone else into a
bathroom. 'Private parts are private parts,' Mum says. I'd kind
of like to see another boy's thing though, because I only have
sisters so I don't know if all boys' things look the same. I've seen
Dad's a few times in the shower a long time ago, but it's way too
hairy and saggy.

After a while Digby comes out of the bathroom and says,
'Wanna play a game?'

'Yes, please,' I say, because I've just spotted this huge marble
chess set on the coffee table in the lounge. The kings are
wearing long robes and the queens have real jewels in their
crowns and the bishops look like executioners and all the
pawns are carrying scabbards like a proper medieval battle.

'Do you want to be white?' I ask Digby, because white
always starts.

Chess is the only game Mum lets me play online because
Dr Louisa says I shouldn't have too much screen time. If I do,
my brain beans start exploding like fireworks and everything
speeds up inside until I start doing headstands. I *really* want to
play chess with Digby, but he's busy messing around with his
laptop and headsets in the kitchen. I don't think he has brain
beans like me.

'Nah, chess sucks itself sideways.'

I'm too embarrassed to ask what that even means.

Digby waves me over to the big black bench and points at
something that looks like Nanna Pam's birdwatching binoculars
crossed with a swimming cap.

'Let's play Alt-World,' he says, fitting the binocular cap over
my head. 'It's HAIR tech. We can go inside together.'

'What's HAIR tech?' It sounds like an app Ruby might like, because she loves playing hairdressers and makeup artists.

Digby looks at me like I'm an idiot.

'Hyper-Augmented Integrated Reality,' he says. 'It's realer than real. Dad got it from work. There's real people in Alt-World. I can go inside whenever I want.'

'Cool.' I've heard a bit about Alt-World from the kids at school. First it was Minecraft and then it was Fortnite and then it was Joglo and Fusion-X and Bandidos and Gigabitten and now it's Alt-World. Mum never lets me play those types of games though, she says living in the real world should be enough for everyone.

I adjust the goggles to focus on the big purple Alt-World symbol floating on the laptop screen.

'This is where I went down yesterday,' says Digby, pulling his own cap down over his ears and fixing his goggles. 'But no dobbing, Jackson. If you dob, I won't be your friend any more.'

Ruby says that a lot, especially when I catch her raiding the biscuit barrel at home. I never *ever* dob though, because I like eating Oreos as much as Ruby. So we usually make a deal and take three cookies each, then we eat them together behind the laundry room door where no one else can find us.

Digby presses play on the laptop and we both stand there wearing our goggles, waiting for the scan. It's going to take a few minutes to load, so we eat half a blueberry muffin each. Digby goes to the big silver fridge and takes out a tub of white stuff he calls *mask-a-pone*. He spreads some of it onto his muffin and offers me some too, but I can't figure out if it's cheese or cream so I say, 'No, thanks.'

'You can try it in Alt-World, without really eating it,' he says. 'There's heaps of stuff you can try with HAIR tech. You can see anything you want, too. Have you ever seen a lady naked?'

Suddenly the scanner beeps and flashes red and then the game starts. *Whoosh*, the goggles suck me down-down-down into this really long cobbled tunnel and I get a bit puffed because I'm running inside Alt-World, following Digby into the centre of the earth.

When we get to the end of the tunnel there's this big dim room that's a bit like a cave. It's foggy and I can even smell the sea, only it's not the summer saltiness of Queenscliff beach, it's a rotten fish sort of smell. Maybe we'll go hunting for buried treasure down here?

In the shadows I notice there are other people too, adults. There's a short blonde lady wearing floppy rabbit ears who's sort of hiding behind a rock and a muscly man wearing a pig mask who's trying to catch her with a lasso. There are other people hanging around just watching them and some of them are calling out like they're taking sides, so that must be part of the game.

The rabbit-lady scoots out from behind the rock and I get a big surprise because she's not wearing any trousers. She bolts away up another tunnel and the pig-man starts chasing her, swinging his lasso around and making these grunting sounds I don't like. He's much taller than her so he's catching up really easily, then Digby starts following them.

'Come on, Jackson, let's go rabbit hunting!'

I don't want to chase a lady with no trousers, but I don't want to lose Digby in Alt-World either, so I follow him and Pig Man. I jog along the tunnel, but I can't see much through the fog and then I turn a corner and *bang!* Suddenly they're right there in front of me.

The pig-man has caught the lady and he's holding her against the slimy wall and pushing her around a bit, saying, 'Slut-slut-slut.' Digby grins at me and says, 'It's another word for girl.' I've got two sisters and a mum and two grandmas, but I've never heard that word for girl before.

Then I notice my thing waking up inside my soccer shorts, it's started doing that a lot more lately, ever since I started growing hair under my armpits. I get really embarrassed and try to cover it with my hand, but Digby notices it too. Everything looks bigger because of the HAIR tech goggles.

'Look, Curtis! Your dragon's getting bigger and stronger.' He points at the green dragon picture on my soccer shorts stretching tighter and tighter across my thing. 'You'll have to tell Coach about that! He likes big strong dragons.'

Digby laughs like crazy, but I wish I could just fall into one of the lava pits in Alt-World and get vaporised.

I'm getting worried for the lady now. She looks hurt and sad and the pig-man is bothering her and she starts crying and that makes me scared.

I turn to Digby to ask if please-please-please we can just play chess instead?

Then I hear this super-loud knocking sound from further down the tunnel and *whoosh*, suddenly we're being reverse-sucked right back up into the kitchen.

Digby rips the goggles off my head and slams down the laptop screen.

'Someone's at the front door,' he pants.

My heart is beating so loudly, I thought maybe *it* was making the sound.

'Cool, wasn't it?' Digby races across the room to open the door. 'Remember, no dobbing, it's our special secret.'

But it doesn't feel very special. Not when my heartbeat is going doof-doof-doof inside my brain and down in that dark tunnel somewhere, there's a lady who might still be crying.

4

Digby opens the door. Nanna Pam is standing on the doorstep like Mary Poppins, all crisp and neat in her nice woollen skirt and peachy blouse.

I'm *so* happy to see her.

'Hello Jackson.' She waves at me. 'It's home time, darling. I've done a roast lamb.'

Nanna Pam's roasts are the best. She makes crispy potatoes and honeyed carrots and green beans cut up into tiny diagonal pieces that melt in your mouth. She's so good at cooking, she'd definitely win at Kitchen Maestro if she ever went on the show.

'How was soccer training?' Nanna Pam asks, but Digby's already tapping on his dad's office door.

When Digby's dad opens it, he looks a bit cross because he's still on the phone. Then he sees Nanna Pam and waves in a much nicer way, but he still keeps talking.

Nanna Pam just smiles and says, 'Got everything, Jackson? What do you say to Digby and his dad?'

I'm not sure what to say to Digby, because I hated playing Alt-World.

Nanna Pam helps me out. 'Thank you for having Jackson, Digby. Please say thanks to your father, when he's off the phone.'

Digby nods and says to me, 'See you at school.'

He shuts the door behind us, then we're walking down the steps and back to Nanna Pam's car. I want to tell Nanna Pam everything about Alt-World and find out what a *slut* is, but I'm guessing it isn't a nice word. Nanna Pam doesn't even like the word *fart*, so I decide not to ask.

In the car, Nanna Pam starts talking about how Milla got a ribbon at the gymnastics gala and how Ruby got a 'most improved' award, and how Mum's still singing for the Special Ps at the Mother's Day concert at Care Cottage.

I just nod and smile, because that's what Nanna Pam likes. Whenever Dad's overseas we see a lot more of Nanna Pam, especially on Mum's workdays. Nanna Pam comes over after school to help Milla make the dinner or to help Ruby with her homework, or just to sit and drink about six cups of tea and natter away to me. I've learned to nod and smile a lot.

After we've been in Nanna Pam's car a while and she hasn't stopped chatting, I decide to call my *other* grandma instead. I love Nanna Pam, but Granny's still my favourite because she's *always* ready to listen. I have to be careful, because Nanna Pam thinks my shoe-phone is weird. I've heard her ask Dad, 'When will Jackson grow out of his shoe-phone thing?' She doesn't seem to realise that my shoe-phone gets bigger with my feet every year, so I won't *ever* grow out of it.

Super slowly, so that Nanna Pam doesn't notice, I wiggle my foot out of my soccer boot and hold the sole to my ear. It only rings once before Granny answers. Her shoe-phone is in her purple sparkly sandals that match her shimmery kaftan.

'It's still Mother's Day,' I whisper into the heel of my boot.

'Don't I know it, Jack-Jack!' Granny yells back at me, then she's laughing like a crazy hyena and that makes me laugh out loud too.

'Happy Mother's Day, Granny. I really miss you.'

Nanna Pam glances into the rear-vision mirror, so I drop my hands into my lap. She smiles at me and starts talking about when she was the Grand Poo-Bah of Brazil, doing important trade stuff for the government.

When I put my shoe-phone back up to my ear, it's just me and Granny talking in a spacetime dimension that the scientists haven't discovered yet, but one day they will. For now, only dogs and cats can hear our conversations, the same way they know a big storm's coming before humans do.

Nanna Pam turns onto the road back to Queenscliff.

I can hear Grandpa through the shoe-phone now and he's calling out my name, but it's coming out all wrong like *Saxon* not *Jackson*. I laugh because I love this joke – 'Saxon... Taxon... Staxon, ah, I remember – Jackson!' Grandpa's been doing that ever since I was a baby all snuggled up in my comfy blue elephant blankie.

Mum doesn't believe I can remember that far back. She says I've got an 'overactive imagination' but actually, I'm a memory magnet.

Behind Grandpa's jokey voice, I hear a hissing like a huge spitting snake and I know exactly what it is: the big dry-cleaning machine at Kaminski's Dry Cleaners. I can even smell the solvents and spotters and deodorisers through the shoe-phone. All those clothes wrapped in plastic smell so good it makes me want to lick them. Once I did that when I was four, but Mum made me drink a litre of charcoal afterwards, so I never did it again.

My shoe-phone beeps because the videocall is activating

now, and that means I'm actually going to *see* Granny and Grandpa. The screen stays foggy for a moment, then there's a pale outline of Granny. Suddenly she's right there, with her happy smile that's bright enough to power a small toaster. It feels like if I reach out, I could actually touch her.

Granny's wearing her big purple kaftan today with her dangly crystal beads. Her hair's in pink rollers because Granny thinks her hair's too straight, even though it's the nicest hair I've ever seen on a grandma. I don't know why she's always trying to make it curly when it's perfect already, like silvery ribbons streaming down her back.

Grandpa's waving at me from behind Granny's head, wearing a black singlet that's stretched a bit too tight across his belly. His hair is all wavy and stiff from the sticky wax he puts in it every day, and his eyes are big and blue and glimmering. I've never seen the Polish sky in summer, but Granny says Grandpa's eyes are *exactly* that colour.

Granny's porcelain Feng Shui cat is sitting on the front counter, with its golden paw powered by invisible magic that makes money pour in through the front door. The Feng Shui cat sits next to the lolly jar, full of jellybeans and chewy toffees and those rancid spearmint leaves that taste like toothpaste. Granny and Grandpa give out handfuls of lollies to all the kids who visit their shop, even to the rude ones and sometimes to their parents too, so that makes *everyone* come back to Kaminski's.

Behind the front counter, there's a big white wall covered in spools of rainbow yarn. Further back, there's Granny's old sewing machine with the heavy foot pedal that creaks and groans whenever she pushes it. Granny's mum carried that sewing machine in a hard leather suitcase all the way from Poland on a steamboat, right after the Nazis started wasting

Europe with their butterfly bombs and prison camps and evil
ways to torture you for being Jewish or too clever or just a bit
unusual.

Everyone in Great-Granny's family was all of that, so they
had to leave their jobs and homes and friends in Warsaw and
forget the best dumplings and sour soup and jelly pig's trotters
and come to the other side of the world and live in hot places
where no one else wanted to live and eat boring stuff like Weet-
Bix and Vegemite.

Grandpa tells me how many pieces he's dry-cleaned this
week and I say, 'Wow, that's a lot!' They both work at Kaminski's
until after midnight most days because that's what Granny's
parents did. Granny says she 'inherited a migrant mentality',
which Grandpa says means they 'just keep turning up'.

I can never exactly remember what a migrant is, so I have to
ask again. Grandpa doesn't get cranky, his eyes just crinkle up
like jolly old Santa. He tells me again what a migrant is – 'a
person living in a foreign land' – and I reckon *I* might be a
migrant too.

I put down the shoe-phone and lean forward to ask
Nanna Pam.

'Nanna, am I a migrant?'

It takes a while for the words to slide out of my mouth. The
last word gets stuck on the *i* sound, so it comes out like *myyy-
grant*.

Nanna Pam snorts like there's something stuck up her nose.
Maybe there is, so I find the mini box of tissues in the seat
pocket in front of me and throw them onto the front passenger
seat where Nanna Pam can reach them.

'Jackson!' Nanna Pam sounds grouchy. 'Don't you throw
things at me. Especially not when I'm driving.'

I wasn't actually *throwing* the tissues at her, I was just trying to help her sniffy nose. I want to explain that to her, but the words don't come.

I lift up the shoe-phone again to see what's happening at Kaminski's; Grandpa's busy using the steam-iron presser and Granny's just smiling, waiting for me to talk. Granny's got a special way of doing that.

'Something bad happened at Digby's, Granny,' I whisper, moving the shoe-phone closer to my mouth. 'I watched a lady who wasn't wearing any trousers getting chased by a pig-man who called her a slut.'

Granny sips loudly at something, probably the mug of warm ginger tea she's always carrying around Kaminski's as she sprays and steams and presses. Granny's a miracle cleaner, even with super-difficult stains like wine or coffee or blood. Granny can make clothes so clean and bright again, it's actually hard to look at them.

'And how did that make you feel, Jackson?' Granny asks.

Usually it's Dr Louisa who asks those kinds of questions. Granny's voice is like gentle music and she's asking as if she wants to hug me and, suddenly, tears come into my eyes for no reason at all.

I want to wrap my arms around her middle and press my face into her softness.

'I... really miss you,' I whisper. I can't hear myself properly, but Granny understands me anyway. Sometimes I don't even have to use any words and she *still* hears me. 'Please can you come visit, Granny?'

'Oh, Jack-Jack, I'm sorry,' says Granny. 'Queenscliff's just so far away.'

'But I really need you to come,' I say, a bit louder now. 'Dad keeps going overseas and I really miss him, too.'

I notice there's wetness sliding down my cheeks.

'Please, Granny? Or can't you find your way back from the Otherworld?'

And then for the millionth time, my memory download shows me what I saw on Dad's laptop the day after the accident, a great big black crater smoking at the bottom of Cahill's Leap. Then somehow I see the whole thing in slow-mo inside my brain: Grandpa swerving to avoid the truck, the car skidding and flipping across two lanes of highway, smashing through the metal barricade and falling down-down-down into a terrible explosion at the bottom of the ravine.

Mum never told me exactly what happened because I was only nine, but it was on the news and the Council's been having meetings ever since about making the road wider to stop it from ever happening again.

'Were you scared?' I ask Granny. My voice goes all wobbly and there's a little sob I can't keep down.

Granny doesn't answer.

'What's it like in the Otherworld?'

All I can hear is the swishing and spraying of the dry-cleaning machines and Granny mumbling something I can't understand.

'When can I come back to Kaminski's?' I ask, but I already know the answer to that: I'm never going back to Kaminski's Dry Cleaners, and neither are they.

'Are you feeling all right, Jackson?' Nanna Pam asks suddenly. I look up from my shoe-phone to see her staring at me in the rear-vision mirror. Maybe she heard me talking to Granny?

'Car sick,' I say, because it's easier.

'Well, we're home now.'

She parks her car behind the Red Rocket in the driveway.

It's dark outside, but there's light behind the curtains in the lounge.

Nanna Pam doesn't turn off the engine. 'Your mum and the girls are home. The lamb roast's waiting inside. If you're not too car sick, that is.'

'Thanks Nanna,' I say. 'I love your roasts.' It comes out a bit slowly, but she smiles and blows me a kiss.

As I climb out of the car, she lowers her window.

'You're not a migrant, Jackson,' she says. 'You were born right here in Australia, just like me. What would make you think that?'

I want to explain how I feel like a stranger everywhere, but Nanna Pam doesn't wait. She just waves and drives away down Seaview Street.

The taillights of her car look like red robot eyes staring at me, until blackness gobbles them up.

5

There's my wake-up call.

The sound of baroque music warbling down the stairs signals it must be seventeen minutes past five on the day after Mother's Day. I reach for my phone on the bedside table: yes, exactly so. It's been an unrelenting routine for almost five years now, yet somehow I still feel shocked by it *every single morning*. Not always the same music, rarely the same mood, but *always* 5.17 for my clockwork boy.

I spring out of bed, charge down the hallway and take the spiral staircase two steps at a time. Milla and Ruby are still sleeping and it's just not fair on them. Once outside Jackson's door, however, I hesitate. What will his mood be this morning: sombre, hyper or aggro? Whichever it is, I tell myself, I *must* stay calm.

Nudging open the door, I find Jackson suspended upside down from his bunk-bed, doodling on his stomach with a black permanent marker. How long has he been hanging there with the blood rushing to his brain? How long *can* a child hang upside down on a daily basis, without causing some kind of permanent damage?

'Jackson, please get down.'

I move around the room, stepping over the contents of the drawers he empties out every night. When he was younger, I used to insist that he clear away the chaos before breakfast each morning. Overseeing the task like some sort of maternal police officer until every pencil, Lego piece and Pokémon card had been restored to its rightful position. These days, I've lost the will for order. 'Pick your battles,' the family therapist advises.

'Where's the speaker hiding today, hon?' I'm scanning for the source of the music.

Jackson doesn't reply. He secretes it somewhere new every morning, but today it's louder than usual. He's been cranking up the volume since Andy left for New York.

As I move closer to Jackson's bunk, the music grows louder. I check under his bed, between the sheets and, finally, locate the speaker beneath a cushion.

I switch it off with a flourish.

'That's better,' I say, smiling at him. 'Good morning.'

Jackson uncurls his legs from the bunk, somersaults backwards and lands heavily on his knees. The impact doesn't seem to register.

'Are you okay, Jackson?'

He staggers to his feet and takes several steps towards me. 'Muuum.'

I recoil at his tone, backing towards the door. I've heard it before, on difficult days. 'Let's not start the day like this, Jackson.'

It hasn't happened in recent months, but he's hurt me inadvertently in the past. Dr Kelleher points out that Jackson's outbursts aren't personal, they're merely symptomatic of deep frustration. And they can be minimised, apparently, by Andy and me 'modelling parental containment'.

'Muuum.' Jackson launches himself at me.

Instinctively, I raise my hands to cover my face.

A moment later, his arms encircle my waist and I feel his cheek pressed against my chest.

'Oh, darling boy.' I lower my hands, ashamed of my instinct to protect myself from my eleven-year-old son. 'Is everything... okay, Jackson?'

He jerks his head up to look at me. 'I'm just really really hungry, Mum.'

'Well, we can fix that,' I say. 'What about a bowl of porridge the way you like it? You need lots of energy for school today.'

'Yum.' Jackson smiles.

I wish Andy was here to witness this tiny triumph of what Dr Kelleher calls 'de-escalation'.

As we move down the stairs and along the hallway, I notice the kitchen light is on already. We enter the kitchen to find Milla at the island bench, looking effortlessly stunning in a white silk kimono, bent over her notebook. The neat lines across the page suggest she's writing another poem.

Snickers is curled up in her lap. He leaps hopefully to the floor as soon as I enter the kitchen. For a dachshund of such meagre proportions, Snickers has the appetite of a Saint Bernard. He trots towards me, his belly almost brushing the tiles, then begins gnawing at the sisal mat.

'Naughty, Snickers.' I reach down to fondle his ears, then gently extract the rug from his teeth.

Snickers gazes up at me with a look that says, 'Feed me or I'll die'.

I tip some dry doggie biscuits into his bowl.

'How are you, Milla?' I ask.

'Tired,' she replies. Her weary smile suggests her patience is dwindling with Jackson's early-morning music-blasting.

Jackson raises a hand of greeting, then pulls up a chair so close to his sister that their shoulders touch. Milla endures this encroachment of personal space with characteristic good humour, until Jackson leans over and tries to read her poem.

'Stop.' She snaps her notebook shut.

'What is it?' he asks.

'Haiku,' she replies. 'Seventeen syllables and three verses, like the one I gave Mum for Mother's Day yesterday.'

'Tricky,' I observe, taking the oats from the pantry.

Jackson begins fidgeting with the glass cannister containing his bread-clip collection – 387 and counting – watching the coloured tabs slide across each other as he rolls the tube beneath his palms.

'Want some porridge, Milla?' I ask. 'I'm making some for Jackson.'

'It's way too early.' She pulls a face. 'Can't I just have breakfast at Nanna Pam's?'

I think for a moment. Today's logistics are more complicated than usual, with Andy away. Pamela will arrive at 7.15 to take Milla to her regular gymnastics training, while I take Jackson and Ruby to school, then rush to work by nine.

'Okay,' I relent. 'But promise me you'll eat something before school.'

'I'm going outside,' announces Jackson.

'What for?' I tip water from the kettle into the oats. 'It's cold out there.'

'Snickers is going to poop on the rug again.'

'Wow, how do you know that?' Milla asks with wonder. 'You're, like, the Dog Whisperer, Jackson.'

I glance at Snickers, trying to gauge the urgency of the situation.

Jackson takes Snickers by the collar, guiding him out of the kitchen and into the back yard.

A moment later, I hear Snickers barking and Tom Lovell's voice drifting over the side fence.

'That man is always up at unnatural hours,' I mutter, stirring the porridge.

'Just like us.' Milla smiles.

'Mu-um!' calls Jackson urgently.

Setting down the spoon, I hurry outside to find Jackson in the herb garden, holding a headstand among the French lavender. He's chatting amiably to Tom, while Snickers noses around the lemongrass.

'Morning, Julia.' Tom grips the top of the palings, peering over them. 'I was just telling Jackson about those palm berries. Tracey's not happy about them.'

He points at the culprit palm in our yard. 'It's dropping fruit all over our place and attracting bats. Palms are classified as weeds, you know. We could call the Council about it.'

I mime seriousness, trying to ignore the visual and olfactory assault delivered by Snickers' morning bowel motion dispensed over the rosemary.

'Snickers, you're a stinker!' yells Jackson, still upside down.

'Can we talk about this... a little later, Tom?' I ask, wincing at the stench. 'Breakfast's on the stove and Andy's overseas. He won't be back until Wednesday week, I'm afraid.'

'He's away *again*?' Tom glances skyward, as if he might spy Andy's aeroplane returning from New York.

'It doesn't make things easy.' I tug at Jackson's ankles, but his excellent core control means that forcing him out of a headstand is much harder than it should be.

'Tracey won't stand for it,' Tom warns.

'I'm so sorry.'

Jackson rights himself at last.

'Sorry isn't a substitute for action,' admonishes Tom.

'We'll get onto it,' I promise. I force a smile at our neighbour, then shepherd Jackson and Snickers back into the house.

'What was that all about?' asks Milla, her eyes still trained on her notebook.

'It was Tom being pedantic. "Tracey won't stand for it" ... Over a few berries on his lawn! How would they cope living with something *really* challenging?'

My eyes stray to Jackson, now sitting on the rug petting Snickers.

'Tom Lovell has way too much time on his hands.'

What would life be like if palm berries were *my* biggest concern?

I resume my position at the stove, checking on the porridge.

Jackson moves back to the island bench, taking Snickers with him. Balancing the dog in his lap, he stares at his hands. 'Is time... heavy or light?'

'Whoa, deep question,' says Milla.

When the porridge is just the right consistency for Jackson's sensitive palate, I pour some into a bowl and fetch the prune juice from the fridge. As I tip the carton over the bowl, Snickers leaps from Jackson's lap and slips through my legs, causing me to douse the porridge beneath.

'Oh, Snickers, naughty!' I push the bowl in front of Jackson. 'There's a little more juice in there than usual, sorry.'

Jackson stares into his bowl, then stoops forward to sniff the contents.

Snickers begins to whimper.

'Want your breakfast, too?' I bend down and scratch him behind the ears.

Suddenly Jackson's bowl of porridge spins wildly across the bench and into Milla's lap, the contents splattering in all directions.

'Ouch.' Milla's response is remarkably restrained.

I rush to help her, applying an icepack from the freezer to the angry red scald mark appearing on her thigh, then dabbing at her robe with a cloth.

I wheel around to face Jackson.

'What were you thinking?' I want to yell.

'Go to your room,' I say instead, deploying the calm-but-firm tone that Dr Kelleher claims is most effective. 'You need some time out.'

Jackson bares his teeth and hisses. White flecks of spittle land on the bench.

Right now, Dr Kelleher would say: 'Love the boy, not the behaviour'. But psychological truisms can't rectify the unpredictability of life with Jackson, which I've been forced to accept as *our* version of 'normal'.

'Go to your room, please, Jackson.'

'It's wrong wrong wrong!' Jackson shouts, and I can only assume he's referring to the excessive prune juice I poured across his porridge.

'Please, Jackson. Ruby's still asleep.'

At nine years of age, Ruby sleeps soundly through most noises: the garbage trucks and sirens of the street, Andy's late-night homecomings, Jackson's tirades.

'I don't care about Ruby!' he bellows, bounding off the stool and booting the flip-top bin across the kitchen. It smashes against the wall, causing our family rules sign to fall, then ricochets away sending eggshells, half-eaten toast and last night's lasagne across the floor.

Where is the boy I stood arm-in-arm with on the Queens-cliff dunes only yesterday, planning a surfing safari for summer?

'I know for a fact that you care about Ruby,' I say, manufacturing confidence. 'You packed her school lunches every day last week, remember? You're a very caring big brother.'

Jackson sinks down onto a stool, his eyelids twitching.

Milla moves across the room, stooping down to salvage the family rules sign. She brushes off the scraps before refastening it to the wall. 'I think the rules just got broken all at once, Mum.'

I stare at the sign's directives. *Be Polite. Be Considerate. Gentle Voices. Remember Your Manners. Think First.* Five family rules developed years ago, after I'd spent hours in the Emergency Department with Jackson yet again. At Andy's suggestion, we'd all sat down at the kitchen table with coloured markers, conjuring words and pictures that depicted a calmer family life.

It was madness, of course. A desperate attempt to control our environment, at a time when we were still insisting to ourselves that Jackson was *rambunctious* or *spirited* or *headstrong*. Those five simple rules offered reassurance that our chaotic lives were amenable to order, somehow, if only we tried harder.

'Everything's okay, hon.' I put my arm around Jackson and escort him down the hall and up the stairs to his bedroom. 'Just take a moment for yourself, until you've calmed down.'

Closing the door behind me, I brace for the barrage of objects Jackson usually hurls against it. Remarkably, all is silent bar the cooing of the top-knot pigeons nesting in the branches beyond his window.

Loitering a moment, I lean my ear to the door.

'Mum?' Jackson calls out softly. 'Are you still there?'

He's listening too.

Gently, I push open the door.

Jackson hails me from his bed. 'I'm calm already, Mum.'

'You are,' I agree, smiling in spite of myself. 'What upset you, Jackson?'

He fingers his nostril for a moment. 'Are angels real, Mum?'

Over the years, I've learned to adapt to the sometimes startling directions of conversations with Jackson.

I move into the room again.

'Well, I've never seen an angel myself, but that doesn't necessarily mean they don't exist.' I sit down on the edge of his bed. 'I've never seen oxygen either, but I'm breathing it now, right?'

Jackson's eyes encourage me to keep talking.

'Granny believed in angels; do you remember? Her family had seen so many bad things during World War Two, she decided to believe in the good things.'

After her parents escaped the horrors of the holocaust, my mother had been happy to turn to all and any symbols of luck, prosperity and spirituality.

Jackson nods. 'She told me about St Jhudiel, my birth angel. The guardian angel for Friday.'

'Did she?' I'm surprised by this detail.

Jackson looks wistful. 'Granny gave me a little statue of St Jhudiel wearing a green cloak. He had a halo and a golden sash. He was holding a big bunch of flowers.'

I have no recollection of my mother ever giving such a statue to Jackson.

'It was beautiful,' he continues. 'But it was so little that I...

lost it. On New Year's Day in Erskineville. It fell down the drain in the gutter outside our old house.'

'Which New Year's was that, Jackson?'

Jackson's eyes are dejected. 'When I was three.'

I raise an eyebrow. Jackson often 'remembers' things that simply cannot be corroborated. While I've always considered it an imaginative by-product of his unusual brain chemistry, Andy suspects Jackson of out-and-out lying.

'Granny told me St Jhudiel has special powers to help me if ever I'm in trouble. I should never have lost that statue.'

He looks so upset that I reach for his hand.

'Have you been thinking about... Granny and Grandpa and the accident again?'

Jackson throws his arms around me, hugging me tightly. I stroke the back of his neck, until I feel his body beginning to relax.

After a while, he slumps down onto the bed again.

'Why don't you go back to sleep?' I whisper. 'It's still really early.'

'I want to start today over,' he murmurs. Then, like a much younger child, he closes his eyes and rolls over.

'You can, hon.' Gingerly, I tiptoe out of the room.

Downstairs, I pause in the kitchen doorway to watch my eldest daughter write.

'You're amazing,' I observe. 'Thanks for being so patient with Jackson.'

Milla sets her notebook aside. 'Ditto, Mum. Jackson's tough. You never give up.'

A wave of gratitude washes over me, for the sympathy of a sensitive daughter.

'How's the poetry?' I ask. 'Finished your competition entry yet?'

She shakes her head. 'I'm still working on it.'

'Can I read it?'

'Not yet.' Milla looks conflicted. 'But I've finished three haiku for Dad, for when he comes back from New York.'

She flicks through the pages in her notebook.

'I'm sure he'll love them, Millsy.'

Milla's face crumples. 'Why can't he stay home for a change? When's Dad going to... come back to us?'

I sense she doesn't mean just from New York.

Resisting tears, I move across the kitchen and take her in my arms. My eldest girl, almost as tall as me now, poised on the cusp of womanhood. Old enough to understand the complications of adult life, but young enough to crave a happy-ever-after.

'His job is... really important. For him and for us,' I say. 'But it's hard when he's gone so long.'

When Andy's been away for a while, I even start to miss the minor irritants of married life; debating politics over dinner, raking up nuisance palm berries in the back yard, arguing over whose turn it is to take out the rubbish.

'It's still dark outside, Millsy, so...' I glance towards my bedroom. 'I'm going to lie down again. I'll be up in about thirty minutes, okay?'

'Sure, Mum.'

As an almost daily witness to Jackson's early-morning shenanigans, Milla doesn't need an explanation. She smiles wanly and returns to her poetry.

Wandering back into the bedroom, I pick up the photo frame on the bedside table, containing a family portrait taken on Jackson's second birthday. A much younger Andy, with a handsome head of salt-and-pepper hair and a relaxed smile, cheerfully restrains Jackson from plunging his hands into the birthday cake. Five-year-old Milla sits on my lap, wriggling with delight as a still energetic version of myself kisses her cheek.

In those early years, when our good humour was still intact, Andy and I referred to Jackson's differences as NQR – *not quite right*. Jackson's chainsaw-like cry as a baby was NQR. The way he resisted nappy changes – smearing faeces across the wall, between his fingers and often on us – was definitely NQR. As a toddler, his capacity to scale bookshelves, benches and fences was within developmental parameters, but still NQR.

It was his kindergarten teacher, Mrs Craig, who queried whether Jackson had ADHD after he started biting his classmates. While the child psychologist we consulted dismissed the ADHD theory, she was more alarmed by Jackson's response to a Rorschach inkblot test.

'What do you see, Jackson?' she prompted, pointing at a black-stained page.

'A prison,' he replied.

'Who's inside?'

'People who hit other people's heads with hammers.'

'Why do they do that, Jackson?'

'They want to find out where the memories are.'

This interaction catapulted Jackson into a consultation with a paediatric psychiatrist who, after conducting his own assessments, proceeded to apply various labels to *parts* of Jackson's experience.

Multiple tic disorder, for the nose-fingering and blinking. *Vulnerability to intrusive thoughts*, describing the unusual ideas that assaulted Jackson's brain, prompting him to cackle with glee or weep with despair. *Sensation-seeking*, explaining his tendency to climb higher, dive deeper and stay upside down longer than any of his peers.

With these assessments complete, the psychiatrist opened a drawer and produced a small packet of medication.

'Try a sample pack of Protazen,' he said, passing the box to me. 'Just to settle Jackson down a bit. If you notice a difference, I'll write you a prescription.'

With no diagnosis and no treatment plan.

'But why would I... medicate Jackson, when we don't know what's wrong?'

The doctor leaned back in his chair, smiling as if we were old friends.

'In my experience, Mrs Curtis, children like Jackson often respond well to low-level medication. Until hopefully, they grow out of... whatever it is they're going through. If they're not over it by the time they're teenagers, then typically we look at something stronger.'

We kept clear of the mental health profession for a long time after that, despite the fact that Jackson's second year at school was marked by a decline in verbal communication and an increase in physical risk-taking. By the third grade, Jackson had endured two broken arms, a shattered femur and a dislocated collarbone, mostly incurred in our own back yard.

When my parents died in the early months of Jackson's fourth grade, a trauma I could barely process myself, a sympathetic hospital social worker suggested that family therapy might serve to help us all. And *that* was how we met Dr Louisa Kelleher, a paediatric psychologist.

'The complexity of Jackson's issues goes beyond a single, unifying diagnosis,' she announced, after our first session together. 'Jackson's inner thoughts are probably more developed than his outer expression allows. We'll work on some practical strategies for better communication across the family system.'

Dr Kelleher has been a critical support for our family ever since.

I place the photoframe on the bedside table again and collapse onto the bed, gazing at the empty side of the mattress.

Over the years, Andy's travel has increased in tandem with the complexity of Jackson's issues. Not by design, I realise, but enough that I've sometimes felt abandoned by Andy. It's seemed indulgent and unfair, with Andy busy breadwinning overseas, so I've always tried to suppress it.

But it can't continue, I recognise now, this unrelenting toll on me.

On *us* as a couple.

Never quite attending to the steady corrosion of unresolved resentments between us.

My gaze lingers on the faded bedsheet strung up as a makeshift curtain across the window, where the Venetians once were. Beyond it, the sunrise is touching the world with its galvanising colours of gold, orange and pink.

I'm not nearly ready to face my Monday morning, so I close my eyes instead.

Just like Jackson, I want to start the day over again.

6

It's the day after Mother's Day, and the sixty-fourth day of school this year. That number reminds me of Dead Granny, because she was only sixty-four when she went to the Otherworld, about twenty years too early.

I'm on my way to school in the Red Rocket with Ruby, she's listening to her music and shimmying in her seat. She's always dancing and humming wherever she goes. Sometimes Ruby's words even come out like a song because she's 'got the family music gene', Mum says.

Mum's driving the Red Rocket, she's got her smart work clothes on and loads of makeup. I didn't get to talk to Dead Granny much in Nanna Pam's car last night, so I decide to try again now. I slide my school-shoe off and press the invisible buttons that usually connect us, but she doesn't pick up.

If Granny's not home in the Otherworld, where *else* can she be?

Mum steers the Red Rocket into the left lane, then reaches forward and turns up the radio. Her eyes are a bit sad this morning, so maybe she's thinking about Granny and Grandpa again, or about Dad in New York. Even though we videocall with him almost every day, it's not the same as hugging him in his pyjamas and sniffing his morning-Dad smell and watching him fix broken stuff with the toolbox that *his* dad made.

There's a loud ad-man yelling out of the radio about 'limited stock' and 'prices can't last' and 'terms and conditions may vary' and the sound is so ugly, I close my eyes. When I do that, suddenly Dead Granny appears right in front of me, pointing down at my shoe-phone.

'Hello, Granny!' I open my eyes and pull my foot over my knee. 'I thought you weren't home.'

Ruby's so focused on her music, she doesn't even notice my shoe-phone.

'I was just taking a bath,' says Granny. I didn't think dead people had bodies to wash, but maybe they give you a new one in the Otherworld? 'How are you, Jack-Jack?'

I decide to tell Granny all about what happened this morning, when the top-knot pigeons were making weird noises outside my attic window. How I turned on my music to drown out the alien-bird sounds, then I hung upside down from my bunk to stop the intruder-thoughts. I dangled there for a long time, looking at my treasures spread across the floor. My fingers could *just* reach the black marker under my bed, so I started drawing on my stomach until suddenly Mum was in the room, all topsy-turvy and telling me I could hurt myself hanging like that and my room was a big mess and didn't I realise how early it was?

'She wasn't happy, Granny,' I say. 'I had to start the day over.'

'Well.' Granny sighs. 'You just need to get your beans out in the morning, don't you?'

Granny really gets me. She understands that every morning

when I wake up, my beans are flying around inside me like popcorn in a pot. They bounce me out of bed and make me want to jump and dance and do a hundred push-ups, even when the rest of the world is sleeping. When I do, Mum gets cranky. And she'd be even crankier if she knew what I did at Digby's house yesterday afternoon in Alt-World.

'I'm itchy,' Ruby whispers, so close to my ear that my shoe-phone screen flickers and Dead Granny vanishes.

Suddenly my shoe-phone is just a shoe, and it's 8.37 on an ordinary Monday morning again.

I turn and look at Ruby. She's knotting up her hair with both hands, scratching. Mum notices this in the rear-vision mirror and brakes so hard, my head almost hits the seat in front.

'You were itchy yesterday too, weren't you?' says Mum. 'I guess we'd better go back and get you something for it. Have we got any antihistamine at home?'

Mum's talking about medicine, but she sounds like she wants to murder someone.

I close my eyes and scan the first aid cupboard with my memory download. I see capsules for headache and syrup for chesty coughs, spray for sinusitis, chocolate tablets for worms and stretchy tape for sore muscles. But there's definitely no antihistamine, only those pills the Bad Brain Doctor gave me when I saw him a few years ago.

I really liked that Bad Brain Doctor, but Mum didn't. He looked a bit like a movie star with bright blue eyes and a black beard and he asked me cool questions like, 'If your dad was an animal, what would he be?' I told him 'A frog,' because I'm learning Mandarin and frogs mean money and hard work in China, and our dad works hard all the time.

The Bad Brain Doctor liked my answers so much he gave

me a packet of blue Smarties and Mum a tiny packet of pills. Afterwards, Mum got into an argument with the lady at the front desk about those pills, then she marched me out of the waiting room and said, 'We're never going back to that doctor again.'

Ruby whimpers and her little hand touches my arm. She's pretty small for a third-grader, which makes her awesome at gymnastics.

'I'm itchy, Jack-Jack.' She's whispering so Mum can't hear.

I'm worried that maybe Ruby's like Cooper in 5T who gets super-itchy when he eats prawns and his face puffs up and he starts to choke and he has to stick a needle in his thigh to breathe again.

'You'll be okay,' I whisper back, then suddenly we're pulling into our driveway. Mum's parking the Red Rocket under the carport and she's in a big rush because all the sick people at Care Cottage are still waiting for her songs.

'Come on, kids!' she yells, so we hop out of the van and go inside to sort out Ruby's itch.

In the kitchen, Mum flings opens the medicine cabinet and starts touching all the bottles and packets. There's no antihistamine, so she grabs a tube of eczema ointment instead.

She turns to Ruby. 'Where exactly does it itch?'

Ruby points to the top of her head. Mum looks worried and parts Ruby's curls with her fingers, then she spits out a single word.

'Nits.'

I look at where she's pointing. There's a bunch of little brown eggs in Ruby's hair and some behind her ears too.

'Where there are nits, there are lice,' says Mum. 'Are you itchy too, Jackson?'

I shake my head, even though I'm imagining gazillions of

little blood-suckers crawling all over me. Then I feel my eyelids
start to twitch and that means I'm *definitely* going to start
motor-blinking. Whenever that happens at school, a lot of kids
laugh and call me *Indicator*. They ask me, 'Are you turning left,
or right?' and I get really embarrassed then, because I can't stop
the blinking.

'Bath time,' announces Mum and we all troop into the
bathroom.

Mum turns on the taps and steam starts floating and
twisting into cool shapes in the air, like the mist that hangs over
Queenscliff beach on cold mornings. I've watched surfers in
that mist, turning their boards across the waves like magic
water-dancers.

'I don't want a bath!' whines Ruby. 'It's not night-time yet.'

'But you've got nits, hon,' says Mum. 'We have to comb
them out with a special conditioner, remember?'

We've done this loads of times before. So Ruby sits down in
the bath and I sit on the toilet seat beside Mum and she
squeezes the conditioner onto Ruby's hair.

'I'm sorry, Rubes,' says Mum, scraping the steel lice comb
through her hair.

'Ouch!' Ruby shrieks so loudly, it reminds me of the lady in
Alt-World.

Mum opens the tissue in her palm and shows us the lice
floating in the cream, six-legged bugs all fat with Ruby's blood.

Ruby screams. 'Get them out, Mummy!'

'I am, hon,' says Mum, but it takes forever because Ruby's
curls are tricky like Goldilocks. I try to help Mum, but she just
keeps saying, 'Wait, Jackson!'

Eventually, Mum hands Ruby a towel and says, 'Done,
Rubes.'

Ruby stands up in the bath and I lean forward to see if her private parts are like the lady's in Alt-World.

'Stop it, Jackson,' snaps Mum.

Ruby doesn't care, but Mum looks really cross and embarrassed and a bit sad too, so I'm guessing she won't be any happier if I tell her about Alt-World.

Mum reaches into the bath and pulls out the plug, and it's like the whole world's being sucked down to hell. The water's wailing and guzzling, I have to squeeze my eyes shut and cover my ears to stop the sound. By the time I open my eyes again, Mum's rinsing out the lice comb.

'You're a bit young for puberty, Jackson,' she says in a disappointed sort of voice.

I learned about puberty in term one when this big friendly giraffe called Healthy Harold came to visit our school. A lady called Sheila rolled a plastic wrapper called a condom onto a banana and it was hilarious. Then Healthy Harold told us about all the human flavours, like lesbian and gay and intersex and bisexual and transgender. I think maybe Anohni who sings 'Hope There's Someone' is one of those flavours, her voice is so different and wonderful.

'Get dressed, hon,' says Mum, waving Ruby out of the bathroom. 'I need to check your hair now, Jackson.'

'I don't have nits.'

Mum just ignores me because she's *always* worried about stuff that never happens. Like strangers in cars who kidnap kids, or housefires that start in the night, or Milla wearing skirts that accidentally show her undies when she bends over, or letting me go into the men's toilets by myself at Beachcomber Mall, even though I always remember to close the seat and flush every time.

'Lice spread quickly, Jackson.' Mum takes up the comb again.

I sit down on the bathmat and it doesn't take her three seconds to spot some.

'Bingo.' Mum sighs. 'Take off your shirt, please.'

I unbutton my school shirt and she squeezes out a big slop of conditioner, then she massages my head a bit, just like Karen our hairdresser who's got super long fake nails that feel really nice.

But it's not so nice when she starts using the comb.

'Too hard!' I yell, but Mum just keeps on scraping like she's raking up palm berries in the back yard.

'Think about something else,' says Mum. 'How was your playdate with Digby yesterday afternoon?'

'It wasn't a playdate. I'm in Grade Five now.'

'Okay,' she says. 'Nanna Pam said you had a nice time. Who picked you up after soccer training, Miranda or Will?'

'Coach dropped us home,' I explain. 'Coach drops Digby home every Sunday night after training.'

'Oh.' Mum sounds surprised. 'No one mentioned that to me. Well, that's very nice of Steve. And who was at home when you got to Digby's?'

'Will,' I answer.

She wipes more nits onto a tissue. 'And what did you two do together at Digby's?'

Mum's always grilling me like this, especially after school. She always wants to know what I did at lunchtime, who I played with and what I ate.

'Nothing much.' My head stings a lot.

'But you must've done something. Did you have a snack after training?'

'Will gave us muffins,' I say. 'Then he had to go to work.'

'What, he left the two of you by yourselves at home?' Mum's voice turns high-pitched.

'No, he just went into his home office, so we played on Digby's laptop.'

Mum doesn't look too happy about that either.

'We didn't play shoot-em-up games,' I say, trying to make her feel better.

'How long did you play on the computer?'

'Not that long. Digby's lucky, his dad lets him play games online all the time.'

Mum's face tells me that she's about to go into a frenzy.

'It doesn't matter what other children do, or their parents for that matter. You know what Dr Kelleher says about screen time. What exactly did you play on the computer, Jackson?'

My mouth's gone dry and I feel a bit sick. She's already cranky about the laptop, so there's no way I can tell her about the lady with no trousers.

'Kirby's,' I say. That's Ruby's favourite game, about a big bouncy ball of yarn that bobs around a maze collecting interesting things like marshmallows and gemstones and crystal goblets on twenty-seven different levels.

'That sounds a bit young for you.' Mum looks at me hard. Maybe she knows I'm not telling the whole truth, she's pretty good at reading minds.

I say nothing.

After a while, Mum breathes out super slowly. A nice man called Andy from Headspace taught her that.

'Well, overall, did you have a good time with Digby?'

I want to tell her that I liked Digby for his quietness and his soccer skills and his big Google house, but I didn't like how he bossed me around and told me not to tell anyone about what happened in Alt-World.

'Sort of,' I say.

Mum's combing my hair really fast now and muttering about getting to Care Cottage by 9.30.

'Get changed please, Jackson,' she says, tossing the comb into the bath.

She heads out into the hallway, humming a tune that she's planning to sing to the Special Ps.

I dry off and pull on my uniform and sprint down the hallway to the front door where Mum's already waiting for both of us.

'Ruby!' Mum barks. 'Where are you?'

'Mummy!' Ruby runs out of her bedroom. 'It's Pyjama Day!'

Mum blinks a few times, which sets me off too. The only way I can stop it now is to do a headstand for a while, but I can't do that because we're already running late.

'What's Pyjama Day?' Mum's voice is spooky-calm.

'Here's a note,' says Ruby. She's waving it around like a white flag and then I remember the announcement Crazy Daisy made about it at last Friday's assembly.

'It's only for Year Three,' I tell Mum. 'It's a fundraiser.'

Mum snatches the note out of Ruby's hands and begins to read.

'All right, go get your pyjamas back on,' she says, but her lips are all pinched-up.

Ruby's eyes turn watery. 'I'm... sorry I forgot, Mummy. Jackson would've remembered.'

The sight of Ruby crying does something to Mum.

'No darling, I'm the one who should be sorry.' She lets out this really big breath and her face goes all droopy. 'Lateness can't kill us. Don't be too hard on yourself, you've got a lot on.'

Ruby smiles at Mum, then disappears into her room.

Usually we're running late for school when we've forgotten

our lunches or Ruby's slept in or Dad calls from New York five minutes before we're due to leave. But we've never been late because of nits and Pyjama Day.

'This is atypical lateness,' I tell Mum.

Mum looks at me for a moment, then laughs out loud. She sounds a bit like a chicken squawking, which makes me laugh too.

'You're right, Jackson.' Mum chuckles. 'In this family, we even run late in unusual ways. Thanks, hon, I needed that.'

Ruby trots out of her room in a fluffy pink dressing gown and sequined purple Ugg boots. She looks like she's ready for bed again, only her school bag's strapped to her back.

We all march out of the house and into the Red Rocket for the second time. I check the clock on the dashboard: it's 9.22 and school started at 9.05, so we'll definitely need a late note from the front office.

'Did you pack your lunches?' Mum asks, as we drive along Seaview Street. 'Please say yes.'

'I packed them,' I tell her.

'What's on our sandwiches?' asks Ruby, plugging her headphones into Mum's old iPhone. 'Salami?'

'Egg,' I reply.

Ruby wrinkles up her nose. Salami is her favourite and she *hates* curried egg.

'Thanks for packing them, Jackson,' Mum says. 'Little things like that make a big difference to me.'

Her smile in the rear-view mirror makes me feel toasty inside.

'What are you listening to?' I ask Ruby.

'Antony,' she replies, so loudly it makes my brain jangle. Ruby speaks too loudly whenever she's wearing headphones.

'Antony who?' Mum asks.

'Antony and the Johnsons,' says Ruby. 'It's Jackson's favourite song.'

'But that singer's not Antony any more,' I correct her. 'It's Anohni. He's become the she he was, all along.'

Ruby ignores me, she's too busy listening to 'Hope There's Someone', the song I'm dancing to at the Winter Eisteddfod.

'What's that?' Mum's accelerating so fast that the dashboard alarm beeps. Mum set that up after the police caught Dad speeding last time.

'Antony was a migrant girl inside a boy's body,' I explain. 'So she changed her name to Anohni to find her way home.'

'I have absolutely no idea what you're talking about, Jackson.' Mum shakes her head.

I can't explain it any better, so I just stare out the window, wondering how all those birds sitting on telegraph wires don't get deep-fried by the electricity. It's dangerous up there, and as high as I'll be flying on aerial silks at the eisteddfod.

We pull into the Kiss-N-Go zone. There's no one else there, because the bell rang ages ago.

'It's okay, you're just a few minutes late,' says Mum. She looks a bit happier now.

I start telling her that we'll need a signed late note, but she's already waving us out of the Red Rocket and blowing kisses and saying 'Bye-bye darlings' and the door of the van's shutting behind us and then we're both standing cold on the footpath with our hair still wet from the lice shampoo.

Ruby starts to blubber.

'What's wrong?' I ask, watching Mum drive away.

'I want a proper kiss and a hug.'

I put my arm around her, just like Mum does. 'It's okay Rubes.'

We walk through the school gate.

'Take me to class please, Jack-Jack?'

I don't bother about late notes, I just walk with Ruby to Mrs Reilly's room. We look through the window first and I see the kids from 3R listening to a story from a chapter book.

I turn to Ruby and fix up one of the plaits she's tried to braid herself on our way to school, it's already unravelling a bit. Then I knock on the door because Ruby's feeling a bit shy and Mrs Reilly calls out, 'Come in!'

'Good morning, Ruby.' The teacher has this beautiful smile that sort of hugs you without touching you. I'm thinking that maybe *I* could stay in 3R for today and Mrs Reilly could use me as a helper or something, but she turns to me and says, 'Thanks, dear,' in a way that tells me I have to leave.

I don't want to go to 5T, with Mr Thompson who's super-strict.

As Mrs Reilly shuffles me out the door, I turn to wave at Ruby but she's not looking at me any more, she's already chatting to her best friend, Tessa.

I walk really slowly across the playground.

When I get to 5T, I knock on the door and Mr Thompson calls out, 'Yesss?' I push open the door and he's standing at the front of the class like a praying mantis, with his stick legs and arms and bug eyes.

'Where's your late note, Curtisss?'

Mr Thompson calls everyone by their surnames even though we're not allowed to call him just 'Thompson' – I found that out in my first week at Queenscliff Public.

'Mum said I didn't need one.'

Mr Thompson looks peeved. 'Perhaps your mother needs to reacquaint herself with the school handbook?'

He points to my desk, which means I should sit down.

I kind of fall into my seat and try not to look at April

Kennedy. Her desk is diagonal to mine and if I move my eyes a bit to the left, I can see her long black hair and skin that's white as a cloud. It's much softer than mine, I touched her hand last term when our pencil cases got mixed up. Her skin was so soft it made my stomach go all buzzy.

Mr Thompson is teaching science and trying to be interesting and funny, but it's not working. He's doing a rhyming rap about 'Earth's place in space as a base for the human race' and waggling his head in an uncool way. Then he starts talking about 'celestial motions' and because 'motion' is the word Nanna Pam uses for poop, I laugh out loud.

'Something amusing you, Curtisss?' Mr Thompson hisses in his snaky voice.

You're teaching us about heavenly poops, I want to say. Only angels can do those.

My lips keep wobbling, even though I've asked them to stop.

'What's the earth's daily rotation called, Curtisss?' Mr Thompson's eyes are slaughtering me now.

I scan my memory download from the last lesson, about the line that runs through the north and south poles. That same line makes water go down the plughole in different directions depending on where you are in the world and then – *bang* – suddenly I remember the name for the earth's daily rotation.

'Di-urinal motion,' I say.

Mr Thompson's eyes bulge even more.

The class falls about laughing and I'm confused but kind of pleased because everyone's giggling in a good way, even April Kennedy.

Then suddenly I figure out what I've actually said.

'Diurnal! I mean, diurnal motion!' I'm trying to make it

right but it's too late, Mr Thompson's face has turned a wicked shade of purple.

'So now you're the class clown, Curtisss?' Mr Thompson's voice is so dangerous I want to dive under my desk. 'Take yourself off to the urinal then, since you're so clever. It's a shame your mother hasn't toilet-trained you by Year Five.'

The class is deadly quiet. My hands are slippery and my eyelids are twitching and I want to kill Mr Thompson for mentioning Mum again.

'Go on, Curtisss, off to the toilets,' he says. 'You can think about your behaviour on the way.'

I stand out of my chair so quickly it tips over backwards and hits the floor with a clang. April Kennedy gasps, which is strange because she's not the one in trouble.

'Watch it, Curtisss,' Mr Thompson growls. 'Or you can go straight from the toilets to the principal's office.'

I try not to look at anyone as I walk to the door, then I notice Digby's hand shoot straight up in the air.

'Yes, Bianco?'

'I'm sorry, sir, but I need to go to the toilet too.'

Mr Thompson looks suspiciously between Digby and me.

'Fine, go with Curtis.'

Trying to get out of that classroom is like wading through wet sand. Just when it feels like I'm going to be stuck there forever, my fingers reach the door handle and I'm pushing it open to freedom and then I'm out in the clean eucalyptus air where I can breathe again. Digby grins at me and suddenly I know he's the best friend I could ever ask for.

We walk under the Moreton Bay Fig, dodging the sticky lumps of fruit on the asphalt. As we pass the canteen, the whiff of raspberry muffins and hot cheese rolls and meat pies makes my stomach rumble even though a moment ago, I was feeling sick. The delicious smells don't last long though, because soon we're getting closer to the toilets. Walking along in the opposite direction is a third-grader all dressed up for Pyjama Day.

She looks a bit like Ruby, with a pink nightie and tan Ugg boots and a fluffy white robe with a floppy hoodie. She's got a long blonde ponytail and she's wearing spectacles with really thick glass inside them. I recognise her face from somewhere, but she's not in Ruby's class. Her Ugg boots make this squeaky sound as she walks into the girls' side of the toilets.

We're right outside the toilet block now and I don't actually need to pee, so I just stop and wait for Digby to go in. I'm remembering how Mr Thompson thought I was being rude on purpose, when actually I just got the word *diurnal* mixed up with *urinal*. That happens a lot. All the words I've ever seen, even the foreign ones, are stuck in my memory download and get jumbled, especially when I try to move them out of my mouth.

Digby turns to me and says, 'Come on, Curtis.'

He sounds a bit like Mr Thompson. I don't like that very much, but I follow him anyway because he's my friend. Then I notice that we're walking into the *girls'* side of the toilets.

'It's the girls',' I say, in case he's forgotten.

But Digby doesn't hear me, he's too busy looking inside each cubicle. I'm wondering what he's lost in there.

There are pink-coloured tiles on the wall above the hand-basins, and the pattern they make looks a bit like a chess board. If I put a rook at h1 and move my queen to f5, I'll checkmate the white king at h5. It smells a lot better in here than the boys' toilets, but there's a strange whining in the pipes that sounds like cats yowling.

Digby stops walking and I almost bump into him from behind.

'Let's play a trick on her,' he says.

I blink a few times, wondering who *she* is, then I remember the third-grader who's in here too. She must be in the cubicle at the end of the row, that's the only one with the door closed. I'm wondering if Digby can remember her name, then I feel a massive blinking attack coming on.

'What's wrong with you?' Digby whispers, staring at the blink-blink-blinking.

'Nothing,' I say, trying to control my eyelids.

He screws up his nose as if he doesn't want to be my friend any more.

I follow him to the end of the row of toilets and Digby points at the closed door of the last cubicle. 'I'll play the trick. You guard the door.'

I can hear the gushing sound of the girl's pee and I don't like it, so I cover my ears with my hands. Digby pulls them away from my ears as the toilet flushes.

'Stand there,' he whispers, pointing to one side of the door. 'I'm going in.'

He creeps forward, maybe because he's going to jump out at the girl and yell 'Boo!' I do that to Ruby at home a lot. I just hope the girl won't scream as loudly as Ruby, because sometimes she's as screechy as an ambulance siren.

Digby nods at me like we're secret agents waiting to pounce.

The door opens and Digby jumps forward and bundles the girl back into the cubicle. He's so quick I don't even see her. The girl gives a little yelp but it's much softer than Ruby's, then the door slams shut behind them.

I just stand there, looking at the pink chessboard tiles and pulling martial arts poses and making cool 'Hwaaa!' sounds. Suddenly I remember the girl's name: it's Sienna Wilson-Brown, she's Tommy's little sister. Tommy is the best striker in our Under-Eleven Dragons team, I've seen his sister at the soccer field before with their super pretty mum.

I'm wondering if Digby's tickling Sienna, but I can't hear any laughing. After a while, I crouch down to see what's happening. All I can see is four legs and the edge of Sienna's nightie, it's got gold stars on the hem and one of her Ugg boots has slipped off and turned over in a puddle near the toilet. I reach under the door to stand it up because no one likes wet slippers. As I do, I accidentally touch her leg.

My eyelids are going nuts now, so I pull myself up again and put one hand on the door and the other over my eyelids. I'm stretching the skin tight to stop them blinking, when suddenly I hear the girl cry out, 'Stop, I don't like it.'

She sounds scared so I push hard at the door, then I start banging on it. I don't stop until Digby yanks it open and shoves me backwards, knocking me onto the wet floor.

He stands over me, scowling. 'Let's go.'

I turn to check on Sienna, but the cubicle door has swung shut.

We leave the toilets and start walking back across the playground to 5T, but

I'm wondering why Digby pushed me over and what Sienna didn't like.

'Didn't Sienna like the trick?'

'You wrecked it before the good bit.' Digby snorts. 'She was just a cry-baby. Don't tell anyone, okay? It's our secret.'

That's the second time he's asked me to keep a secret, and I didn't like the first one. I want to ask why this is a secret too, but Digby's already talking about soccer on Saturday and how we're playing a super tough team called the Tornadoes.

We move around the back of the canteen and suddenly Miss Marion the dance teacher is standing right in front of us.

She smiles like a real Fairy Godmother. 'Hi boys.'

Today her crazy socks are stripy green with a little black bowtie behind each ankle. She's carrying a clipboard and a KeepCup full of coffee because it's almost time for recess.

'Don't forget, Jackson, dance rehearsal this Saturday afternoon in the school hall. Only four weeks until Winter Eisteddfod.'

I nod, even though I still haven't told Mum or Dad about my dancing yet and I don't know how to before Saturday's practice.

'Good.' Miss Marion twirls on her flat black ballet slippers and walks off in the direction of the staff room.

'What dance rehearsal?' asks Digby, as we start out across the playground again. 'Is your sister dancing in something?'

Digby's favourite sports are soccer and rugby, so he definitely won't be interested in my eisteddfod.

I pretend I didn't hear him and Digby doesn't care.

He's already talking about Saturday's match again, but I'm not listening to his words.

I can't stop thinking about Sienna's wet slipper.

7

I'm standing shivering on the soccer sideline on a chilly Saturday morning, counting my blessings. It's all part of the *gratitude practice* prescribed by our family therapist. Most days, it's easy enough for me to summon appreciation for a job that I love, three energetic kids, and a quaint fixer-upper near the beach. Other days, I feel like ripping the Master of Psychology (Clinical Child Psychology) off Dr Kelleher's wall and hurling it, Frisbee-like, from her second-storey window.

'Hi Julia.'

Recognising the voice, I turn to greet Jackson's soccer coach.

'Hi Steve. How are you?'

Steve and his family relocated to Sydney from a small rural town in South Australia five years ago, but his country characteristics remain. He's chatty and laconic and, with two daughters who play only netball, he's chosen to channel his passion for soccer into coaching other people's sons. This season, he's a lucky windfall for our Under-Eleven Dragons team.

'Not bad, thanks,' he says, propping up a freestanding sign that reads:

This is a game. The players are children.
The coaches and referees are volunteers.
Please respect others.

'Ready for another big game?' he asks.

'Another big game of cheering,' I reply.

'You'd do all right on the field.' He looks me up and down. 'You're sporty enough for it. Ever played?'

I shake my head, aware that I'm blushing. Aware too that I shouldn't be.

'Thanks for dropping Jackson back with Digby after soccer training last Sunday,' I say, steering the conversation towards more comfortable territory. 'I hope you didn't go out of your way?'

'Nope.' Steve shrugs. 'Digby's place is five minutes from the oval. I drop him back most Sundays, Miranda and Will are pretty busy with their work.'

'Everyone's busy.' I sigh. 'Life didn't feel this frantic when I was growing up.'

'I reckon.' Steve presses a wayward divot of turf into place with the toe of his trainer. 'We all do too much, then we totally over-schedule our kids. It's crazy.'

I nod, rather guiltily. Sometimes when I'm reversing the seven-seater out of our driveway, scrambling to get to some trifling activity, I wonder if *this* will be my children's core memory of *mother*. A weary, snippy woman, screeching random orders from the driver's seat: 'We're late, strap in, let's go!'

My own childhood couldn't have been more different. Spending lengthy weekends at Kaminski's Dry Cleaners, scratching out imaginary lands on the shop floor with ragged stubs of chalk. Helping my parents clean, press and steam our way to a better future, one collared shirt at a time.

'How's Jackson doing at the moment?' asks Steve, laying out rope ladders across the grass.

I don't have to manufacture my gratitude now. When I first told Steve about Jackson's neurodiversity – explaining that his verbal skills lagged his age by roughly four years – Steve simply observed, 'Well, he doesn't need to be a good conversationalist on the soccer pitch, does he?'

Other parents have been less forgiving, including at Jackson's old school where we were progressively shunned by parents variously irritated or disturbed by Jackson's unusual behaviours.

'Thanks for asking, Steve,' I reply. 'Jackson's settled in pretty well. But he loves his soccer more than school, thanks to you.'

Steve looks slightly embarrassed. 'Where's the rest of the family today?'

'The girls have gone to gymnastics with my mother-in-law,' I say. 'She helps out a lot when Andy's away.'

'Right.' Steve extracts a set of plastic cones from the equipment bag. 'And will Andy... be okay to coach in my place on Monday arvo? I've got that conference in Melbourne I told him about. I won't get back in time.'

I vaguely recall this arrangement, but Andy's still in New York.

'Andy's away, I'm afraid. But don't worry,' I add, feeling responsible somehow that Andy has failed to organise an alternative. 'If you need someone to take the training... then I will.'

'Really? Good on you.' Steve seems impressed by this false bravado. 'What are your plans for tomorrow, Julia?'

For one wild moment, I imagine that Steve is about to ask me out.

'Probably just taking the kids to visit my mother-in-law,' I say, after a pause. 'We do that most Sundays.'

Steve laughs heartily, and I realise I grimaced.

'Daresay you're not the first woman to feel that way about her mother-in-law.' He rubs the lenses of his sunglasses with the hem of his t-shirt. 'Clichés are usually based on something.'

'Indeed.' A music therapist from Sydney's western suburbs hadn't quite been Pamela's idea of a perfect match for Andy, I suspect. She'd been frosty for the first few years of our marriage, thawing only when Milla came along.

'She adores the kids,' I say, attempting a positive reframe. 'And I'm sure I haven't been the perfect daughter-in-law.'

Steve motions at a stack of plastic cones. 'Could you lay these out for me, Jules?'

'Of course,' I say, pleased to have a task.

More soccer parents are streaming onto the sidelines now, but I can't remember all of their names. It's hard keeping track when the only thing we have in common is the fact our children play soccer together. If only I had Jackson's powers of retention.

I cast a fixed smile in their direction as I move across the pitch.

'Hi, Jules!' calls Hannah Wilson-Brown, whose name no one *ever* forgets. With a mane of auburn hair, limbs cling-wrapped in active wear and hefty marquise diamonds adorning her earlobes, Hannah delivers improbable levels of glamour to the role of soccer mum.

I smile and wave at Sienna, her daughter, who holds tightly to her hand. Despite the thick-lens spectacles perched on her nose, Sienna is as eye-catching as her mother. The little girl seems uncharacteristically solemn this morning, however, and doesn't wave back.

'All righty, Dragons!' Steve snaps the players and parents to attention. 'Warm-up!'

The boys assemble in two lines and Jackson begins a passing drill with his friend, Digby.

Setting out the final cone, I jog back to the sideline where Lola, the Brazilian-born mother of goalie Eddie, is now standing next to Hannah.

'Hellooo, Julia!' Lola pronounces my name 'Yulia', which sounds far more exotic than I feel on a Saturday morning. She air-kisses me three times. 'How are you?'

'Good, thanks.' I admire Lola's luminous skin, charcoal eyes and fine, arched eyebrows. 'How are things with you, Lola?'

'Well, you know. Eddie never wants to get out of bed... I call and call until I have to drag him out, then he just floats around the house looking for his football boots, his socks, his jocks...'

'Oh, I hear you,' Hannah chimes in. 'Tommy's the same. We turned the house upside down looking for shin pads this morning, then Sienna started crying for no apparent reason. I barely had time for a shower and I hate going out with wet hair...'

I mime frustration, secretly coveting *exactly* this kind of Saturday morning. A baseline level of parental wrangling with an average pre-teen boy, where the only negative consequence of failure might be a 'bad hair day'.

How would Lola and Hannah cope, I wonder, if exposed to *my* brand of difficulty with Jackson, every single day? I'll never know, of course, because I can't reveal any of it. If Jackson's condition was physical – a rare disease, childhood leukaemia or even a clear psychiatric diagnosis – it might be easier to talk about.

Lola and Hannah bow their heads over Hannah's phone, scrolling through images of her Mother's Day luncheon at an exclusive yacht club six days ago.

I try not to feel envious. Even now, I couldn't possibly take Jackson anywhere involving white linen and fine glassware.

'Righto Dragons!' Steve's voice draws me back to the football pitch. 'Into positions!'

The Dragons take to the field facing the Tornadoes, a rough-looking mob of boys who appear built more for rugby than soccer.

One long blow of the referee's whistle signals kick-off.

Almost immediately, a pug-faced father on the opposite sideline begins to holler at his son. 'On your player, Cooper! Kick it up the field!'

Lola, Hannah and I exchange glances.

'Rip into 'em, Tornadoes!' the vocaliser bellows.

The first half of the game is played mostly in mid-field. Despite valiant attacks on both sides, neither team manages to convert. At half-time the Dragons walk off the pitch, sweaty and red-faced. They huddle around a tub of frozen oranges, sucking loudly at the rinds. Several fathers loiter at the edges as Steve speaks, listening to his advice to 'pass early' and 'take chances', before taking their boys aside for further personal pointers.

I hear Digby's father, Will – a tall, well-groomed financier – exhort Digby to 'kick it like I showed you'.

It's not the World Cup, I think.

A long sharp whistle signals recommencement of play. As the boys run back onto the pitch, the outspoken Tornadoes father moves closer to his fellow supporters. Even at a distance, his words are still audible.

'Stay on your player, Cooper!'

Hannah's son, Tommy, intercepts at kick-off, booting the ball towards the centre circle. Jackson sprints to reach it first. He deftly passes it into open space in front of Digby, who powers forward and shoots. The Tornadoes' goalie leaps left as the ball soars right.

'Goal!'

The Dragons whoop and cheer, crowding around Digby and slapping him on the back. The Tornadoes' goalie lies on his stomach, thumping his fist into the dirt.

'Great goal, Digby!' calls Steve. 'Killer pass, Jackson!'

Steve turns and gives me the thumbs-up sign, while Lola and Hannah continue clapping. Suddenly little Sienna bursts into tears.

'What's the matter, sweetie?' Hannah crouches down next to her daughter.

The girl throws her arms around her mother's neck.

'Shhh,' says Hannah. 'What's wrong?'

Sienna shakes her head and says nothing.

Over the top of her daughter's hair, Hannah rolls her eyes at me. 'Let's stand up and support the team, Sienna.'

Digby and Jackson are still cavorting around the field. Digby lifts his shirt over his head and runs across the pitch, his arms outstretched. Jackson copies him, exposing – to my dismay – the black thatching of his early-morning stomach art.

Sienna scowls at her mother. 'I want to go home.'

'We have to wait until the game's finished, darling.'

'I want to go home now.'

'Well, we can't.' Hannah tries to extricate herself from her daughter's grip, prising at her fingers. 'Let go of me.'

Sienna shrieks and falls onto the grass, weeping.

'What a tantrum about nothing.' Hannah steps around her daughter and leans toward me. 'I don't think she likes it when other children get all the attention.'

'Muuummmy,' whimpers Sienna.

'You're too old for this,' Hannah groans. 'What's gotten into you?'

'Look!' Lola points at the field, where a player is dribbling the ball at speed towards the Tornadoes' goal.

'Shoot, Cooper!' his father yells. 'For God's sake, shoot!'

Jackson tackles the boy head-on, swiftly relieving him of the ball.

Cooper's father explodes from the sideline. 'Hey ref, call the foul!'

The referee ignores him.

'That was a foul by number nine!' The man points an accusatory finger at Jackson. 'Are you bloody blind?'

Instantly, the game grinds to a halt. The referee strides off the field and speaks with the spectator, gesticulating at the sign.

Children. Volunteers. Respect.

'It wasn't a foul,' mutters Lola. 'Jackson's been playing so well.'

The referee is shaking his head, while another parent implores Cooper's father to settle down.

On the field, Jackson's fists are clenching and unclenching as he stands observing the altercation. In that moment, I want to run onto the field and explain to Jackson that this loud-mouthed father is behaving like a child himself. But how can Jackson learn to self-regulate if I constantly intervene in complicated situations?

I send all my telepathic encouragement instead.

Jackson doesn't seem to absorb it, scuffing at the ground with his boots.

Steve appears at my side.

'Out of respect for the ref, Jules, I'm keeping my cool. But if that idiot doesn't back off soon, I'll go over and fight for Jackson.'

I realise I've been holding my breath. 'Thank you, Steve.'

A minute later, Cooper's father retreats.

'Bloody selfish,' says Steve. 'I'm going to report that guy to his own club.'

'I'm glad,' says Hannah. 'There's way too much testosterone at these matches.'

'But I've seen women do it too,' counters Steve. 'It's just stupid bloody parents convinced their kid's going to be the next Socceroo. Look, both sides have completely lost their mojo now because a parent wrecked the magic.'

Steve's right; the final few minutes of the game are a lack-lustre affair. When the referee signals time, the boys shake hands mechanically. The Dragons' victory feels hollow, somehow.

As the players move off the field, Steve calls the team over.

'Well done, boys.' He crouches down among them. 'That was a tough game, but you held on.'

Digby's father, Will, suddenly tosses an open packet of jelly snakes into the huddle and the boys fall on it, snatching up as many as they can.

Steve waits for the commotion to settle.

'I'd like to present Dragon of the Week.' He lifts a colourful toy dragon, the team's mascot, from the kit. 'This week's award goes to a player who kept passing to his team mates and put up with some unfair abuse from a parent. Congratulations, Jackson Curtis!'

Jackson stands to accept the mascot. Grinning, he thrusts it into the air.

This is real progress for Jackson, I think, snapping several shots with my phone.

'One last thing, Dragons,' continues Steve. 'Training is on as usual tomorrow, but I can't be here for Monday's session. Jackson's Mum will take the training instead. Let's give her a round of applause.'

One of the Dragons casts a disbelieving look in my direction. 'A mum?'

'Yes, mate. Her name's Julia and she's just as sporty as any Dad. So you'd better listen to her, or there'll be consequences.'

The other mothers of the group titter. I can't help but wonder whether Steve's wife realises how lucky she is.

'All righty, boys,' Steve grins. 'Well done to you all. Enjoy your Saturday arvo.'

The parents and boys clap, then slowly begin to disperse.

'Have a good weekend,' Lola calls to me as she moves off with Eddie.

'You too, Lola,' I call back.

'What are you up to this weekend?' Hannah asks, studiously ignoring the still snivelling Sienna.

'Oh, nothing much. You?'

'We're doing lunch at Miyaki today,' Hannah enthuses. 'It's got an eighteen-month waiting list! Can you imagine?'

I certainly can, especially Hannah's social media feed tomorrow: #blessed #spoiled #envymylife.

'Come on, kids.' Hannah rounds up Tommy and tugs at Sienna's hand. 'See you at training on Monday, Julia. If you need any help, let me know?'

'Thanks, I might take you up on that.' I wave at Sienna, who hides her face behind her mother's waist.

Picking up Jackson's water bottle, I hold it out for him as he barrels down the sideline. When he reaches me, he throws his arms around me.

'I'm so proud of you, Dragon of the Match.' I kiss the top of his head. 'Dad will be, too.'

Jackson looks up at me. 'Will you always be proud of me, Mum?'

'Always.'

'No matter what?'

I study his face. 'Is something wrong?'

Jackson gazes at the ground. 'Mum, I...'

Digby materialises next to us, hopping from one foot to the other. 'Can Jackson come over please, Mrs Curtis?'

Instantly, Jackson pulls out of our embrace.

'You two had a playdate last Sunday after training,' I smile at Digby. 'Aren't you sick of each other by now?'

Jackson's elation evaporates. I've said exactly the wrong thing, it seems.

Digby motions at his father. 'My dad said it's okay.'

I look over at Will, who's busy kicking a soccer ball around with Rory, Digby's younger brother.

Jackson sits down on the grass and turns over his soccer boot, fingering the studs on the sole. It's clear to me exactly where this is headed.

'Enjoy your weekend.' Steve walks past us, hauling a bag of equipment over his shoulder.

'Bye, Coach,' replies Jackson dully.

'Hey, Jackson.' Steve drops the bag and turns. 'I think I saw something interesting on your stomach earlier. Can I see it again?'

He crouches down next to Jackson.

'Oh, it's just...' I begin, but before I can prevent it, Jackson raises his shirt.

Steve studies the jumble of numbers and letters on Jackson's belly, tracing his forefinger in the air. 'Checkmated the King at E6,' he observes. 'You like chess?'

Jackson beams. 'Yes, Coach.'

I squint at the black markings on Jackson's stomach, incredulous that Steve has deciphered something intelligible – even inspiring – there.

Steve turns to me and smiles. 'They all learn differently, huh?'

'I... had no idea,' I falter.

He stands up and hoists the bag back over his shoulder again. 'See you next weekend, Julia.'

Open-mouthed, I watch Steve walk towards the carpark.

'Can Jackson come over, Mrs Curtis?' Digby presses. 'Please?'

Jackson almost never receives such invitations, yet Digby seems keen to develop the friendship. Meanwhile, Jackson's soccer coach just detected a chessboard on his stomach when I, his mother, could see only graffiti. Maybe it's *me* who's NQR.

'All right Digby,' I say, overriding my natural reticence. 'I'll pick you up at two o'clock, Jackson.'

Digby whoops and throws an arm around Jackson's shoulders. Four hours is a generous playdate, compared to the hour they spent together last Sunday evening.

Digby races over to tell his father, half-dragging Jackson with him.

Will looks up as I approach. 'Is Jackson coming over?' he asks, a little brusquely.

'Thanks for having him again,' I smile. 'My mother-in-law said they had a lot of fun last Sunday.'

In all truth, Pamela had said more about Will's appearance – 'Digby's father looks just like a Renaissance sculpture!' – than anything else.

I hesitate, considering how to couch my concerns. 'I should let you know that, er... Jackson can be quite... rambunctious at times.'

Will cocks his head. Perhaps *rambunctious* isn't a word he hears frequently in financial services.

'He... gets a bit wild if he has too much sugar,' I explain, 'so we don't let him eat much junk food at home.'

I don't disclose how Jackson once consumed an entire block of chocolate, donned a Spiderman outfit and ended up on the neighbour's side of the fence, with a gash to the scalp that needed nine stitches in emergency.

'We also... don't let Jackson have much screen time at home, it revs him up too much. If they go on the computer again...'

'I'll keep an eye on it,' says Will, humouring me.

All the other parents have gone home now, replaced by a throng of unfamiliar faces congregating for the next game.

If Andy was here, he'd tell me to stop over-sharing. But he isn't, so I don't.

'The thing is, Will,' – I glance around to ensure that Jackson is a distance away, still playing with Digby and Rory – 'Jackson can be a bit of a troublemaker, without even trying.'

Will sniffs. 'Can't be any more trouble than Digby.'

'Are you certain Miranda doesn't mind us imposing on your weekend?'

Will snorts. 'Miranda's going out with her mothers' group today, so I'm the one on duty. It's a belated Mother's Day celebration for them.'

'Oh.' I attempt to process this. I'd simply *assumed* that Miranda, Digby's mother, would be at home as a benign presence, if not actively overseeing the boys. But how can I revoke my permission now, on the basis that Will is a father? On the assumption that mothers are somehow more responsible, more aware, more capable than their menfolk? It's exactly the kind of discrimination I object to when directed at women.

'Come on, you three,' Will calls out to the boys. 'Let's get going.'

What would Andy do?

Children spend time at other people's houses all the time, he'd tell me. Jackson is in the fifth grade and making new friends; we cannot monitor his every move or manage every aspect of his neurodiversity. It's time to embrace small steps towards independence for Jackson.

Will turns to me. 'I'm happy to drop Jackson home later if that helps?'

'That's all right,' I say. 'I'll collect him at two o'clock.'

I turn back to Jackson. 'This is going to be the longest play-date you've ever had in your life!'

The smile Jackson returns me is half-hearted, and I cannot fathom why. He's just been granted more time with a friend than he's ever been allowed.

'Bye, sweetheart. See you at two.'

As Jackson walks away at Will's side, he looks so small that I feel an overwhelming urge to call him back.

'Remember the family rules, okay?' I call after him instead.

8

I'm the salami in the sandwich between Digby and Rory in the back of Will's car. I don't even *want* to be going back to Digby's, I just want to call Dead Granny. It'll be tricky using my shoe-phone though, because Digby's trying to show me his dad's new Mercedes. He's telling me how much bigger and way cooler it is than Coach's car, it's even got silver screens that fold down from the back of the seats like an aeroplane.

I've only been in an aeroplane twice before. The first time I was a baby and my ears hurt so much I cried and couldn't stop, Mum had to stand in the emergency exit rocking me almost the whole way to Singapore. The second time I was eight and Mum took me to Perth to see a *karmic kinesiologist*. He wore a cape like a wizard and burped when he pressed different bits of my body. Even though his magic couldn't stop my blinking, I really liked the aeroplane ride because the smiley Qantas lady gave me a deck of Flying Kangaroo cards and six choc-chip cookies in four hours.

Rory's making heaps of noise next to me, his chipmunk voice is starting to hurt my ears. Not the aeroplane kind of hurt-

ing, more a tired sort of hurting, but I can't ask Chipmunk-Rory
to stop because that wouldn't *Be Polite*. Maybe I should stop
caring about our family rules? Mum was so busy reminding me
about them after the soccer match, she didn't even notice I
didn't want to go to Digby's again.

Digby doesn't have any family rules, but he definitely needs
them. He's talking too loudly in my ear now about all the
special things he wants to show me in Alt-World, he really
needs to use his *Gentle Voice.*

Will pulls up in the driveway and, as soon as the engine
stops, the front door swings open and out steps this skinny
blonde lady who looks a bit like a nervous Christmas elf.
She's wearing a long red dress and I'm pretty sure I've seen
her somewhere before, maybe in a photo in Digby's lounge
room. My memory download tells me maybe it's Digby's
mum.

We hop out of the car and walk closer to the Christmas elf.
She's got these big eyes the colour of rockpools and short black
hair and pixie ears and long dangly earrings. She smells all
buttery and a bit lemony too, like a freshly baked cake. Maybe
she's been making blueberry muffins, just like she did last
Sunday?

My stomach grumbles because I didn't eat much breakfast
today. I haven't been eating porridge after I hurt Milla by accident, when the bowl slipped out of my hand and made a
massive mess. Mum thought I did it on purpose, so I went
ballistic with the bin. I said sorry afterwards but I've decided
just to eat bananas for breakfast. Fruit isn't as good as porridge
though, I get hungry super quickly.

'Why are you still here?' Will asks the Christmas elf.
'Weren't you going out with your mothers' group?'

The Christmas elf looks at Will like he's a dog, not a dad.

'I messaged you earlier,' she says. 'I decided to cancel. I don't think I'm ready... for all that again.'

She looks super-ready to me, all spangled up like that.

'I've decided to take myself for a massage instead,' she says. 'You didn't see my message?'

'I got a bit distracted at soccer,' says Will. 'Did I reply?'

It's pretty funny he can't remember if he replied, so I laugh out loud. They both turn and look at me and Digby does too, but Rory just keeps kicking a little white pebble around their driveway.

'No, you didn't reply.' The Christmas elf sounds crankier. 'I said I'd need a lift to my appointment, straight after soccer. Now I'm going to be late.'

She walks down the stairs and when she gets to the bottom, she pulls out a big brown kombucha bottle from her handbag and sucks at it like she's super thirsty.

Will glares at her. 'Have you been...?'

Christmas elf cuts him off. 'You were running late.'

'It's not Dad's fault, Miranda,' says Digby, pointing at me. 'Jackson took ages asking his Mum if he could come over.'

So that's her real name: Miranda. But why does Digby call her that? Should I start calling my mum 'Julia'?

Miranda takes a step closer to me and I smell something that's not buttery lemon-cake, something a bit like Dad's aftershave.

'Did we really have to agree to this?' she asks.

My face goes all hot and sweaty because she's looking straight at me.

I want to tell Miranda that *I* didn't agree to this either. No one asked me if I wanted to come to their house, it just sort of happened.

'I thought it might help... dilute the dynamic between Digby and Rory.' Will sounds unsure and a bit grumpy too now.

'Help you get more work done, you mean?'

Miranda takes another step forward.

'Hello, Jackson.' Her eyes aren't smiling the way her mouth is. 'There's been a bit of confusion. Digby's dad needs to take me to an appointment. Is it okay for you and Digby to stay here on your own for a while?'

My eyelids start to twitch. *A while* is how long Mum told us Dad would be in New York, but it's been a week. I don't want to be left alone with Digby for *a while*.

Miranda's smile is frozen and she's staring at my blinking. I want to say, 'Stop, I don't like it,' because I don't like the way she's looking at me and I don't like Alt-World.

Finally, I get some words out. 'Not... Alt-World?'

'Sure you can, buddy,' says Will, as if he's doing me a big favour. 'I'll set you up on the kitchen bench. Those HAIR tech goggles are pretty cool, aren't they? One of the perks of the finance industry.'

That makes me want to cry.

Will bounds up the steps of their big cold castle and through the heavy front door. He disappears inside – probably turning on Digby's laptop and getting the goggles and pulling out two stools at the kitchen bench – then he's galloping back down the stairs again.

Will, Rory and Miranda pile into the car.

As they're pulling out of the driveway, Will slides down his window. 'Make sure you lock the front door when you go inside. Don't answer the door if anyone knocks, okay? Stranger danger. I won't be long, but you can always call me on the mobile.'

Digby nods and I do the same to *Be Polite*. But inside, my

brain beans have turned into the Bongo Drums of Death. They're drumming so loud I can't think or move and I definitely can't talk.

Digby turns to me, his lips pulled into a weird thin line.

'Ready, Curtis?' He's talking like Mr Thompson again.

No way, I think. My heart feels like it's going to kamikaze-dive out of my chest and explode on the driveway.

'Come on, Curtis.' Digby walks up the stairs, but I'm stuck on the front lawn like a stupid old scarecrow.

'Let's play Alt-World,' he says. 'We can start where we finished last Sunday.'

When I don't move, Digby walks back down the stairs and jerks my arm. He's yanking me to the door but my bongo-brain is screaming, 'Nooo waaay.'

It's only when Digby freezes, then turns around with this snarly dog look on his face that I realise I've screamed it *out loud*.

'What did you say?' He steps so close to me that our chests touch. His breath smells like he had eggs for breakfast.

'What did you say, Indicator?'

I don't wait any longer, I just turn and run.

I don't look over my shoulder either, because if I do Digby might use his Darth Vader mind to pull me back again. I just keep on running and with my arms out wide, I can feel the air rushing under them like wings. If I run just a little bit faster, the wind might catch hold of me, lift me up and carry me far, far away. Then I remember it's Saturday afternoon and Miss Marion's holding her special dance practice in the school hall *right now*.

Mum would probably need Google Maps to get there, but I don't. I just keep running past the twenty-four-hour medical centre, across the road at the bus stop, and turn the corner at the fried chicken place that Milla calls Kids Fattening Centre.

It feels so good to get away from Digby, I'm not even puffed. My soccer boots are slippery on the concrete though, which makes me stumble a bit. Suddenly I'm falling, and the footpath's rising up really quickly, but I just roll onto my side like a circus clown and hop straight back up again. Miss Marion taught me how to do that. She always says 'It's safety first in aerial silks', so I've learned to roll properly and check my foot locks and never, ever use silks around my neck.

After the tumble I'm covered in heaps of dust and fuzz, but I'm still flying like a rocket through the school gate and across the playground. When I land at the school hall, I have to pull up really quickly because Miss Marion is standing just inside the doorway.

'Jackson.' She looks surprised and pleased.

The music stops and all the girls in navy leotards turn and stare at me just standing there, panting. Some of the girls smile too, and one of them is April Kennedy. That doesn't help me breathe any better, so I decide not to look at her at all.

Instead I look at Miss Marion's crazy socks, which are red with silvery sequins and big yellow hearts all over them. They're so bright and fun and cheerful, they help my bongo-drum beans to calm down inside my brain.

'So glad you could join us,' says Miss Marion. 'Take off those soccer boots, please, you can't possibly dance in those. We've been through the routine once, but we need to add your aerial work. Would you like a drink? You look a little hot and bothered.'

I shake my head.

'You missed the costuming earlier,' she says. 'Here's yours.'

She passes me a coat hanger with clear plastic over it, like the ones Dead Granny used at Kaminski's. Inside are two white leotards, two pairs of skin-coloured dance undies and one set of arm bands with white feathery wings on them. I recognise all of it, because Miss Marion and I have been talking about costumes for weeks.

I already know that dance undies are designed to keep my thing pressed flat on stage, because that's what real male dancers do in their shows on Broadway. And my white leotard is different to all the other navy leotards, because in the routine I'm a flying boy angel who visits April Kennedy because she's really sick in hospital.

Miss Marion shows me to the boys' bathroom and I spend some time figuring out the dance undies. They feel a bit like the nappies I used to wear when I was little, only thinner and not so scratchy. I try on the white leotard and arm bands too, but I have to climb up onto the toilet seat to see what I look like in the mirror.

I surprise myself because I really *do* look like an angel, maybe even an Archangel. And with my thing pressed flat inside the dance undies I almost look like a girl on the outside, which is interesting and sort of beautiful.

When I come out of the boys' toilets Miss Marion says, 'Wonderful, Jackson!' Then she gets me to stretch a bit while the others finish their snacks. Over the rustling and chewing and chattering, Miss Marion claps her hands and everyone goes quiet.

'All right, everyone. Ready to fly, Jackson?' She smiles and points above me. 'Look, all installed and tested. A theatre friend helped me out.'

I tilt my head back and my mouth just falls open, because there's brand new rigging up there. Not like the wall-hung silks

I've been using for practices over the gym mat, but pro rigging like in Cirque du Soleil, with huge beams and bolts.

There's a silver figure-eight ring sticking out of one beam, with a swivel for all my twisting and spinning. Flowing out of it are the longest silks I've ever seen, all soft and black with sparkly diamond studs like stars at midnight.

I'm so amazed I want to say 'thank you', but my words are all glued up. Maybe my face says it anyway because Miss Marion just grins and says, 'Excellent! Dancers, splits please.'

Everyone slides down onto the floor like ballerinas. The girls push so low into their splits, some of them drop their foreheads to their thighs. That's easy for girls to do, but it took me a whole month. I still have to practise every day now, stretching out my hamstrings by hanging off my bunk.

'Stage positions!' Miss Marion calls, spinning twice on the spot.

I love how Miss Marion does crazy things that other adults never do, like random cartwheels in the middle of dance practice. Sometimes she just sits down and meditates for a few minutes and we all have to chant 'om shanti shanti' while she clears away her 'mind clutter'. That makes me wonder if maybe she's a memory magnet like me, but I'm too shy to ask.

Miss Marion walks over and puts her hand on my shoulder.

'You're going to be amazing up there, Jackson,' she says.

My face goes all warm and tingly because I think maybe she's right.

9

'This is it,' I say to Milla, sipping at my tea.

She glances up at me from across the island bench.

'This is the day we build our street library,' I announce. 'As soon as we've finished lunch, let's do it.'

Milla smiles and closes her notebook. 'I didn't think it was ever going to happen.'

'Neither did I, if I'm honest.' I gnaw at the end of my sushi roll.

'Where's Jackson?' asks Ruby, through a mouthful of peanut butter sandwich. 'Can't he help too?'

'Not today,' I say. 'He's at a friend's house until two o'clock. A second playdate.'

'Two in one week,' says Milla, clearly pleased for her brother. 'Jackson's getting... better, isn't he Mum?'

'Well, there's nothing... wrong with him.' I shrug. 'But some of his behaviours are definitely improving.'

'I like Jackson,' declares Ruby, twirling the tassels on her gymnastics leotard. 'He's different and that's good. He's not a boring brother.'

'There's no one else like Jackson, that's for sure.' I smile. 'Why don't you go and get changed out of that gym gear, Rubes? Put something old on, so we can build the street library together.'

'But I don't have anything old,' objects Ruby.

'What about the worst of your best?'

Ruby thinks for a moment. Then she leaps off the stool, pirouettes across the room and down the hall.

'You seem a bit different yourself, Mum.' Milla sips at her mug of green tea. 'Happier.'

This surprises me, given Dr Kelleher deemed me 'flatter than usual' at our last appointment; but I challenge *anyone* to feel perky after waking up at 5.17 for five years.

'I'm certainly... relieved that Jackson's playing soccer and finding some friends in Queenscliff, doing things he never did in Erskineville.'

Milla stands to stack her plate in the dishwasher.

'What books will we put in the new library?' she asks. 'We'll have to start it off, then passers-by will just keep swapping them.'

Months ago, Milla spent hours researching the history of the Street Library movement around the world.

'Just quietly, I'd like to get rid of those silly romance novels Nanna Pam gave me last Christmas,' I say. 'Too many heroes called Wade or Blake or Shayne. I can't fathom why she reads them...'

Milla sniggers. 'I'm throwing out *Science and Scepticism*.'

'I don't think you can, hon,' I say. 'It's one of Dad's all-time favourites. He used to talk to Granny about it.'

'Taunt' would be another word for the conversations Andy liked having with my mother about religion and spirituality. Along with regularly gifting her books like *Science and Scepti-*

cism and interrogating her veneration of saints, whenever she said grace before a meal he'd observe: 'But God didn't make the dinner, Teresa.'

'Dad doesn't believe in God, does he?' Milla asks.

I shake my head. 'He's a science man.'

'Do you believe in God or science, Mum?'

I think about this for a moment.

'Well, Granny used to say "Only God knows what the future holds". But if God knew about Granny and Grandpa's car accident and didn't do anything to stop it, then I think I hate His guts.'

Milla laughs, rather guiltily. 'Sorry, that's not funny, is it?'

'It kind of is.' I smile at her. 'I understand Dad's scepticism about religion, I really do, but science doesn't have all the answers either. Humans are bigger than our biology. We're more creative, more dynamic, more complicated. We're capable of incredible things that science can't measure. Like music and dance, art and empathy, compassion and love.'

I stand up and add my plate to the dishwasher.

'Those are the things that bring us closest to the divine. Maybe "God" is just a made-up word to describe the most creative and noble parts of humanity?'

Milla smiles. 'That's beautiful, Mum. You should be a poet.'

'I'm a singer, not a poet,' I laugh. 'Or a builder, for that matter.'

Ruby shuffles back into the room, looking uncharacteristically drab in a pair of faded shorts and a crumpled t-shirt.

'Ta-da,' she says, in a glum voice.

'It's only temporary, Rubes.' I put an arm around her shoulder. 'You'll be back to your stylish self in no time.'

I turn to them both. 'Let's put on some tunes and build, my

girls! Why don't you go get the materials out of the shed? I'll organise the music.'

The girls head out into the back yard. It's a rare sight, I realise, Ruby and Milla spending time together without Jackson nearby. As they fetch the materials from the shed and carry them into the front yard, I connect my phone to a portable speaker and set it down on the veranda.

'My playlist!' demands Ruby, seizing my phone and scrolling through the music album. 'My songs!'

Inspecting the materials the girls have hauled down the driveway, I'm uncertain of whether I *will* be able to build a street library without Andy's brute strength. For a passing moment, I consider calling Steve; I'm sure he would help me, in his rural gentleman way. Then I recall what I told my daughters on Mother's Day – 'girls can do anything' – and determine to prove myself right.

'Here's the plan, Mum.' Ruby waves the Build Your Own Street Library instructions at me.

We sit on the front steps and study the leaflet before setting to work, sanding down timber surfaces, affixing corner hinges and hammering together the Perspex door. With the woodwork complete, we take turns digging out a five-foot hole for the library's base.

It's much too tiring for Ruby. After several concerted attempts with the shovel, she sits down on the steps again and serenades us with her favourite Taylor Swift songs.

Milla and I continue digging, until we're drenched through with sweat.

Soon bored of singing, Ruby starts scooping handfuls of palm berries off the driveway and tossing them into Tom and Tracey's yard.

'Don't!' I call.

'Why not?' asks Ruby. 'Jackson does it all the time.'

'He does?' I groan. 'Come here, Rubes. We need your help.'

It takes the combined strength of Milla, Ruby and me to stand the library upright in its newly dug hole. Once in position, we mix a large bucket of wet cement and pour it into the base.

When the cement is partially dry, we cover it in soil. For a finishing touch, Ruby spray-paints the library's walls in a cheerful palette of gold, pink, electric blue, orange and lime green.

As the spray paint dries, we sit together on the front steps and admire our new little library. Milla makes us all a cup of tea, while Ruby fetches some unwanted books from the house.

'Ni hao ma?' says Ruby, tossing a Mandarin title onto the front step next to me, about a magical white horse that brought the seasons to the farmers of Old China.

'But that's such a wonderful story,' I object.

'It's like school work,' replies Ruby. 'Why do we have to learn Mandarin before school anyway, Mum?'

'It's the language of the future,' I say. 'It was a choice of either Mandarin or Arabic.'

'But why *before* school?' Ruby sighs. 'I hate going to school early.'

I'm reminded of the conversation I had with Steve on the soccer field this morning. Maybe I *am* guilty of over-scheduling my children, jamming their lives full of opportunities they never asked for. What do *I* know of the future, after all, and the type of skills they might need? Next year I'll probably be replaced at the hospice by a singing robot, delivering personalised playlists to the dying.

'If we got rid of Mandarin before school, what would you do with all that spare time?' I ask.

'Learn surfing!' enthuses Milla, the colour in her cheeks deepening. 'And write more poetry.'

'Singing lessons,' says Ruby. 'But only from you, Mummy!'

'Right,' I laugh. 'Sounds like more work for me, then.'

'When will someone swap the first book?' Ruby asks.

'After we post to Insta,' replies Milla.

'Let's take a selfie, then!' Ruby seizes my phone and takes a snap of the three of us, in front of our new little library.

'Hashtag girlsinbooks,' says Milla, slipping an arm through mine. 'Thanks for building it with us, Mum.'

Ruby leaps up and tests the spray paint for smudges. 'It's dry!'

She begins arranging the titles spine-out in the library.

A tall bearded man in a wetsuit, with wild blonde hair and bare feet, jogs past our front gate with a surfboard under his arm. He stops, backs up a few steps, then leans over the fence to inspect the library.

'What's this?' he smiles at Ruby.

'It's our new street library,' she explains. 'You take a book and swap it for one of yours, for free.'

'Great idea. Did you build it?'

The man reaches out and prods the library's thick centre post, as if testing its stability.

'It won't ever move,' says Ruby earnestly. 'We poured concrete under the soil.'

'That's really something.' The man glances at Milla. 'And you must be... Milla, I guess?'

Milla's eyes widen in surprise.

'My son's told me a lot about you. All good, of course.' He

grins at me. 'I'm Malcolm, Riley's dad. We live over in Addison Avenue.'

'Oh.' I'm unsure if I've ever met a 'Riley' before, but the name is familiar. 'Hello, I'm Julia.'

We shake hands. His calloused palm suggests a man accustomed to manual work.

'Well, the ocean's calling,' says Malcolm. 'Nice to meet you. I'll drop in a few books later for your rainbow library.'

He jogs off in the direction of the beach.

'Bye!' Ruby calls after him, then turns back, her face flushed with excitement. 'Did you hear what he just said? It's our... rainbow library!'

'Has a nice ring to it, doesn't it?' I say.

Milla reaches for her notebook. 'I've just finished a poem about rainbows.'

'Read it!' shouts Ruby. 'Go on, Millsy, please!'

'Is this your competition entry?' I ask.

Milla nods. 'Do you... really want to hear it, Mum?'

Her voice is strangely shaky.

'Of course.'

Milla exhales. '"Rainbows", dedicated to my little brother, Jackson.'

> the singers have said it
> the dreamers and poets
> the artists and sculptors
> the teachers all know it
> we're rainbows, all colours
> the spiritual seekers
> the Quakers and Shakers
> the mystery keepers
> everyone sees it

we're rainbows, all flavours
the harlots and husbands
the tax men and wives
the Rabbis and Buddhas
saving our lives
we're rainbows, all countries
living this kaleidoscope
together

Milla hugs her notebook to her chest, not daring to look at me.

'Brilliant,' I breathe. 'I need you to... read it again. Slowly.'

Milla begins to smile.

'What did it mean?' asks Ruby. 'What's a harlot?'

Milla laughs. 'Well, it's about... how special we are, Rubes. Even though we're all different, we're actually the same on the inside. The judges probably won't like it though, they're all proper poets.'

'What's a proper poet?' I ask.

'Someone who's had their poems published somewhere.' Milla shrugs.

'You're a proper poet, too, Millsy,' I say. 'Even if no one publishes your work, or you don't win the competition. "Proper" is a very subjective term. One person's hate is another's love.'

'Well, Daddy will *definitely* love it,' says Ruby, leaping up and twirling on her toes. 'And so will Jackson, because he loves rainbows.'

'Oh!' I glance at my watch. 'I almost forgot to pick up Jackson from Digby's. Do either of you want to come along for the ride?'

Ruby shakes her head. 'I want to wait for someone to swap a book. Can't I just stay here with Milla?'

'Sure,' I say. 'But don't wander off, okay? I'll be ten minutes.'

In the van, I plug the address into Google Maps and wend my way through the back streets of Queenscliff. Digby's family home is on the other side of the headland, overlooking the ocean. It's a triumph of modern design, a rectangular prism with exposed steel rafters, a slatted timber façade and spacious internal voids visible through high windows. Testament to both a sophisticated aesthetic and enviable levels of disposable income.

I tap on the door.

Miranda opens it. I've only ever seen her at soccer, but today she looks stunning in a glamorous red dress.

'Nice outfit,' I say. 'Been out to lunch?'

She smiles, totters forward on her strappy heels and kisses me on the cheek. It's a slightly over-familiar gesture, but the smell of alcohol hanging about her suggests it's been a boozy lunch.

'I just went for a massage.'

Even stranger, I think.

'I've come to collect Jackson. Have they had a good time?'

Miranda's face drops. 'Jackson's... not here.'

'What do you mean?' I gaze into her kohl-lined eyes. 'Where is he?'

'He went home earlier.' She glances nervously over her shoulder.

'Home?' I repeat. 'But he's... not at home. Not yet, anyway.'

Miranda stares at me, then calls down the cavernous hallway. 'Digby! Come here!'

The boy emerges from the rear of the house and dawdles down the hallway.

'Tell Julia what happened with Jackson,' she commands.

'He went home.' Digby's gaze doesn't quite meet mine. 'He said he was feeling sick.'

'Sick?' My mind whirls. 'What time did he go?'

'Maybe an hour ago.' Digby shrugs. 'Maybe two.'

'But he's not at our place yet,' I say, panic rising in my chest. 'Did he leave on... foot?'

Digby nods.

'If it's been... two hours already, then maybe...' My voice is shaking now. 'Maybe we should call the police?'

Miranda stares at me like an animal trapped in headlights.

'But you know what boys are like. He's probably just...' She trails off.

I try to slow my breathing. There have been so many unexpected incidents with Jackson over the years, I've had to learn to think calmly in the moment.

'He... can't have gone far,' I say. 'I'll just drive around the streets a bit and see if I can spot him. Did he say he was definitely going home?'

Miranda looks to Digby for confirmation.

'He didn't say,' the boy replies.

'I'm really so sorry about this,' says Miranda. 'And Will's not here, or I'd get him to help. I can't... I can't drive right now.'

Her eyes fill with tears. I'm struggling to understand why, given *her* son is standing next to her.

I pull out my phone. In Andy's absence, who should I call?

It comes to me in an instant.

Steve answers within two rings.

'Jackson's missing,' I blurt. My alarm intensifies as I describe the situation.

'It'll be okay,' he soothes. 'I'm getting into the car right now.'

'I've got no idea where he's gone, Steve. We agreed I'd pick him up at two from Digby's but he's just... disappeared.' My eyes begin to tear up.

'We'll sort this out, Jules. Trust me, I'm onto it.'

'Thank you,' I murmur, hurrying back to the van.

As I reverse out of their driveway, Miranda and Digby stand together in the doorway like silent sentinels, watching me.

When I'm standing on the stage, I get wriggles in my stomach like just before a soccer match or whenever April Kennedy looks at me in class. April is in position already, lying on a big white hospital bed which is actually a gym mat covered in a sheet. The blank expression on her face makes me worry that she really *is* sick, even though I know she's just pretending.

Miss Marion nods. That's the signal for me to grab the silks with both hands and do a Russian climb. At the top, I curl my feet into a double foot lock and loop a silk around my thigh for a hammock, then I swing about in the air with no hands. All the girls' faces are shocked. They've never seen me do my aerial silks before, so if they're this scared already, they'll probably faint when I do the *really* tricky stuff.

Miss Marion claps her hands to tell us the music's about to start. The dancers turn face-down on the stage except for April Kennedy, who lies on the hospital bed with her eyes shut. From the ceiling, I can take a good look at her beautiful oval face and long black hair fanned out over her white arms. April's mum is from Korea and moved to Australia to marry

April's dad, so I guess that means she's a *migrant* like Dead Granny's family. A shiver shoots up my spine because it feels good watching April from the ceiling, but a bit weird too because she can't see me.

When the music starts, I feel it creeping inside me like it always does. The gentleness makes my brain beans melt away, then my body starts moving all by itself. The girls below me are moving too, like ripples on the dark surface of a pond.

> *Hope there's someone who'll take care of me*
> *When I die, will I go?*
> *Hope there's someone to set my heart free,*
> *Nice to hold, when I'm tired...*

The first time Miss Marion played this song to me, I stopped breathing I wanted to hear it so badly. It was eerie and strange because, behind the sound of the cello and the violins and the piano, I could actually hear Dead Granny singing in the Otherworld. The sound was so lonely and lovely, I started to cry.

When the song finished and everything turned ordinary again, tears were dripping down my face. All the other dancers crowded around me asking, 'What's wrong? What's wrong?' and maybe because I didn't know how to answer them, April Kennedy said in this really brave voice, 'Nothing's wrong with Jackson. That song would make anyone cry.'

That's when I knew that April Kennedy was my special friend.

I watch the dancers moving through their routine below me, waiting for the moment I turn into a boy angel. At exactly two minutes thirty, the music changes and I grip the silks tighter, even though the double foot lock means I can't fall. I've practised so many times over the mat with Miss Marion, I know *everything* about aerial safety.

I twist and swing exactly as we've practised, in exactly the right order, until it's time for the finale. Then I start my descent, spinning faster and faster. The silks are unravelling but holding me firm, and the music's getting louder.

Suddenly, the music just stops.

The silks pull tight across my hips like I've slammed on the brakes. I'm hanging upside down above April, my face positioned perfectly in front of hers.

The music starts up again for the final bars, but it's as soft as a stream in a rainforest. The other dancers drop silently to the floor and reach for one another, holding hands wherever they fall.

April and I stare at each other under the dimmed lights, our lips so close they almost touch. Her eyes are glowing like dark gems in the shadows. I've never kissed a girl before, but I really want to now.

I place my hands over April's cheeks, just as Miss Marion showed me, and April puts her hands on mine. We lean our foreheads together and, as the music ends April's breathing does too. The silence is heavy, but I'm going to stay with her until the very end, because that's what angels do.

My heart is beating like wildfire, and not because I just did the best descent ever.

'Bravo! Brava!' shrieks Miss Marion from the edge of the stage. I open my eyes at exactly the same time as April. We both laugh because it feels a bit weird, but so right, too. It's the first time we've ever put the routines together and it worked like magic.

'I got goose bumps,' whispers April.

Me too, I want to say, but my beans make me do a headstand instead, right in the middle of the stage. My face is sweaty and I'm trying to catch my breath, but it's harder than usual. If I wasn't barefoot, I'd call Dead Granny and tell her all about it.

'We've got a fighting chance at the Winter Eisteddfod!' Miss Marion is still clapping. 'I've never seen anything so visually stunning!'

Suddenly I notice that April isn't there any more. She's climbed off the hospital bed and gone to talk to some of her other friends. I wish I could think of a good reason to follow her, but I can't.

So I just stay in my headstand, until my beans stop moving completely. Maybe Anohni's music and April Kennedy vaporised them together, somehow?

Then Miss Marion tells us we have to do the whole routine again. I'm so happy I roll out of my headstand, grab the silks and swing across the stage like Tarzan, beating at my chest. A bunch of girls scatter across the stage giggling. I wish April Kennedy was one of them.

Miss Marion tells us to take off our costumes and store them in their special bags and hang them up in the hall storeroom. We're not allowed to touch them again until the day before the eisteddfod.

Then we all change back into our ordinary clothes and Miss Marion makes us do the whole routine again – four times more and 'one for good luck' – until we're all super sore and tired and hungry for afternoon tea.

Finally, Miss Marion yells, 'Break time! Hydrate and refuel!'

Everyone in the room cheers.

I'm climbing down the rigging when someone calls out, 'Jackson!'

I turn to see April Kennedy waving. I check behind me to see who she's waving at, but there's no one else in the air behind me. April laughs and shakes her head, then she's holding up a packet of rice crackers. Does she really want to share them with me?

I'm a bit shaky climbing down the rest of the way, then I'm walking towards her in what feels like slow-mo. April looks friendly but also a bit shy. I'm trying to think of something clever to say to her when suddenly Coach Steve speeds into the hall.

'Jackson?' He skids to a stop near Miss Marion. 'Is Jackson here?'

Coach sees me and charges over, saying things I can't catch in my brain. He grabs hold of my shoulders and shakes me, but all I can think of is sitting close to April Kennedy and sharing her rice crackers. After a while Coach looks frustrated and starts waggling his finger at me, then he turns and talks to Miss Marion instead.

Then they're both standing in front of me, frowning. I've got no idea what to say, but I remember Dr Louisa's advice about faces and feelings: 'If someone's frowning, Jackson, it's a signal that you need to stop and apologise. If they're smiling, keep going.'

So quickly I say, 'Sorry.'

Coach sighs. His shoulders sink down a bit.

'That's all right mate, but I'm afraid you've got some serious explaining to do at home. Your mum has no idea you're here. She's worried sick about you.'

Miss Marion ushers us towards the hall door so quickly, I can't even look back and wave at April.

'Great rehearsal, Jackson.' She pats me on the back. 'But you've got some serious explaining to do for me, too... about why your mother doesn't know you're here today. Given she's signed a Parental Permission Note for it.' Miss Marion's right eyebrow arches up so far, it's like an arrow pointing to the Otherworld.

My cheeks are burning and my eyelids are itchy. I know for sure I shouldn't have faked Mum's signature, but I don't know how to explain it.

Coach puts an arm around my shoulders. 'Can it wait until Monday, Marion?'

I'm so happy I could hug him.

Then he's guiding me out of the hall and into the carpark and asking me stuff about what I was doing at Digby's house and why I left. It's hard to focus on what he's saying with my bongo-beans battering inside my brain.

In the car, Coach sends Mum a message from his phone.

After a while there's a little ding and Coach turns to me and says, 'Well, she's very relieved. Put your seatbelt on, please, Jackson.'

I strap in and start watching the busyness outside the car. There are loads of adults pushing prams and mowing lawns and walking dogs and carrying shopping bags, and loads of kids on bicycles and playing handball and basketball in drive-ways. They all look so normal, I wonder if any of *them* ever get into trouble, or can't get their words out, or think about people in the Otherworld?

Suddenly I see this teenager skateboarding on the road ahead of us, he's not on the footpath where he's supposed to be. He's wearing this bright yellow Hawaiian shirt and these great big gold headphones and a silky green jacket that flaps behind him in the wind. He's carrying a huge bunch of sunflowers and he's not wearing a helmet. When he looks back to check the traffic behind him, he's got this big gleaming smile spread right across his face. He looks so happy that I start smiling too. He veers across the road right in front of Coach's car, forcing him to brake.

Coach says something rude under his breath.

Suddenly I realise it's Riley, Milla's friend from the bus stop, only he's not wearing his school uniform because it's Saturday. I try to open the window and call out to him, but I can't. Coach's car is super high-tech and he's always in control of all the buttons.

Riley crouches down and holds onto the edge of his skateboard with one hand, cutting left into a side street and whizzing around the corner.

'Wow,' I say. Riley looks like he's having heaps of fun, probably the most fun anyone's having in Queenscliff today.

I wonder if Mum and Dad will ever let *me* skate without a helmet like that, but I reckon I know the answer already. Mum probably wouldn't and Dad probably would, so they'd argue about it for hours. Some weekends Dad comes skateboarding with me, but Mum doesn't like that much. Maybe he's at home already, waiting to take me to the skatepark?

I wiggle forward and tap Coach on the shoulder. 'Is my dad at home?'

'Isn't your dad still in New York, mate?'

'Oh, right.' I remember everything else, but somehow I forgot that.

Coach glances at me in the rear-vision mirror. 'Is your dad away a lot, Jackson?'

I don't want to say 'yes', so I just say nothing.

'That must be hard for you.' Coach is still looking at me. 'And for your mum, too.'

I grind my teeth together to stop my chin from wobbling.

'Are your mum and dad... still together?'

I don't know how to answer that, and I wish he hadn't asked.

A moment later we're turning into Seaview Street and parking in the driveway behind the Red Rocket. Mum's waiting for us on the veranda with her head in her hands. I feel like the biggest idiot in the world because I can see how worried she's been.

As soon as I climb out of Coach's car, Mum flies down the steps and hugs me like she hasn't seen me in three years. I lean into her softness.

Mum doesn't say anything for a long time, she just strokes the back of my neck. After a while she takes my face in her hands.

'I was so worried, Jackson. I almost called the police.' Her eyes are glistening. 'Why did you leave Digby's without telling his parents where you were going?'

Mum goes foggy in front of me because I'm crying too.

'Digby's parents weren't there,' I whisper. 'I couldn't tell them.'

Mum blinks. 'Then why did you leave Digby's at all? We agreed that I'd pick you up at two o'clock. Don't you remember the conversation we had at soccer?'

I *can* remember that conversation. I can remember *every* conversation. But I also remember Digby standing in his driveway tugging at my arm, trying to make me go inside and play Alt-World again.

'Can you imagine how I felt when I got to Digby's and Miranda said you'd already gone home, Jackson?' asks Mum.

Her waterfall tears are telling me that she was really scared.

'Why did you leave Digby's, Jackson?'

My eyes start to twitch. 'I needed to... get some fresh air. Like you needed to, last Sunday in the café with Nanna Pam.'

'But why?'

'I need to tell you something, Mum.'

'Okay.' She's frowning so hard now, I can count five deep lines across her forehead.

We sit down on the steps together. I glance over at Coach, wondering how I'm going to tell Mum about playing Alt-World with Digby and the lady with no trousers when *he's* standing right there, listening.

'I haven't told you before, because... I didn't think you'd like it.'

Why isn't Coach leaving, anyway? He's not joining us on the steps and he's not getting into his car, he's just standing in the middle of the lawn like he's playing musical statues.

'What is it, Jackson?' Mum's voice sounds a bit scared.

I'm pretty sure Coach likes Digby because he drops him home every week, or at least he doesn't *not* like him. So I *can't* tell Mum about Alt-World, not right now with Coach so close. But she's standing there waiting for me to tell her *something*, so I decide to tell her my other secret.

'I've joined a girls' dance group.'

'What?' Mum looks confused.

'At Queenscliff Public. I'm the only boy in it and I've learned aerial silks.'

The words come out easily, maybe because I love dance so much.

'I've practised for three-and-a-half months and Miss Marion is the best teacher. She's given me a special role on stage at the town hall for the Winter Eis... Eis...'

My brain gets stuck on the word 'eisteddfod', which is a super tricky word to say out loud.

Coach moves forward and sits down on the other side of Mum.

'That's where I found him,' he explains to her. 'At dance practice in the hall. I went over to Digby's straight after you called. Digby told me that he'd heard Miss Marion mention it to Jackson at school yesterday.'

Mum looks irritated. 'Well, I wish someone had bothered to tell *me* about this. Why did the school know, Jackson, and I didn't?'

Her voice is prickly.

If I tell her about the fake signature on the permission note, she might not let me do dance again. No more aerial silks, no more flying angels and no more April Kennedy.

Mum keeps staring at me.

'I didn't tell you because I wanted to make it a surprise.'

That's sort of true, but my eyelids start to flicker. Mum looks doubtful.

'And I didn't think Dad would like me dancing.'

That part's definitely true.

Mum rubs a hand over her face, which looks about a hundred years older. 'Right. Well, thanks for telling me. We can talk to Dad about this when he gets home from New York.'

The invisible Dad-hole in my chest rips open even wider, because that's still half a week away.

Mum turns to Coach. 'Thanks for all your help this after-noon, Steve. I couldn't have coped without you. Not with Andy overseas and everything.'

'No worries,' says Coach, patting Mum on the shoulder. 'It was a bit of a fright for all of us. It's amazing how you manage to keep going, Julia. What with a job and three kids and...' He nods at me, but I'm not sure what he means.

Mum lets out a massive sigh. Coach just keeps patting her shoulder.

'This calls for an old-fashioned rural remedy,' he says after a while. 'Got any whisky, Julia? I'll pour you a stiff drink. Need one myself, as a matter of fact.'

Laughter explodes out of Mum's mouth. Suddenly she's not so scared and cranky any more, she's smiley and a bit silly.

'We don't drink the hard stuff, Steve, but there's a bottle of Pinot in the pantry.' She waves a hand in the direction of the kitchen. 'I'll get some glasses.'

'Nah, I'll find 'em.' Coach stands up and moves to the front door.

It's sort of strange that he's letting himself in, when he's never been inside our house before. The wire screen door bangs shut behind him.

I watch Mum's face, waiting for her to roast me. But she just sits there, looking worn out and disappointed.

'I'm so glad you're safe,' she murmurs. 'When I went to pick you up at Digby's house and Miranda said you'd been gone for hours, I just felt... so scared, Jackson.'

Maybe she felt as scared as I did when I ran away from Digby's house today.

'Mum, there's something else I want to tell you...' I start, but the wire screen door opens again. Coach Steve's muscly footballer's bottom pokes out of it first, then the rest of his body follows. He's carrying a bottle of wine in one hand and two glasses in the other.

'Here we are,' he says, sitting down next to Mum again. 'Doctor's orders.' He pours her a glass so full, wine slops over the side.

I watch them clinking their glasses together and I'm thinking of fixing myself a Milo, when suddenly a boy on a skateboard veers into our driveway.

He's skating so fast he's definitely going to crash into the Red Rocket, but then he leaps off the board like an acrobat, flips it up with his toe and catches it in his left hand.

It's Riley again, only he's holding the bunch of sunflowers

behind his back now. Up close, he's got suntanned skin and snowy-white teeth and curly long blonde hair like Ruby's.

He grins as if he expected to find us all on the front steps like this.

Mum and Coach just stare at him.

'Hi, I'm Riley,' he says, fidgeting with the drawstring of his big green jacket. 'Is Milla home?'

'Oh,' says Mum, setting down her glass. 'And you are...?'

'Riley,' the boy says again.

'You said that.' Mum looks a bit embarrassed. 'And you know Milla from...?'

'School,' he says. 'We do Pilates together.'

Coach Steve snorts into his glass so hard, wine spurts from his nose. I run to the Red Rocket and grab the mini box of tissues and pass them to him for politeness.

'Sorry. Second shock of the day, mate.' He dabs at his face with the tissue. 'School sport's not what it used to be. Do you two do any other sport, apart from... Pilates?'

Mum laughs again and takes another long sip of her wine.

'Well, I've just done my Bronze Medallion,' Riley replies. 'I'm a volunteer lifesaver down at Queenscliff.'

'Good on you, mate,' says Coach. 'That's an important skill.'

'I think you met my dad earlier,' says Riley, looking at Mum now. 'His name's Malcolm. He was going for a surf.'

'Oh... yes,' says Mum. 'We talked about the library.'

Suddenly Milla's standing at the front door, tugging at her braids and looking really nervous and pleased and embarrassed all at once. She opens the screen door and steps onto the veranda.

'Hi,' she sort of squeaks, which doesn't sound like Milla at all.

'Hey,' says Riley. He's fidgeting with the cuffs of his jacket, then he passes her the sunflowers without really looking at her. 'Want to check out the waves?'

'Sure,' Milla-Mouse squeaks again and it makes me giggle. I press my teeth together, because that helps with crying *and* laughing.

Milla turns to Mum, super excited. 'Can I go down to the beach, Mum?'

'Okay,' says Mum, glancing at Coach.

'Thanks, Mrs...' Riley starts, but Mum says, 'Call me Julia. Don't stay out too long, please.'

Milla practically bounds down the steps to Riley, hugging the sunflowers to her chest. She reminds me of those lovesick top-knot pigeons outside my bedroom window.

Milla props the sunflowers against the post of our library, then she and Riley head off down Seaview Street. I scale the front fence to watch them go. I'm wondering if they're going to hold hands or kiss or something, and if maybe *I* might walk like that one day with April Kennedy? The idea makes my stomach go all fluttery and my beans start bouncing, so I do a headstand on the fence.

'Jesus,' says Coach, which must mean he's a Christian. 'Has Jackson ever done gymnastics, Julia?'

'Get down before you fall down,' Mum calls.

I somersault off the fence and start walking back to Mum and Coach. They're talking about Dad now and all the cool places he visits in the world, and how hard he's working because he doesn't want to be 'made redundant'. That sounds a lot like the word Nanna uses for chewing gum – 'repugnant' – which means extra nasty.

Mum's eyes are glossy and her cheeks are pink now, she looks much younger and definitely more relaxed.

'Top up?' She waves the bottle of wine at Coach.

'Don't mind if I do,' he says.

Mum tries to pour more wine into his glass but manages to slosh it over the step.

'God, I'm an idiot!' Mum giggles, but she didn't laugh like that when I spilled my porridge last week.

I wish Dad would come back from New York right now.

I pass Mum the box of tissues and she takes one and dabs it against the top step. Some of the wine has leaked into the wood and Dad won't like that; he's always rubbing special oil into the steps to protect them from wind and rain and salty sea spray. I'm not sure how to get wine out of wood, but Dead Granny would know because she's the spotless specialist. I've been waiting for her to call all day, so I decide to call her now and ask.

'I'm going inside,' I say, without explaining why. Mum doesn't like me talking about Dead Granny and my shoe-phone, even in front of family friends.

'Okay,' says Mum. 'We won't be out here too long. Ruby's watching a movie inside. You might like to watch it too?'

'Which one?'

'Oh, uh... *The Devil Wears Prada*.'

Ruby's watched it at least fifty times. 'When's Dad back?'

'Wednesday night,' says Mum. She picks up her phone. 'He's texting me his arrival time in a while.'

If it's going to be *a while*, we might be waiting weeks.

As I'm walking to the front door, Coach stands up and tries to shake my hand.

'You're a good kid,' he says, pumping my palm in his. It feels a bit strange, but adults do strange things when they drink wine. 'And that was an incredible headstand on the front fence.'

It's the second time I've shaken Coach's hand today. The

first was when I got Dragon of the Match at soccer this morning, which feels like *forever* ago.

'Thanks, champ,' says Coach, finally letting go of my hand. 'Get some rest. You've had a big day. I'll take care of your mum out here.'

Mum smiles at Coach. She looks so much calmer and her face is lighter.

'See you soon, mate,' he calls, as I head in through the front door.

I really like Coach. And he's being so nice to Mum, I like him even more.

There's an uncanny silence in the house even though it's already 5.33 am on an ordinary Monday morning. In the absence of music, my body clock has woken me up anyway. Could Jackson *really* be sleeping in?

I reach for my phone on the bedside table and check my messages: nothing in from Andy overnight. The hollowed-out feeling I carry inside whenever he's away is morphing into something far more toxic. Irrespective of the time difference, surely he's read the message I sent last night?

Bit of an incident with Jackson this arvo – went AWOL for a few hours. All okay, found him at school. Let's chat about it when you get back?

Maybe it sounded too casual, too in control. Re-reading the message, I certainly didn't frame it as the emergency it felt like at the time. But couldn't Andy have read between the lines and simply *imagined* how it might have felt for me? Even sending the briefest reply would suffice.

But *silence?*

My thoughts are galloping like unbridled horses through hostile terrain. *Andy doesn't care. He's wedded to his job. His work trips are a convenient way of checking out of family responsibilities. He finds living with Jackson so challenging, he heads overseas for respite. Maybe he even finds comfort there, in someone else's arms.*

I shake my head, as if to physically dislodge the thoughts. Then, recalling Dr Kelleher's advice to Jackson – 'distract yourself a bit, you don't have to believe every intrusive thought you have' – I decide to make myself a cup of tea.

Slipping my phone into the pocket of my robe, I pad down the hall towards the kitchen. Pausing at the bottom of the spiral stairs leading up to Jackson's room, I detect a sound – but it's not music.

I step out of my slippers in an effort to mute my footfall, then steal up the stairs. At the top, I lean my ear against Jackson's door.

'Granny?' I hear him say. 'Granny, please can you come?'

He sounds so vulnerable, it's heart-breaking.

I nudge open the door.

With the sun rising later now as winter approaches, the room is still cloaked in darkness. I creep across the carpet to Jackson's bed, expecting him to greet me. In the dimness, I can just make out the shape of him. He's tucked under the duvet, even his head concealed beneath.

Gently, I peel back the covers.

Jackson screams so loudly, I scream too.

'Oh my God,' I gasp, pressing a hand to my chest. 'You almost gave me a heart attack.'

Jackson scrambles upright. 'And I thought you were Dead Granny! I'd just asked her to come.'

'Of course.' I let out a deep breath. 'That must've been frightening for you. I'm so sorry. Here, let's turn on the light.'

Groping for his bedside lamp, I flick on the switch.

'You're crying, Jackson.' I brush his tear-stained cheek with the tips of my fingers. 'What's wrong?'

A delayed reaction, perhaps, from Saturday afternoon's trouble.

Jackson sniffs. 'Dead Granny's not... talking to me... any more.'

His words are slower than usual this morning. It's hard to know how to console him, when I hanker to talk to my mother as much as Jackson.

'Oh, darling. Could the problem be... a technical issue with your shoe-phone?' I venture, feeling rather foolish.

Jackson tilts his head to one side. 'Maybe. But who could fix it, Mum?'

'I'm not sure.' I scramble for a solution. 'The IT guy at work says most technical glitches can be fixed by a simple shutdown-reboot. Maybe turn off your shoe-phone, leave it off for the rest of today, then reboot it tomorrow?'

I have no idea how Jackson might react to this suggestion. Or what I'll say to him tomorrow if the 'reboot' doesn't work.

'Rebooting my shoe-phone,' Jackson grins. 'That's funny, Mum. Okay, I'll turn it off now.'

He pulls out a sneaker from under the duvet, presses the heel with his thumb, then places it on the floor.

Flopping back onto the mattress he asks, 'Can you remember everything about Dead Granny, Mum?'

'Not as much as I'd like,' I admit. 'But luckily we've got some videos of her and Grandpa. Scoot over, I'll show you one.'

Jackson slides towards the wall, leaving ample space for me to snuggle in next to him. It feels like a throwback to his toddler years when, in order to send three-year-old Jackson off to sleep, I'd have to climb under the duvet wearing my pyjamas, pretending I was ready for bed too. Then I'd sing him 'Summertime' on loop until the wriggling stopped, his body relaxed and eventually, I'd start extricating myself from his bed. More often than not, however, I'd simply fall asleep beside him, waking up at some unearthly hour entangled in the sheets.

I remove the phone from my robe pocket.

'Screentime?' Jackson grins.

'Not quite,' I smile, then begin scrolling through countless thumbnail images in my digital albums, some from years ago. When I find the video I'm looking for, I lift up the screen so we both can see it. 'Watch this, Jackson.'

I sigh with nostalgia at the sight of our Erskineville home. In the clip, I'm standing outside Jackson's bedroom door with my mother, who'd taken the day off from Kaminski's to visit her only grandson on his first birthday. As I film through the phone, my mother's hand pushes open the bedroom door. Baby Jackson lies gurgling in his cot after his afternoon nap, sunlight streaming through a gap in the curtains.

The camera takes in a tall white bookcase, jammed full of stuffed toys, then pans to a stack of books piled next to an old rocking chair.

'That was your favourite as a baby.' I point to a book entitled *Where is the Green Sheep?*

Jackson shakes his head. 'No, it wasn't. *Tough Boris* was my favourite, about a big grungy pirate who really loved his parrot.'

'Oh, right.' I vaguely recall that title. 'You remembered that well.'

The camera moves to the cot now and we see the infant Jackson, wrapped up in a blue baby blanket with embroidered elephants on it, and my mother's arms reaching in to pick him up.

'There's Granny,' I whisper. 'Look how she adored you.'

Mum cradles Jackson against her chest, beaming with grandmotherly pride. 'Who's my gorgeous boy?' she coos. 'What a special little one we have here.'

I wince at the prescience of her words. Little did my mother know that barely three years later, doctors would be trying to determine exactly how 'special' Jackson was.

She wrinkles her nose at the camera. 'I think he's done a poo-poo.'

'No I didn't,' objects Jackson. 'My nappy wasn't dirty. Where's Incy?'

'Where's what?'

'Incy,' he repeats. 'My pull-toy with the music. Incy-Wincy spider climbed up the water spout...'

I look blankly at him.

'You put Incy on the change table before my afternoon nap,' he says. 'I remember.'

The camera follows my mother, still holding Jackson, as she walks to the other side of the room where the change table stands. 'Come on, let's get you a fresh nappy.'

Perched on top of the change mat, exactly where Jackson predicted, is a fluffy spider pull-toy.

'There's Incy.' Jackson points at the screen. 'See?'

My mother passes the toy to Jackson, then lowers him onto the change table.

'Have you watched this video before, Jackson?' I stare at him hard.

He shakes his head. 'You never let me touch your phone. Look at my flubbery cheeks!'

From a close-up of Jackson's face, the camera whips sideways and the screen pixelates. When it reforms, it's clear that I've swapped places with my mother. Changing Jackson was always a difficult task, due to his penchant for rolling in his own poo.

'Mum! You look like a princess,' says Jackson, gazing at the footage. My hair was much longer, my face plumper.

'Do you still have your tree bracelet?' he asks suddenly.

'My what?'

'It was gold with a red jewel,' he continues. 'Was it a real ruby?'

I say nothing for a moment, then pause the video.

Rolling onto one side, I prop a hand under my chin. 'Do you mean... my Tree of Life bracelet with the garnet at the centre?'

He nods.

'I haven't worn that bracelet for nine years, Jackson. I lost it at the beach when you were two years old.'

It's getting much lighter outside. The sun has risen and the top-knots are cooing and everything is signifying a normal Monday morning, except for this.

'How did you even... remember that bracelet?' I ask. 'I wasn't wearing it in the video.'

'I remember everything,' he says. 'I'm a memory magnet.'

I'm reluctant to repeat the judgements he's heard before.

No one can remember that far back. It's just a fertile imagination. You're using creative licence. Don't make fibbing a habit.

Instead, I try a different tack. 'Tell me, Jackson, what else can you... remember?'

His eyes light up. 'So much, Mum.'

'What's your very first memory?'

'Well... I'm lying on the rainbow mat in the lounge room in the old house,' he starts.

'The rainbow mat?' How could he recall the foam playmat he rolled around on for the first nine-months of his life? He *must* have seen it in photos.

Jackson ignores my incredulity. 'I'm on the rainbow mat and I'm kicking my feet at that big bunny mobile hanging above me,' Jackson continues. 'I really wanted to get to that smiley green bunny circling in the air... but I never, ever could.'

I'd forgotten about that rabbit, and I'm quite sure we have no photos of it.

'Okay,' I say. 'What's your first memory of Dad, then?'

'It's hard...' Jackson shakes his head.

'Just try.'

It takes him a while to form the words. Once they start flowing, he doesn't stop.

'Dad was driving and... everything went dark. The thunder hurt my ears and the lightning frightened me. I cried and cried until Dad pulled over. Then he climbed into the back, took me out of my baby seat and held me until I felt better. The rain just kept pouring down. We sat there for ages, watching the windscreen wipers.'

'Wow,' I say. 'That storm was a once-in-twenty-years event. Our back yard was flooded. You were... tiny, Jackson, but we talked about it for years afterwards. What else do you remember?'

He looks wistful.

'I remember Dead Granny pushing me in my stroller under the old cherry trees in Erskineville. One day I saw a pink petal falling out of the branches. It twisted and turned as if it was going to miss me, but then it brushed my nose like the softest snowflake and I actually smelled it passing.'

Jackson smiles now.

'Whenever Dead Granny put me down for afternoon naps, I

always dreamed the same dream about a room full of peaches. That dream was so good, because I never had to share any of those peaches with Milla or Ruby or anyone else and when I woke up from it, Granny was right there.'

'Do you remember any other dreams?' I ask.

'I remember all of them.'

'Every single one?'

'My memory magnet's full of them.'

I stare at him for a long time, then attempt to ask something more verifiable.

'What's the first thing you can remember about... me, Jackson?'

Jackson gazes at the ceiling, his forehead wrinkled with concentration.

'You were moving around the room and I was just lying there watching you. I couldn't move my head because it was too heavy. Sometimes you'd disappear and that No-Mum feeling made me cry, but you'd always come back and kiss me and tickle me under my chin. You were wearing this beautiful red dress covered in music symbols.'

'My semi-quaver dress,' I gasp. 'But... you couldn't walk, Jackson. You couldn't even sit up.'

Jackson nods solemnly.

'I can't believe this,' I murmur.

'You picked up a machine with a cord dangling out of it, the roaring sound was terrible. You didn't notice I was crying until the machine stopped. By that time, I was screaming so much my ears hurt.'

'My hairdryer?' I ask in disbelief.

Jackson nods. 'You scooped me up and hummed "Summertime", then you pulled down your dress and the sweetness flowed so fast I couldn't swallow it all. Then I... I vomited on your beautiful dress.'

'That's right! I had to take it off and wear something else that day...'

I'd forgotten the incident entirely. I shift my face closer to Jackson's.

'How do you remember it all?' I whisper, feeling a little frightened.

'I'm a memory magnet,' he answers. 'Like I keep telling you. Do you believe me now?'

'Yes,' I breathe. 'Even if I don't know how it's... humanly possible.'

I knew Jackson had unusual powers of retention, but I had no idea his memories were so vivid and detailed. How did I miss this, over the years? Or have Jackson's developmental challenges prevented him from sharing the full extent of it, up until this very moment?

'I haven't understood you properly, Jackson.' A tear trickles down my cheek. 'I'm... I'm so sorry for not paying more attention.'

Jackson cocks his head.

'Don't be too hard on yourself, Mum,' he says. 'You've got a lot on.'

I laugh at these recycled words of mine, even though he wasn't trying to be funny.

'That's very good advice, Jackson. We've all got a lot on. You do, in particular, with all that dancing you've been doing. Speaking of which, we're going to have to talk to Dad about it when he gets back.'

Jackson stiffens.

'Don't worry, I'm on your side. If you want to dance, that's great. Just don't head off to practices on your own without telling me first, okay? You gave everyone a shock on Saturday, including Digby and his parents.'

'Digby will hate me for... running away.'

Jackson's speech has become suddenly laboured again. Moments ago, recounting his earliest memories, his words were so rapid and fluid.

'I'm sure Digby won't hate you, Jackson. He's your friend.'

Jackson shakes his head vociferously.

'Digby will understand.' I take his hand in mine. 'But if you're worried about explaining what happened, I can come with you to school this morning. We can tell Digby about dance together.'

Jackson looks uncertain. 'Can't we just lie here all day and watch *Baby Me and Princess Mum*?'

I laugh. 'As much as I'd like that, I'm afraid not. You need to get ready for school and I need to go to work. But I want to do more of this, Jackson. I want to hear about all your memories and... well, you.' I give him another squeeze. 'There's a lot you can help me remember again.'

'Okay, Mum.'

Jackson's smile is euphoric.

* * *

We pull up outside school at 8.51.

'Kiss-N-Go?' Ruby points at where we normally stop.

'Not today, Rubes,' I say. 'Jackson needs to talk to Digby about what happened on Saturday, so I'm coming into school to help.'

So much for letting Jackson handle complicated situations on his own: I doubt Dr Kelleher would be impressed with me.

'Hooray!' Ruby claps her hands.

We drive around looking for a parking spot, finding one several streets away.

'That's too far!' grumbles Ruby.

'It's good exercise,' I reply. In the crisp autumn air, I welcome the walk.

We climb out of the van and onto damp turf at the side of the road. Jackson immediately starts clawing at his legs, fussing about the wet grass, while Ruby struggles to hoist her backpack onto her shoulders.

'Let me help,' I say, taking her bag and squeezing her hand.

We're almost at the school gate when I notice Jackson staring at a girl walking towards us. She waves at Jackson, her long black hair glinting like liquorice in the sun, then smiles as if she's about to say something. Jackson lowers his gaze and stares at his shoes, thwarting her completely. When he looks up again, his eyelids are blinking madly.

'Who's that?' I ask, watching her move through the school gate, swinging a small black instrument case in one hand and waving at a group of students with the other.

'April Kennedy,' Ruby answers for her brother.

'Of Thermowhizz fame.' I smile at Jackson. 'She's lovely.'

'April plays the violin,' Ruby informs me. 'She's been learning it since she was three.'

'Is that so?' I glance again at Jackson, who seems paler now than a moment ago. 'Are you all right, Jackson?'

He nods, his eyes still following April.

'There's Tessa!' yells Ruby, pointing to the other side of the playground. 'Can I drop my bag to class, Mummy?'

'Okay, darling,' I say. 'We'll find Digby. Where's your class-room again, Jackson?'

I feel guilty that I've forgotten. When the children first started at Queenscliff, I walked them into school every day.

After they'd settled in, I always found reasons just to drop them in the 'Kiss-N-Go' zone.

Jackson motions at a grey row of demountable bungalows.

'Oh yes, that's right.' I smile. 'Now, where does Digby usually hang out?'

He nods in the direction of the canteen.

We traverse the playground, navigating our way around games of handball and bulrush and kill-tag. The playground is packed with students, small groups of chatty parents and the occasional teacher striding to the staff room.

As we pass beneath a majestic fig tree, Jackson clutches at his stomach.

'What's the matter?' I ask.

He points at the mashed figs on the ground. 'That smell makes my stomach go weird.'

'Let's walk somewhere else, then.' I notice he's staring beyond my shoulder.

Turning to follow his gaze, I see the school principal rushing across the playground. Crazy Daisy, the students call her. I wonder who she's after this time?

To my surprise, she turns and charges towards us, stopping in front Jackson with her hand outstretched like a traffic warden.

'You can't be here this morning,' she says, her chin wobbling. 'I'm sorry, Mrs Curtis, but you'll have to take Jackson home straight away.'

'Why?' Jackson looks as startled as I feel.

The playground bell rings and students begin filing into the quadrangle nearby. It's not winter yet, so still warm enough for assemblies conducted in the fresh air. The parents start dispersing, but I see Lola from soccer approaching. She's accompanied by several other parents I haven't met yet.

'Hi Julia,' she calls out.

'Mrs Curtis, please take Jackson home,' the school principal repeats. 'The police have advised that under no circumstances should he be here.'

'What?' A cold pit gnaws at my stomach.

The world seems to slow down. Jackson's face turns a putrid shade of grey.

'There's been a serious incident, Mrs Curtis.'

'Is everything okay?' Lola calls out, still moving towards us.

The school principal turns and shakes her head at Lola. 'This is not your business.'

Her sharp tone causes Lola to retreat, while other parents cast concerned glances in our direction.

'Mummy!' Ruby materialises next to us. 'Want to meet Tessa?'

I crouch down in front of her and lower my voice. 'Rubes, this is very important. Please just go and sit down for assembly? I'll see you this afternoon.'

'Uh, okay.' With a confused shrug Ruby slinks off, glancing back over her shoulder at us.

In the outdoor quadrangle, a teacher picks up the microphone to commence the morning assembly.

Desperation grips me. 'What's happened, Mrs Bennett?'

'I'll walk you over to the gate now,' the school principal replies.

Jackson stares piteously at me. The other parents remain watchful from a distance.

What the hell is going on? I want to demand.

Instead, I put an arm around Jackson's shoulders and begin walking back across the playground. Our footsteps on the gravel seem intrusively loud, with the entire school gone quiet for assembly. The students sit in obedient lines for the announcements, but I fancy I hear whispering.

Jackson loses all control of his blinking and his feet are dragging in the gravel, so that I have to half-guide, half-push him across the playground.

At the school gate, I turn to speak to the school principal, but she cuts me off.

'This is a police matter now. I'm sorry, Mrs Curtis. I only just received the call. There's been a report filed by a parent about an... incident that happened at school last week.'

'What sort of incident?'

'I haven't been given the details,' she replies. 'All I have is a directive from CAS asking me to make sure Jackson doesn't come to school until a formal interview is conducted. Someone from CAS will be calling you shortly to arrange that.'

Jackson drops to the ground and begins unlacing his right shoe.

'What's CAS?' My mind is a maelstrom of questions, competing in their urgency.

'The Child Abuse Squad.'

Icy panic floods through me. 'Wh-why?'

'Mrs Curtis, all I know is that there's been an allegation from a parent about an incident last Monday. Nothing else.'

'Does that mean Jackson's been...?' The possibilities accost me. I turn to Jackson, but his flat expression offers me nothing. 'Or does someone think we...?'

'The school can't be involved now, I'm sorry.' The woman's tone softens slightly. 'It's being dealt with by the police. CAS will make contact to arrange an interview. I suggest you go home and call Jackson's father.'

I cover my face with my hands. 'He's in New York.'

A teacher's announcements about lost property, labelling

lunchboxes and the second-hand clothing pool are audible from the playground.

I feel I might be going to vomit. 'Should we... take Ruby out of school today as well?'

'We were only instructed about Jackson,' the school principal replies. 'In my view, you should try to minimise disruption for Ruby.'

'I just...' My phone starts to ring before I can finish and I glance at the display. It's a number I don't recognise.

'Excuse me. Hello?' I press a finger to my right ear in an effort to block out the assembly sounds. 'Yes, I'm Julia Curtis.'

The school principal turns and, without another word, walks away.

A monotone voice on the other end of the line advises me of the time and location of a mandatory interview at CAS, which Jackson is required to attend with one or more parents this morning.

'His father's overseas,' I explain. 'But I can bring him there for 10.30.'

The call ends. I stand on the footpath, paralysed by panic.

'Mum?' asks Jackson, after a moment.

I wheel around and seize him by the shoulders. 'What happened last Monday, Jackson? Tell me.' My grip is so firm I can see that I'm scaring him.

'Have you been hurt? Or someone else?'

I'm replaying last Monday in my head: it started with Ruby's nits, Pyjama Day and 'atypical lateness'. After that, only Jackson has the answers.

His face is pained. 'I... don't... know.'

'You don't know?' My heart contracts with every second of silence that passes.

Tears fill Jackson's eyes. This scares me more than anything.

'Well, have a think, Jackson, because we're going to have to go and talk to the police at Chatswood about it now.'

As we move off in the direction of the car, I reach for Jackson's hand.

He clamps his palm against mine, like we're standing together at the edge of a cliff looking down.

12

'Can this be it?' asks Mum, looking up at the tall grey tower.

We're standing outside a building that doesn't look anything like a police station, it's more like Dad's office in the city. Last time I visited the advertising agency, I got to sit at Dad's big desk on the twenty-sixth floor and watch all the ferries on Sydney Harbour. Then I met a super pretty lady called Penelope who does everything for Dad like a servant, only he doesn't ever call her that.

Mum checks her phone again, then we walk inside the skyscraper and press the button in the elevator for the sixth floor.

'Did Dad reply to your message?' I ask.

I'm really hoping he has, because maybe *he* can explain exactly what's going on. Mum doesn't know, and she keeps asking me like I might.

'Not yet. I've tried to ring four times but he must have it on... Do Not Disturb, I guess.' Mum's face looks really strange.

We step into the lift and stand there for a few seconds listening to a song by Taylor Swift piping out of invisible speakers. If Ruby was here she'd start dancing. The lyrics of this song are weird though, about golden tattoos and bedposts and dresses you take off right after you've put them on. When the metal doors slide open a few seconds later, we're already on the sixth floor.

In front of us is a glass wall you can't see through; it looks like the bathroom mirror after I've taken a long shower. There's a small black and white sign near the main door that says *CAS*.

'Did they forget the E?' I ask. 'That's how you spell "case" and that's what the police are always working on.'

Mum doesn't answer me, she's already pressing the intercom and then a lady's voice asks, 'Do you have an appointment?'

'Yes,' says Mum. 'This is the Curtis family.'

'Family' sounds a bit funny, when Dad's in New York and Ruby and Milla are at school, and Nanna Pam's at Rotary and Dead Granny's not here at all.

There's a long buzzing sound as the door unlocks itself. Mum pushes it open and I grab her hand again because she looks like she's about to faint. I don't feel so good either.

On the other side of the door are two white velvety sofas, three pink beanbags, a massive ferny plant, a big television on the wall and a wooden coffee table full of blue kinetic sand.

There's a lady behind a front desk, but Mum doesn't even look at her.

I drop onto my knees and reach for the kinetic sand. I've just scooped up a big handful when a friendly voice says, 'Jackson?' and I look up to see a smiley lady standing near the fern.

'Hello Jackson,' she says, squatting down next to me. 'My name's Annabelle. I work here as a police officer.'

She doesn't look like a police officer. She doesn't look much older than Milla. Her cool red spectacles aren't scary at all, she's got a thick brown ponytail hanging down her back and she smells good too, like vanilla or maybe cinnamon. I'm trying to figure out the flavour, when I notice she's wearing crazy socks like Miss Marion, only hers are pink with brown sausage dogs.

'Do you like my socks?' Annabelle grins at me. 'These are my Monday socks. If you come back tomorrow, I'll wear my Tuesday socks. They're blue with poodles. I've got dogs for every day of the week. Do you like dogs, Jackson?'

I start telling Annabelle about Snickers, who's a sausage dog with longer hair even though he's supposed to be a 'non-shedder'. I tell her how Dad gets cranky when Snickers chews the rug, but how he also knows how to reverse his bum over the garden bed and push out his poop, so we don't ever step in it on the lawn.

'Snickers can do that, I mean, not Dad,' I explain.

'That's clever.' Annabelle laughs. 'Maybe Snickers can come over to my place and teach my Jack Russell to do the same thing?'

'Wow, Jack Russell is a really nice name for a dog,' I say.

Annabelle lets out another tinkly laugh, then she says, 'And that's a really good joke, Jackson.'

I don't tell her I wasn't joking, because there's something about Annabelle that *really* makes me want to make her happy. I have more questions about Jack Russell, but there's a lump in my throat that I need to cough out first.

The noise I make isn't very nice, but Annabelle doesn't pay much attention. She turns and introduces herself to Mum, who's sitting on one of the sofas now. 'Would you like a cup of tea or coffee, or maybe a glass of water, Mrs Curtis?'

Mum shakes her head. That warm ginger tea Dead Granny used to drink at Kaminski's would help my throat, if Annabelle had some in her police kitchen.

'Let me explain how this is going to work.' Annabelle sounds like one of the nice instructors at Ruby's gymnastics club, but Mum doesn't look like she's having any fun at all.

'In a little while, Jackson, we're going to go into a different room to talk about something that happened last week. Someone told us you might know something about that. It's my job to make sure you get your chance to share. Mum can come with you, but it's only going to be you and me talking together for a little while. Is that okay?'

The way she said 'you and me' makes me feel warm inside. 'Okay.'

'And do you mind if your mum comes into the interview with you for support?'

Why would I mind? I wonder, but I don't actually ask.

'Okay,' I say again.

'Great,' she says, sitting down next to Mum on the sofa.

'Why don't you get your hands into that kinetic sand again, Jackson, while I talk a bit more to Mum? You can join in if you want to, but it's probably going to be more fun playing with the sand. I like playing with it on my lunch break.'

She grins at me.

I move back to the table. Do *all* the police play with the kinetic sand at lunchtime, or just the police who work with kids?

I push the sand into a big mound and listen to Mum grill Annabelle about why we're here and what on earth has happened? I'm worried that Annabelle won't like that, but Annabelle just tells her nicely to try to relax.

'Why should I?' Mum argues back. 'We've never been inside a police station in our lives.'

'I understand this is a shock for you, Mrs Curtis.' Annabelle sounds like she really does understand. 'But the sooner you cooperate, the sooner you'll be going home. We both want the same thing.'

Mum sits staring at Annabelle for a while, then she gives a little nod.

It's Annabelle's turn to ask questions now. She asks Mum a whole load of them, like if Mum gives her permission to 'make contact with medical professionals and teachers' and whether I have any 'diagnosed physical or mental health issues'.

'Not diagnosed,' says Mum.

'Tell me more,' says Annabelle, so Mum starts talking about all the boring doctors we've ever seen. Like the child psychologist and the Bad Brain Doctor and Dr Louisa and the karmic kinesiologist who looked a lot like Dumbledore, but he didn't have any magic after all.

Annabelle listens to Mum for a long time. 'You've been working with a family therapist – Dr Louisa Kelleher – for almost two years now. The therapy's been focused mainly on parenting and communication strategies. And Jackson's never been on any medication for a diagnosable condition?'

Mum shakes her head. 'Jackson's just always been a bit... unusual, compared to other children. Not always in a challenging way either. He's got an amazing memory. He can beat his father at chess, hands-down. Dr Kelleher says he's neurodiverse.'

'And what do you think that means?' asks Annabelle.

'Well, I think it means that... Jackson is somewhere on the spectrum, but no one's exactly sure where.'

I've learned about spectrums in science at school. How white light hits a collection of raindrops and turns into a rainbow. Dead Granny always used to say, 'You can't get a rainbow without the rain, Jackson.'

Annabelle asks Mum more questions about whether I can

read and write and what my school reports say about my behaviour and friendships and how I 'manage emotions'. I want to tell her about my dance group at school, but Annabelle's totally focused on Mum.

'Can you help me understand Jackson's challenges a little more, Mrs Curtis?'

Mum looks a bit put out. 'Well, on the physical side, Jackson has multiple tics.'

If I've got multiple ticks, that means I must have done something good. And *that's* the name of a song Mum always sings for the Special Ps at Care Cottage, from an old film called *The Sound of Music*. It should've been called *The Sound of Migrants* though, because it's about people who had to leave their homes in Europe and run away from the nasties, just like Dead Granny's parents. In German I think they spell nasty with a 'z', so it ends up looking like Nazi.

I start humming the tune.

Annabelle glances over at me, maybe she's heard me. She smiles, even though my eyelids are twitching and I can't get the hairball out of my throat.

She turns back to Mum. 'Do you think the blinking and the throat-clearing could be a function of Jackson being nervous today?'

'It happens at other times, too,' says Mum.

If my throat wasn't so jammed up, I'd tell Annabelle about how Dr Louisa is teaching me to 'stop thinking about blinking' by imagining a golden beach with palm trees and gentle waves.

Mum whispers something about me 'never quite fitting into any diagnostic category'. Annabelle seems interested in this, but their sentences are getting longer and longer. *Atypical, nonconforming, not diagnosable, blahdey blah-blah-blah.*

I've heard it all before, so I stop eavesdropping and start

building layers of lava flows in the kinetic sand. I'm making a river of fire down the volcano, turning everything into piles of ash, when suddenly Annabelle crouches down next to me.

'That looks awesome,' she says.

Suddenly I'm feeling shy again.

Then she's taking me and Mum down a long corridor and into a big room that looks a bit like someone's dining room, with a square white table and comfortable chairs with orange cushions on them and a massive mirror along the wall.

We sit down at the table and, because of the mirror, it feels like there's six of us in the room. There's lots of art stuff on the table, like colourful markers and highlighters and glitter pens. I want to try them all out, but I'm a bit too nervous.

Annabelle starts talking to Mum again, saying she's not allowed to answer for me and if any of her questions are 'difficult to understand or unfairly couched', then Mum needs to tell her straight away.

I want to ask Annabelle how a couch could be unfair, but Mum looks edgy, so I don't.

'Any questions?' Annabelle asks.

Mum shakes her head.

'Good,' says Annabelle. 'If you need a break, Jackson, let me know. Also, Mrs Curtis, Jackson is not obliged to say or do anything unless he wishes to do so. Anything that he does say or do may be recorded and given in evidence. Do you understand?'

'Yes,' says Mum. Her voice is all shaky.

Annabelle turns to me.

'Jackson, like I just told your mum, you don't have to answer my questions today. You don't have to do anything you don't want to do. We're just having a chat, okay? And just so you know, our chat today is recorded, because what you tell me is really important. Do you understand, Jackson?'

'Yes,' I say, copying Mum.

Annabelle gives me a little wink, like we're about to start playing Monopoly.

'So, Jackson,' she says, 'how did you get here today?'

'Mum drove us in the Red Rocket.'

Annabelle smiles. 'What's the Red Rocket?'

'Our seven-seater van,' I say. 'It's fire-engine red.'

'Cool,' says Annabelle, smiling even wider. 'So, if I said to you, Jackson, "Today you and Mum came here by train", would that be the truth or a lie?'

'A lie,' I say.

'And what happens if you tell a lie?'

'You get in trouble.'

'Has that happened to you before, Jackson?' she asks. 'Have you ever been in trouble for telling a lie?'

I tell her about the time when I was four and Mum took me shopping to buy a birthday present for Milla. There were these blueberry erasers near the cash register and I asked Mum if I could have one, but she said no. I loved their smell so much, I took one anyway. Later when we got home, Mum asked how I got the eraser and I told her that the lady in the shop gave it to me.

'That was a lie,' I explain. 'Mum made me take it back and say sorry to the shop lady.'

'That was the right thing to do,' says Annabelle. 'Well done, Jackson.'

I feel like buttery toast inside because Annabelle said I did the right thing.

'Can we make a promise here and now, that you won't tell any lies today?'

'Yes,' I say, watching her hair turn a honey colour under the bright lights above us.

'Thank you, Jackson,' says Annabelle. 'First of all, I'd love to find out a little bit more about your family and friends and school.'

I'm pretty sure Mum's already told her everything in the waiting room, but I repeat it all anyway. Annabelle wants to know who's in my family and what Queenscliff Public's like and whether it's different to my old school in Erskineville. She asks about what I liked at school *there* versus school *here*, and if there's anything that worries me at school, and who my friends are.

The questions are easy to answer. I even get to tell her about dance with Miss Marion.

'Great.' Annabelle smiles. 'Now, can you tell me about what happened at school last Monday?'

I tell her that Mondays are always extra busy with dance practice *and* chess club on at the same time.

'What was different about last Monday?' she asks. 'Can you remember anything particular that happened?'

I think a bit. 'On that Monday, we had atypical lateness.'

Annabelle waits for me to say more.

Mum reaches forward and moves a glass of water closer to my hand. I gulp most of it down, hoping that drinking might distract my eyelids. Then I try to imagine Dr Louisa's golden sandy beach.

Annabelle's still waiting.

'Maybe just start by telling me a bit about your day?' she asks. 'What were the good and not-so-good things that happened on Monday at school?'

I finish the water.

'A good thing was... I saw my friend April Kennedy in class.

A bad thing was... Mr Thompson sent me out because I used the wrong words. He thought I was being rude. Digby came with me.'

It takes me a while to get it all out, but Annabelle nods like she's pleased with me.

'Go on, Jackson. What happened after you were sent out of class and Digby came with you?'

'We walked across the playground under the fig tree to the toilets. When we got there, a third-grader was there too. A girl.'

I'm stuttering a bit.

'Do you know the girl's name, Jackson?'

I nod. 'Sienna Wilson-Brown. Tommy's little sister. She's nine, like Ruby. Tommy plays on my soccer team. He's the Dragons' best striker.'

'What did Sienna look like, Jackson?'

I tell her about Sienna's nice blonde hair and bright blue eyes and really thick glasses and how on Monday she was wearing a nightie with gold stars and a dressing gown with Ugg boots for Pyjama Day.

'Pyjama Day sounds like fun,' says Annabelle. 'What was Sienna doing when you saw her, Jackson?'

I swallow hard. It's not easy answering when my throat's closing down.

'She was... going to the toilet.'

'Were you in the girls' toilets or the boys' toilets, Jackson?'

'Girls',' I say, embarrassed.

'And what did you see inside the girls' toilets, Jackson?'

'These pink tiles on the wall that looked like a chess game.'

'Was anyone else in there too?'

I shake my head. 'All the other toilets were empty.'

'Anything else?' asks Annabelle.

'I saw Sienna's boot turned over in a puddle. I set it straight because no one likes wet slippers.'

She waits and waits as if I should say more. My stomach is twisting so much, I think it might explode.

'What did you hear in the toilets, Jackson?' asks Annabelle.

'I heard the water in the pipes,' I say. 'And the sound of Sienna's wee and the toilet flushing before...'

I'm having trouble with my words.

'Before what, Jackson?'

'Before we played the trick on her.'

'What type of trick, Jackson?'

I shrug, because Digby never told me.

Annabelle sits there staring at me for a long time. Then she asks really softly, 'What did you touch when you were in the toilets, Jackson?'

I shake my head.

'Nothing at all?' Annabelle's voice is louder now. 'Let's build a picture together. You're standing in the girls' toilets near Sienna Wilson-Brown and you're playing a trick on her. What exactly are your hands doing, Jackson?'

'I've got one hand against the door...'

'Which hand?' she asks. 'Left or right?'

'Is that important?' Mum asks, like she's suddenly woken up.

Annabelle turns to her. 'Do you think he's misunderstood the question, Mrs Curtis?'

Mum looks uncomfortable. 'No, but I just don't know if Jackson has the ability to answer these questions in the way... other children might.'

Wanting to prove Mum wrong, I think really hard. 'It's my... my left hand on the toilet door.'

'Good, Jackson.' Annabelle turns back to me. 'And what's

your right hand doing?'

I really *don't* want to tell her that it's covering my eyes, trying to stop the blinking. It's embarrassing enough that I'm motor-blinking right now.

'What's your right hand doing, Jackson?' Annabelle repeats.

'Nothing,' I say.

'Jackson.' Annabelle leans forward in her seat. 'Remember your promise to me earlier, about not lying today?'

My blinking speeds up even more, then suddenly there's tears in my eyes and they're spearing down my cheeks and diving onto the table like kamikaze pilots crashing into the sea.

Annabelle just smiles in this really gentle way. 'So you're standing near Sienna with your left hand on the toilet door. What is your right hand doing, Jackson?'

I wish I could just lie down on Dr Louisa's imaginary beach.

'My right hand is... busy,' I say.

'It's busy.' Annabelle nods slowly. 'And what happened, Jackson, while your right hand was... "busy"?'

I let out a big breath.

'I heard Sienna say, "Stop, I don't like it".'

Mum rocks forward and claps her hands over her mouth. I want to try holding one of them, but Annabelle won't stop asking questions.

'Did you stop what you were doing, Jackson?' asks Annabelle. 'When Sienna said, "Stop, I don't like it"?'

'The trick was over really quickly,' I explain. 'We left and went back to class.'

'Who touched Sienna, Jackson?'

I close my eyes and watch my memory download replaying what happened in the toilets last Monday morning. I see myself reaching under the cubicle door to set Sienna's slipper right, and my hand accidentally touching her leg.

'I touched her.'

Mum's crying into her hands in this weird silent way. Annabelle takes a box of tissues from a drawer beneath the table and pushes them towards her.

'Digby was in the toilets with you,' says Annabelle. 'What was he doing?'

Even with my memory download in slow-mo, I can't actually *see* what Digby's doing inside the cubicle.

'I don't know,' I say, because that's the truth.

I sneak a look at Mum, but she's not listening any more. She's just staring like a zombie at the big mirror behind Annabelle's head.

'This morning Digby told us what he remembers about what happened in the toilets last Monday,' says Annabelle. 'Digby said he was following you. He said that you started what happened in the toilets. Is he telling the truth, Jackson?'

I close my eyes and think about this.

If I hadn't made Mr Thompson so cranky that he sent me out of class, which made Digby follow me to the toilets, we wouldn't have gone into the girls' side at all. We wouldn't have tricked Sienna and we wouldn't have missed science. We would have just stayed in class learning about celestial motions and *none* of this would have even happened.

So Digby is right, he *did* follow me last Monday. It all started with my stupid di-urinal motion.

'Yes,' I say. 'Digby followed me.'

Mum makes a gurgling sound. She doesn't even look like Mum any more.

'Thank you, Jackson,' says Annabelle. 'That's enough for the time being.'

I'm wondering if going into the girls' toilets when you're a boy is actually a crime, but Annabelle keeps talking.

'You've been very cooperative, Jackson, I appreciate that. I may have some more questions, but for the time being, I need to have a quick chat with your mum by herself. Can you stay here while we do that? We won't be long, I promise.'

She picks up a pad of paper and a set of glitter pens, then pushes them across the table at me. 'Can you draw a picture while you wait? What will you draw?'

'Snickers being naughty.'

Annabelle doesn't smile.

'Can I call Jackson's father?' asks Mum.

'Not yet,' says Annabelle. 'This is still part of the initial interview process. It won't take more than five minutes.'

Annabelle and Mum stand up and leave the room. The way Mum shuffles out reminds me a bit of Dead Granny, with her shoulders rolled forward like she's carrying an ancient sewing machine from Poland.

The big blue door shuts behind them with a clang. It must be made of steel and maybe even bullet-proof. Maybe prison doors are like that, too?

I try not to think about prison. I don't know much about it, except for the yucky food and hard beds and scary criminals in stripy onesies. I don't want to go to prison, but I guess the police might send me there if being a boy in the girls' toilets is wrong. If it's a crime, they might send Digby too.

The room is really quiet without Mum and Annabelle. I can't hear anything except my memory download ticking over. It's always there, streaming inside my brain, scrolling through all the days and nights I've ever had since I was four months old. Showing me what I was wearing, what the weather was like, what I saw and smelled and touched and in what order, recording every single day that's ever been.

Annabelle said she was recording our interview, but I don't think I want to replay today ever again.

When will Mum come back?

Annabelle said it wouldn't take long, but adults always get time mixed up. *In a moment* means *maybe never*, and *in a while* can mean *next week*. I wish I could talk to Dad right now, but New York is so far away.

I pull my left ankle over my right knee and check my shoe-phone. I really want to talk to Dead Granny, but my shoe-phone's still shut down. I hope it reboots tomorrow, but I'm worried that maybe Dead Granny has her shoe-phone turned to Do Not Disturb, like Dad's phone sometimes. Maybe she doesn't want to speak to me any more? Maybe if I tell her about the police interview today, she won't *ever* talk to me again.

Big tears bubble up in my eyes.

If I can't speak to Dead Granny, I'd better pray to St Jhudiel, my birth angel. Dead Granny gave me some special words to use if ever I found myself in trouble, and being interviewed by the police is the biggest trouble I've ever had.

I bow my head to pray to St Jhudiel because he's the mercy specialist.

'Oh Wonderful Archangel Jhudiel...'

When I finish reciting the words, I open my eyes and stare at the big wide mirror that stretches along the wall. I still look skinny and pale and scared, but I feel a tiny bit better.

So I keep repeating the prayer, closing my eyes like Dead Granny used to before every meal, until the words start calming me down.

Dead Granny was right about a lot of things.

Even though she lives in the Otherworld now, she's still right.

13

'Mrs Curtis, take a seat.'

The detective ushers me into a private room and motions at another bland white table with two chairs on either side. No mirror, no art therapy supplies, no glasses of water. It's just me and her, and *I'm* barely here. I'm utterly overwhelmed, struggling to understand what just happened in that interview room with Jackson. The only thing that's patently clear is that Andy would have been a much better advocate for our son.

'Can I call my husband now, please?' I feel incapable of carrying this burden alone any longer.

'Not yet,' the detective replies. 'You agreed to be the designated support person for Jackson's initial interview and this conversation is an extension of that. You can call your husband afterwards.'

The numbness begins to transform into anger; I feel a sudden urge to slap the woman's carefully arranged face.

The interview earlier was sickening, watching her lure Jackson with all that faux-friendly banter. Reeling him in with her warm smile and casual questions, building trust and empathy for the purpose of ensnaring him.

And Jackson fell so easily under her spell, I *hate* her for it.

But I hate myself more.

Now I find that *I'm* the parent of a child who's hurt another child, a nine-year-old girl who could have been my daughter. Instinctively I seize my phone to message Hannah, then toss it back onto the table in disgust. Who am I kidding? Hannah won't want to hear from me, ever again.

'Mrs Curtis.' The detective folds her hands on the table. 'It's not my job to determine whether Jackson is guilty of the allegation. That's something for the courts to decide. Today's interview was for initial information collection only.'

Fuchsia-coloured lipstick weaving over chalky-white teeth.

'But I do need to advise that Jackson's interview suggests that a serious offence has occurred, which means police investigations will be ongoing.'

The ingratiating charm has vanished.

'To further our investigations, I'm filing for magistrate's permission to conduct a DNA swab on Jackson today. I'd be grateful for your continued cooperation. You can stay here while that application is processed. It shouldn't take long.'

My mind is barely keeping pace with her words. 'Please, slow down. What... DNA are you checking?'

'Evidence has been collected from the victim, Mrs Curtis. A clothing sample has been retrieved. I'm not at liberty to discuss the details.'

'But, uh... what exactly is the allegation?'

'Assault.' The detective's face is expressionless. 'The DNA swab will help us ascertain the precise nature of it and the degree of severity. Potentially a charge under Section 66A of the Crimes Act 1990 for Sexual Intercourse-Child Under 10.'

It's as if an electric volt has passed through my body.

'Digital penetration, if it occurred, is deemed sexual intercourse under the law, Mrs Curtis,' the detective continues. 'The charge carries serious penalties, including imprisonment.'

I gape at her. 'But I didn't hear anything that suggested...'

'An assault of some kind has occurred, Mrs Curtis, that's indisputable. We have the physical evidence. Now we just have to find out what type of assault. That's why we're here.'

Bile floods my mouth. I gag into a tissue.

'Would you like some water?'

I shake my head.

'That's just not... That's not Jackson. He's only eleven years old.'

The detective shrugs. 'The statutory presumption in this state is that a child under the age of ten years cannot commit a criminal offence. Eleven to fourteen is a grey area, but the presumption of *Doli incapax* can be challenged where there is sufficient evidence that a child has formed *mens rea*.'

I have no idea what she's just said to me. 'Dolly-what?'

'Where a child understands the difference between right and wrong, Mrs Curtis, the presumption that a child is incapable of crime under legislation or common law can be challenged. This seems applicable in Jackson's case.'

I stare at her, my mind roiling. Is that why she questioned Jackson about the difference between truth and lies, at the beginning of his interview? To prove that he *was* capable of a crime?

'I suggest you seek legal advice, as soon as possible,' she continues. 'After the DNA swab you're free to go, but the family of the victim has instigated a civil court order to prevent Jackson from contacting her directly, or through a third party.'

'The victim.' The word slices through me. If Sienna is a victim, then Jackson is a perpetrator. An offender. A criminal.

I close my eyes, recalling last Saturday's soccer match. Sienna's sombreness on the sideline, which couldn't be mollified by her mother.

I fight the urge to retch again.

'Where do I find legal advice?' Our family's only prior contact with the law is the occasional speeding ticket.

'I can't help you with that, sorry.'

She doesn't sound sorry at all.

Annabelle stands up and motions at the door.

'I'll take you back to the waiting room, Mrs Curtis. You must be present for the DNA swab once the court order comes through. We need permission to conduct a forensic procedure on a young person.'

'Why, is it invasive?' I'm worried for Jackson now. 'Will it hurt?'

The detective wheels around and faces me. For the first time, I detect authentic emotion passing across her face; something between disdain and incredulity.

'It's just a mouth swab,' she snarls, before regaining her composure.

I follow her out of the room, along the barren corridor and out into the waiting room. 'I'll bring Jackson out shortly,' she intones, closing it behind her.

Tears flood down my cheeks and plummet onto my blouse. I seize my phone and dial Andy. I don't care what time it is in New York.

A small cube materialises on the screen and then Andy appears, smiling. Judging by the low-lit backdrop and audible piano music, he's in a café or restaurant.

'Hi there.' He sounds chirpy. 'Sorry I missed your calls. You'd love it here, Jules. Best cabaret I've heard in years.'

When he sees my face, his smile evaporates. 'What's wrong?'

A strangled cry bursts out of my throat.

'What is it, Julia?'

I tell him everything.

When I finally stop, his mouth hangs open.

'Did you hear Jackson admit to... anything?'

I shrug, feeling thoroughly incapable of dealing with any of this.

'Julia, what did Jackson actually say he did?' Andy's tone is desperate.

I glance around the room, trying to reconstruct the detail of it, but my mind is strangely slippery. Are there hidden cameras in the waiting room too, recording this desperate exchange?

'I can't remember, I'm sorry.'

I listened to the interview earlier with greater attention than I've applied to anything in my life, but now – less than thirty minutes later – I can't recall important details.

Andy's face is stony.

'There was a lot going on,' I stammer. 'I was hearing the story from Jackson for the first time and I was just... surviving it, Andy.'

'We need some help,' Andy's tone is brutal. 'A barrister. I know someone who'll know someone. I'll call you back.'

He ends the call abruptly.

The blue slider opens. Jackson appears in the doorway, standing next to the detective. I've never seen him look so fragile.

'Here we are, Jackson,' the detective says in her syrupy traitor's voice. 'I'll come and get you and Mum when it's time for the mouth swab, okay?'

Jackson shuffles back into the waiting room. For a moment he's distracted by the television, the movement and colour of an animal documentary on mute. Then he bows his head and sinks onto a beanbag. Reaching for the table, he scoops some kinetic sand into his palm and watches it trickle through his fingers.

There's no instruction manual for this, no best-practice parenting tips.

'Are you okay, Jackson?'

He ignores me.

I should have protected Jackson more in that interview, I realise now. Or at the very least, demanded legal counsel in the face of such dreadful allegations. But what if it's true? If Jackson's done what Detective Annabelle Johnson claims he might have, as much as I love him, I can't possibly defend him.

How can I connect with my son right now, not knowing which it is?

Tears fill my eyes. Should I call Dr Kelleher? This situation is more paralysing than all of our previous challenges put together.

What would Mum do?

I look down at my loafers. Wishing I could call her, like Jackson does, through the sole of a shoe. Part of me is relieved she's not here to witness this nightmare, for it would surely break her heart.

I close my eyes and try to imagine the contours of my mother's face, something that gets harder to do with each passing year. But I can never fail to visualise her standing at the stove stirring a huge pot of grochówka, infusing love for her family along with the rest of the ingredients.

'A full stomach fixes anything,' Mum used to say.

My eyes snap open.

'Jackson?' I crouch down next to him. 'What would you like for lunch?'

His gaze drifts away from the television.

When our eyes meet, I see the overwhelming fear in his.

'Oh, Jackson.' I pull him to my chest, rocking him gently.

'I didn't know I did something wrong.' A single tear slides down his cheek.

There *must* be more to this, every part of me insists.

'What should I do, Mum?'

'I don't know, Jackson.' I exhale. 'How about we just start with... some lunch?'

I'm trying to stay focused on Jackson's basic needs, in the here and now, even as I fight a fresh wave of nausea.

I stand up and move towards a surly-looking receptionist barricaded behind a high desk. Somehow I failed to notice her when we arrived this morning.

'Er, hi. We need to get some lunch. Is it... okay for us to go out?'

We're not under arrest, I tell myself.

The woman looks up from her laptop. 'Can you do that in less than fifteen minutes? Any longer can be deemed an obstruction to police processes, as Detective Johnson would have explained.'

Detective Johnson didn't explain anything.

'Okay,' I murmur, then turn back to Jackson. 'Come downstairs. Let's buy some lunch. It won't take long.'

'I just want to...' He motions at the television.

'Please, come,' I croak. 'I can't leave you here alone.'

He looks up at me, perhaps hearing the desperation in my voice.

Wordlessly, he stands up. Threading an arm through mine, he guides me out of the office.

We say nothing to each other in the lift.

Downstairs, the world is betraying us with its glassy sky, warm autumn sunshine and the contented thrum of an ordinary Monday.

We wander along the street, searching for a sandwich vendor.

My phone vibrates in my handbag and a message from Andy appears.

Found a defence lawyer, Jeff Goldstein. Wins at all costs, apparently. Ringing him now. No seats on earlier flight, sorry. Will call from airport tomorrow.

What does *winning at all costs* mean, when no one can possibly emerge from this a *winner*?

I stop abruptly and lean against a telegraph pole. My head flies forward as I retch into the gutter.

'Oh, Mum.' Jackson puts an arm around my shoulders.

I dab the corners of my mouth with my sleeve, then steel myself to continue walking.

So many times over the past six years I've felt defeated by Andy's trips away, Jackson's challenges, and the minutiae of family life. Now I have something far more significant to worry about.

'There's a place.' Jackson points at a delicatessen on the opposite side of the street.

We cross the road and join the short queue inside. The smell of bacon, eggs and grilled cheese is sickening.

Jackson looks poorly too. 'Mum, I need to...' He points at a sign, then bolts towards the lavatories.

My eyes well up.

The young woman behind the counter takes my order, pretending she doesn't notice my tears. It's uncomfortable for us both. I fumble for my sunglasses in my handbag, to protect myself from the scrutiny of strangers.

My phone vibrates again. Exasperated, I riffle in my handbag for it. I don't want to talk about the defence lawyer, I just want to buy a sandwich for our son. It feels like an achievable goal right now, when I've clearly failed in so many other ways.

The message is from Steve, not Andy.

Thanks again for Saturday night. Fun spending time with you! Nicest night I've had in a while.

Drinking wine on the veranda with Jackson's soccer coach only thirty-six hours ago feels like the actions of another woman, in another lifetime.

Just checking you're still okay to take soccer training this arvo? Equipment is in my back yard for collection. Thanks for helping out

I groan aloud and compose a return message.

I'm so sorry, Steve. I can't do training today. Something awful has happened. My apologies.

Within fifteen seconds, Steve calls me.
I try to sound normal as I answer.
'Are you okay, Julia?'
These four words prompt a barrage of my own.
Cupping my hand over my mouth, I move away from the

sandwich counter and lean against a wall, blabbering through my tears. Steve simply listens, offering the occasional comforting sound.

I'm still talking as Jackson emerges from the toilet. It's a relief to be sharing this nightmare with Steve but, as Jackson walks towards me, I begin to feel embarrassed.

'I'm sorry for... dumping all of this on you,' I whisper. 'I really shouldn't have mentioned any names. Please don't say anything, to anyone, Steve?'

The woman behind the counter calls out our order. Jackson accepts the lunch bag, then wanders towards the door. At the shopfront, he stands watching the passers-by on the street.

'No worries,' says Steve. 'I'm so concerned for you, Julia. I wish I could give you a hug right now.'

Such sympathy only makes me cry more.

'You poor thing,' he says. 'Poor Jackson. Poor everyone.'

'Poor Sienna.' I weep quietly into the phone. 'Hannah and her family must... despise us. Jackson can't go near Sienna; he'll have to resign from the Dragons. Digby will too. No one will want anything to do with us.'

I'm sobbing at the growing realisation of the likely ripple effect. What will *other* mothers – my friends, like Lola – think of me and my family now? My school-based friendships can't survive this.

'You're at Ground Zero,' says Steve. 'It's appalling, but this is day one. I know it's of little comfort, but you'll never have to go through this day again.'

'But there'll be more days,' I wail, stifling the sound with my hand. 'More and more days. It's a nightmare that's never going to end...'

Steve listens as my sobbing subsides.

'You're right, there will be more difficult days, but... you still have friends for support. People like me. Things will shift. They won't stay like this forever. You've got to believe that, Julia.'

I don't think I truly can right now.

'Thank you, Steve.'

'Anytime,' he says. 'And with your permission, I'd like to come over and visit Jackson, too. He's going to be needing some friends. Maybe I could just kick the soccer ball around with him in the back yard?'

I glance at Jackson, still loitering in the doorway.

How will our family survive the coming weeks of collective outrage – from soccer families to the school community to the world at large?

'You there, Julia?' Steve asks, after a moment.

'Yes,' I whisper. 'You're a wonderful human being, Steve.'

'Well, that's overstating things,' he says. 'We don't know each other very well, Julia, but... you're a good person. Can I pop over later tonight, just to check you're okay? I'll be flying in from Melbourne around six o'clock.'

'I don't think so,' I say, walking towards Jackson. 'I just...'

'No worries,' he says quickly. 'But listen, if you ever need to talk, day or night, just call. Promise?'

'Promise,' I say, ending the call.

Joining Jackson in the doorway, I shield my eyes from the disorienting sunshine.

'Here's the order.' He passes me the lunch bag, then turns and sets out in the direction of the CAS office.

'But it's for you,' I murmur, as I follow him back along the street.

14

'Your cheese toastie is getting cold,' I say, gesturing at the brown bag sitting untouched on the waiting room table.

Jackson looks pained. 'I'm still not hungry. Maybe after the... What's the test I've got to do, Mum?'

My gut clenches. 'A DNA test.'

'What's it for?'

'Did the detective explain?'

'I can't remember. It's weird, I usually remember everything.'

'I know,' I say. 'I can't remember much of the interview either. Maybe we're both in shock.'

I've seen it happen at the hospice: the uncanny amnesia of the traumatised. Grief-stricken carers and patients confusing shock with early onset dementia.

Jackson's eyes are glassy. 'What happened to Sienna in the toilets, Mum?'

I stare at him. 'You told the detective that you... touched her.'

'I did.'

I swallow back the bile rising again.

'Is a DNA test for legs?'

'No, Jackson.' I squint at him, wondering what he's driving at. 'The police officers take some cells from your mouth, not your legs. They'll put a cotton swab in for a few seconds, then it'll be over. It won't hurt.'

'Why do they want my cells?'

'Well, DNA is sort of like a fingerprint. There's a set of genetic characteristics that are specific to you. Everyone's DNA profile is different.'

'But why do the police need it, Mum?'

I'm floundering. If only Andy was here right now, to relieve me of this burden of responding to Jackson. I've felt like this for a long time, I realise suddenly.

'The police want to compare your DNA with... the DNA they've collected from Sienna's clothes. It will help confirm exactly what happened in the toilets last Monday.'

The detective didn't name the item of clothing retrieved from Sienna, but I think I can imagine. The thought makes me nauseous all over again.

'So... the inside of my mouth will help show the police what happened in the school toilets?' Jackson looks astonished.

'Yes. I'm not exactly sure how, but it's a very accurate scientific process.'

'Good,' he says, curiously. 'I'll have to tell Mr Thompson about that when I go back to school.'

The naivety of this statement annihilates me.

Jackson's gaze returns to the television again, distracted now by a children's programme on guinea pigs. I join him on the giant fluffy bean bag because what else can I do?

Minutes or hours later, when my legs are cramping and

there's still no sign of the detective, my phone rings. I flinch at the caller notification while realising I must answer it.

'Hello?'

'Hello there,' says Pamela cheerily. 'Are you stuck at work? Need any help with school pick-ups?'

I glance at my watch. It's almost two-thirty, yet I've completely forgotten about my daughters. 'Oh, yes, thanks Pamela.'

'I noticed you weren't at home when I drove past earlier... so I thought something must've come up.'

I can't bring myself to set her straight.

'It'd be great if you could pick up Ruby. Milla will just catch the bus home.'

'Okay then,' she chirps, 'see you at home a bit later?'

As the call ends, an agonising thought lodges in my mind: I'm going to have to tell all *three* of them what's happened.

I turn back to Jackson.

'Are you hungry yet?' I ask, pointing at the sandwich bag.

Jackson shakes his head, his eyes still fixed on the television.

The detective reappears at the slider.

'Thanks for waiting.' She smiles at Jackson. 'Have you had any lunch?'

You couldn't care less about our lunch, I think.

'Yes,' says Jackson, even though he hasn't. 'Mum bought me a toastie.'

He sits up straighter as the detective moves towards us. It's confounding how eager he is to please this woman.

'Good.' The detective smiles. 'Come through for the mouth swab, Jackson. Your Mum is going to come along too. Is that okay?'

Jackson nods.

We follow the detective down the empty corridor. It's a much smaller room this time, with a desk, three chairs and a metal chest of drawers.

'Sit down, please, Jackson.' She motions to a chair, then opens a drawer and removes a sealed plastic bag.

She holds it up for Jackson to see.

'This is called a buccal test,' she explains. 'We asked the magistrate for permission to take a DNA sample from you, Jackson. The magistrate approved our application. What we collect will be stored in a DNA databank and analysed. No one will have access to it apart from authorised forensic pathologists.'

The detective snaps on a pair of latex gloves as she delivers her spiel by rote. How much could Jackson possibly be understanding, when I'm struggling to take it in myself?

'The results will be returned in about four weeks. The sample will be stored until the investigation is closed. Your Mum is here as your support.'

The detective peels open the swab kit.

'We're going to take a quick mouth swab now. I'll put a cotton swab in your mouth and brush the inside of your cheek a few times. Are you all right with that?'

Jackson nods.

'Let's pretend you're at the dentist.' The detective smiles. 'Open wide!'

The sing-song tone of her voice makes me want to slap her, but Jackson complies. The procedure is over in ten seconds.

'Done,' says the detective, sealing the bag with the sample inside. 'You can go home now, Jackson. I've spoken to your Mum about what you need to do while we wait for the test results. There are a few rules. First, you won't be able to go back to school.'

Jackson's eyes fill with tears.

'Second, we're going to need to speak to you again, in all likelihood. For a second interview.'

I put an arm around him.

'Third, FACS will be wanting to conduct a home visit within the next few days.'

'FACS?' I ask.

'Family and Community Services,' she replies. 'They'll need to ascertain the likely risk of harm in the home.'

'Harm to who?'

'Siblings and so forth,' says the detective. 'They'll explain it all.'

I blanch. I don't want FACS or CAS or any other acronym invading our home.

'We're all finished.' The detective stands. 'Would you like to go home, Jackson?'

Jackson leaps to his feet.

She walks us along the corridor, ushers us through the slider and into the waiting room.

'You're free to go now,' she announces. 'If you have any further questions, you know how to contact us.'

'Bye, Annabelle,' says Jackson. 'Say hi to Jack Russell for me.'

The detective looks momentarily confused. 'Oh... yes. Goodbye, Jackson. Mrs Curtis.'

As the door slides shut behind us, my phone rings.

Jackson peers at the handset and beams. 'Can I speak to Dad? Please, Mum?'

'Sure,' I say. 'Just let me speak to him first.'

'Hi Andy.' We watch the video cube materialise on the screen.

'Where are you?' asks Andy, as the picture clears.

'With Jackson. We're just leaving the CAS office now. They did a DNA swab.'

Andy's expression darkens. 'Without a lawyer present?'

'Yes, but... it was an extension of the interview earlier.'

'Jesus, Julia!' He rakes a hand through his hair. 'You should have waited.'

'I'm sorry. I didn't know if...'

'It's too bloody late for sorry,' he snaps. 'We need to know exactly where this puts us. I'll call the defence lawyer.'

I nod as the video cube vanishes.

'But... I wanted to talk to him,' says Jackson.

'I'm sorry,' I say, as the elevator doors open.

I may well spend the rest of my life apologising.

We stare at the panel above door, counting down the floors.

I put an arm around Jackson, as much for me as for him. I've never felt lonelier in my life.

On the street again, we retrace the route to the van. Within metres of reaching it, Jackson races ahead and lifts a small white ticket from beneath the windscreen wiper. 'Oh no, it's a parking fine!'

'That's the least of our worries, Jackson.'

'But you cried last time we got one, Mum.'

I shake my head at the irony of it all. A hefty fine incurred for a twelve-minute parking infringement, and my even heftier overreaction at the time. What I wouldn't give now for a thousand parking fines, in lieu of a sexual assault allegation.

'It wasn't worth worrying about. I needed to get some perspective, Jackson.'

Jackson nods thoughtfully. 'We've been studying perspective in art.'

I've needed perspective the whole damn time, I realise. Parenting a child with special-yet-undiagnosed needs has been challenging, but I never considered how much *worse* it could be. Now that I'm in a newfound nadir, I'm rapidly seeing how good things once were.

'Can I ride in the front?' asks Jackson.

Normally, I'd say no.

'Sure.'

We climb into the van.

'Can I go back to school tomorrow, Mum?'

I shake my head. 'You heard what Annabelle said. You won't be able to go back to school for a while.'

'What does "a while" mean?'

'I don't know, darling.'

'But I can't miss the Winter Eisteddfod. I'm the boy angel.' His eyelids start to flicker and his fingers stray to his nose. 'Miss Marion's made a special role for me.'

I reach for his hand.

'I'm sorry, Jackson, but this situation is... very serious. Whatever happened last Monday means that for now, there can't be any school. Or dance. Or soccer. Until the police give us permission to... go back to all that.'

I'm holding both of his hands now, far too tightly.

Jackson's face is so despondent, my heart feels as if it's being wrung-out like wet washing.

'It won't be forever. We'll have to take it one day at a time. Right now, we're just waiting for Dad to come back from New York.'

I put the keys into the ignition and glance out of my window. A polished black Jeep is parked across the road, a 'My Family' sticker collection displayed on the rear window, depicting five cutesy stick-figures – Dad, Mum and three kids.

We *were* that family, until this morning.

Pulling my phone from my bag, I tap out a quick message to Pamela.

On our way home now – ETA 45 minutes.

As I close the message, a headline pops into my news feed: *Attack in primary school toilets.*

The breath escapes my lungs as I click on the link.

Two boys in Year Five at a Northern Beaches primary school are undergoing questioning in relation to an alleged assault of a third-grade student in a school toilet block last week. The nine-year-old girl reported the incident to her parents on Sunday, Murdoch Media has been told. The boys have been suspended from school as police investigations continue.

How has this reached the media already? I glance over at Jackson. He's picking at a scab on his knee, oblivious.

Checking the home screen again, I scroll through the Year 5 Facebook Group; there are forty-eight posts in a discussion thread entitled *Incident in the girls' toilets last Monday.*

My stomach churns as I piece it together in reverse order:

Sarah Ferguson: There's no way they'll let those boys back in school. They'll be suspended for sure. [22 likes]

Dell Pearce: Bryony told me a few boys were off 'sick' today. I've got their names. Happy to share if anyone wants to know. PM me. [7 likes]

Troy Roberts: Mrs Bennett said the school's sending an email tonight about counselling for the kids. [40 likes]

Maria Browning: Will the kids be offered counselling? [43 likes]

Jayne Adams: Let the police do their job first. [32 likes]

Lisa Jensen: It's assault but we don't know the full details. [7 likes]

Terri Edwards: No sympathy for those boys or their parents!!! A 9-year old girl has been assaulted. Naming names keeps our schools safe. [26 likes]

Jo Mack: FFS. Why put up names? We don't know the full story. I don't even know what the allegation is. Let the police do their job first. Think of the parents. [22 likes]

Terri Edwards: Jackson Curtis got sent home by Mrs Bennett before assembly. A few parents saw something happening in the play-ground. [15 likes]

I stop reading. I'm barely out of the van before I'm dry-retching into the gutter.

Lola was one of those parents this morning.

'Are you all right, Mum?' Jackson's shoes materialise in my line of vision.

I stand up slowly. 'Any water, hon?'

Jackson scrambles back into the van and finds a water bottle.

'Poor Mum,' he murmurs, passing it to me. 'What's wrong?'

I pour water into my palm, then wipe it across my face.

We stand in the gutter, looking at each other. I don't know how to answer him.

'Let's go home,' I say.

I position a plastic bag between my knees all the way.

We're passing through Allambie Heights when Jackson turns on the radio.

'Not now,' I say, turning it off. What if the incident has reached news radio?

He switches it back on.

'Please, Jackson,' I say, snapping it off again.

We travel home in silence.

As we pull into the driveway, I see Pamela's car parked on the street. I don't think I have the mental strength to talk to her.

The wire screen on the front door swings open. Ruby stands on the threshold.

'Did Jackson do a bad thing?' she calls out, her little chest heaving.

How can I answer that, when I don't know myself? Like the rest of today, I'm entirely unprepared.

'They said you hurt Sienna.' Ruby stares at her brother with accusing eyes. 'What did you do, Jackson?'

I'm wondering who *they* are.

Jackson's face crumples. He pushes past Ruby, bolts down the hall and up the attic staircase, slamming his bedroom door.

Pamela materialises in the doorway and places her hands on Ruby's shoulders.

'Let's read another story, Rubes,' she says. 'There's plenty of time for questions. Is it *Penny Patchett's Party* or that very rude David Walliams book?'

Ruby's face lights up. 'Ooh, David Walliams!' She races off towards the lounge.

Pamela holds the screen door open. 'Are you all right?'

My eyes fill with tears. 'Do you know about...?'

'Ruby shared what's being said at school.'

I move into the hallway and hang up my coat.

'Dinner's in the oven. Milla's done her homework. Ruby's

had a shower.' Pamela shadows me along the hall. 'I've made the school lunches for tomorrow but' – she nods towards the lounge – 'judging from the nasty rumours flying around, you might like to give the girls the day off tomorrow?'

I realise I've given very little thought to Ruby or Milla.

'I'll just read a chapter to Ruby,' says Pamela, 'then I'll pop on a film for her to watch before bedtime. If there's anything else you need...'

'Thank you,' I say, tears sliding out of my eyes.

'Or I can stay over tonight, if you need some company?'

'That's very kind of you, Pamela, but...'

'I understand,' she says, retreating towards the lounge. 'I'd feel the same.'

'You've been a huge help this afternoon,' I call after her.

I move to Milla's room and tap lightly at the door.

'Who is it?'

'Mum.'

I hear the bed creak as Milla climbs off it, followed by her footsteps on the floorboards.

The door opens. 'It's bad, isn't it?'

I'm feigning a poker face, but Milla sees through it.

'Tell me, Mum.'

'The police are still gathering evidence, but... it's not looking good.'

'Will Jackson go to prison?'

'I don't know, Millsy. Let's not jump to conclusions.'

She wraps her arms around me, resting her head against my shoulder.

'Do you want to... have a cup of tea together?' I ask.

'I'm sorry, Mum, I can't.' Milla looks conflicted. 'I promised I'd go for a walk with Riley. I just need to... get some fresh air.'

Under ordinary circumstances, I wouldn't allow my fourteen-year-old daughter to walk the streets at night with a boy I've barely met. 'Can we talk more when you get back?'

'Will talking change anything, Mum?'

'Probably not.' I sigh. 'But you need to know what happened today.'

Milla's phone beeps.

'Riley's out the front,' she says breathlessly.

'I'll walk you out.'

Riley is loitering near the rainbow library in the front yard, his skateboard in one hand and a bunch of ludicrously cheerful orange gerberas in the other.

I open the wire screen. 'Hello, Riley.'

'Hi, Mrs C.' He thrusts the flowers at me. 'These are for you.'

'Oh, that's very nice.' I move onto the veranda to take them.

'We're just going for a walk on the beach,' he says. 'We'll be back by 7.30.'

I glance at my watch; it's just gone six o'clock. What will they be *doing* on the beach for an hour and a half? But I can't begrudge Milla some respite as the world implodes around her.

'Have fun,' I say, waving them off.

As I watch them wander away hand-in-hand, I feel a tiny, unbidden pang of envy for those intoxicating moments of new love.

Alone on the veranda, I pull my phone from my pocket. Scrolling through my contacts, my thumb hovers over the keypad.

Hi Steve. Are you around tonight? Sorry for the late notice.

The reply is instantaneous.

Hey there, just landed. I'll be over ASAP.

Moving back inside, I pause for a moment in the lounge doorway to watch Pamela in the final throes of reading to Ruby. She's pulling out all stops to entertain – impersonating a monstrous, fanged dentist – and Ruby is guffawing with delight. It's an infectious, comforting sound after such an appalling day.

'No one compares to a former diplomat in a time of crisis,' I observe.

She looks up at me and smiles.

'Bedtime, Rubes,' she announces, snapping shut the book.

Ruby tugs at her sleeve. 'One more chapter! Please, Nanna!'

'I can sing you a revolting rhyme, if you like? My singing voice isn't quite as good as your mother's, though.'

I smile at the compliment, but Ruby groans.

'Goodness, you're hard to please. What about a movie, then?' Pamela asks. 'If you get changed into your pyjamas right away, I'll loan you my new iPad overnight and you can watch the movie in bed. How does that sound?'

'Whoa.' Ruby's eyes are round with wonder. She leaps off the couch, dashes across the room and plants a kiss on my cheek. 'Night-night, Mum. Is Jackson all right?'

'Yes, he's doing okay.' I resolve to check on him. 'Enjoy the movie, Rubes. I'll come and tuck you in later.'

'Come on, Nanna!' she yells, running down the hallway to her bedroom.

Pamela turns to me. 'Don't worry, a nice young man from Tech2U installed all the family filters my iPad needs,' she assures me. 'There'll be no more inappropriate content on my watch.'

It's a reference to our interaction in the café on Mother's Day, I realise. 'Thanks for making an effort, Pamela.'

I'm both touched by her support, and at the same time

reminded of how harsh my thoughts about her were at the time.

Trying to extend a peace offering, I say, 'A friend of mine's coming over for a cup of tea shortly. You're welcome to stay if you'd like?'

'Thank you, but no.' She stands to go. 'I'll just put the movie on for Ruby and let myself out. Today must have been difficult for you, especially with Andy away.'

She lays a hand on my arm.

I can't trust myself to say anything without bursting into tears.

'If any of what Ruby heard at school is true, then... you and Andy might be in for a tough time. I know you've both been struggling lately. Marriage is difficult enough, without additional pressure like this.'

I'm unsure what to say.

'If there's anything I can do, I'm here for you. For *all* of you,' she stresses. 'Not just... for my son.'

I'm overcome. 'That means a lot to me, Pamela. Since Mum died, I... I've really missed her.'

I'm not sure why I'm telling her this.

'I'm not surprised,' she observes. 'I miss Andy's father every single day. I'd only been married to Edward for twenty years when he passed. I'm sorry you never got to meet him. He was a remarkable human being.'

It's the first time I've detected vulnerability in Pamela. For the first time, too, I consider her position as a widow. With two sons overseas, one of them permanently, it must be a lonely existence at times in her big old house in Balgowlah Heights.

Pamela looks thoughtful. 'Edward would have loved you, of course. He was very musical, you know. Taught himself the piano. He could play the national anthems of thirty-two different countries by the time I retired from the diplomatic corps.'

I step forward and, rather awkwardly, place my arms around her diminutive frame.

Pamela doesn't pull away.

Eventually, she steps back from our embrace and straightens her linen shirt. Pale pink today, with white polka-dots.

'Right, well then.' She clears her throat. 'You'd best check on Jackson. I'll go set up Ruby and say good night. I'll see you tomorrow, Julia. If you need anything, just shout.'

She turns on her heels and strides down the hall.

'You're wonderful,' I call after her.

I'm surprised to realise I mean it.

15

I tiptoe up the stairs and push open Jackson's door. The bedside light is on, casting a soft glow over the room. It's not quite 6.30, but he's asleep already. Relieved of the torments of the police interview, his face is remarkably peaceful.

The contents of his drawers are strewn across the floor as usual, but I barely register the mess. I should never have cared *at all*, I realise now. A messy room can be *tolerated*, while an assault against another child cannot. Why did I obsess about such trivial things?

I pick my way across the room and perch on the edge of Jackson's bed, watching the rhythmic rise and fall of his chest.

A dull ache rises up in mine, forcing its way out as hot tears.

If I didn't have two other dependants – two brave, beautiful daughters – I might simply disappear with Jackson. Relocate somewhere rural, assume a new identity and try to start afresh. Filling our lungs with air, our minds with sunshine, and our hearts with some kind of hope for the future.

Jackson stirs and rolls over.

I lie down next to him, curling my body around his.

My mind revisits the day's events, despite my exhaustion. Being turned away in the schoolyard by the principal, the interview in the CAS office, a DNA test conducted without a lawyer present, Andy's outrage at my inaction.

He was right, of course. But with Detective Annabelle Johnson bulldozing me through the interview process, it simply didn't occur to me to seek legal support – and I don't remember declining it.

Jackson was confused too, poor boy. By the end of the day, he couldn't even remember the reason he was there at all. 'What happened to Sienna in the toilets, Mum?' he'd asked, genuinely mystified.

This, from a boy who remembers everything.

A feeling of disquiet settles over me. What *were* Jackson's exact words about what happened in the toilets?

Hoisting myself up on one elbow, I gaze at my sleeping son. What did Jackson actually confess to?

I reach for my phone and type out a message to Andy.

When will the lawyer call me? I want to talk to him ASAP about the interview while it's still fresh.

Even if I can't trust my own powers of recall, a lawyer might be able to help me reconstruct the interview.

A faint tap-tapping drifts up from the veranda.

I slide out of bed and tiptoe back across the room. Closing Jackson's door behind me, I don't bother to conceal my dishevelment as I walk down the stairs.

'Oh dear,' says Steve, as I open the front door.

I unlatch the wire screen.

He holds a bottle of wine in one hand and a block of chocolate in the other. 'Which do you need more of right now?'

I can barely rally a smile.

He steps through the door and I collapse against him, desperate for human comfort. I lean my head against his chest as the tears slide down my face.

'Come,' he says, gesturing to the kitchen.

Numbly, I follow him.

'Sit down,' he orders. 'I know where everything is.'

He finds two glasses and opens the wine, then fills the kettle and places it on the stove. Opening one end of the chocolate, he slides several rows in front of me.

'This will help.'

I shake my head, lifting the wineglass to my lips instead.

If Andy stepped off his flight from New York right now, what would he make of this?

Beyond caring, I gulp at the wine.

Andy wasn't here when I needed him today and, when he finally answered his phone, all he had for me was judgement about how poorly I'd handled the situation. He was justified in that assessment, but it still hurt.

Steve pulls out a stool and sits down, close enough for me to be aware of the scent of his aftershave.

'Want to talk?'

I shrug. 'I'd rather you do the talking.'

'Okay, sure. What will I start with?' He smiles brightly. 'Um... Julia, even though you've been crying, you look lovely tonight.'

'Please,' I object, but I register the compliment all the same.

'I was just trying to lighten things up a little.' Steve looks embarrassed. 'I'm sorry if that was out of line.'

He's trying so hard.

'No, it's not out of line. I just... Okay, you look nice, too.'

I can't believe I actually said that.

'Well, cheers to that,' says Steve, clinking his glass against mine.

He takes a sip of wine, then leans closer. 'Julia, I've got something to tell you.'

His blue-grey eyes are pensive.

'Miranda called me tonight. You know, Digby's mum? She sounded a bit... tipsy.'

I watch his lips form the words.

'You're a newcomer to the Northern Beaches, so you might not know that... well, Miranda Bianco has a problem with alcohol. She's been in and out of rehab for years. Whenever she falls off the wagon, she starts carrying vodka around in Evian bottles.'

I'm not entirely surprised by this revelation, given the strong smell of liquor about Miranda when I collected Jackson last week. But if I'd known the extent of it, I wouldn't have accepted the play date opportunities so readily.

'And... what?' I'm uncertain why Steve is sharing this now.

'Miranda rang about an hour ago and told me about Digby's police interview this morning. They had to go to Chatswood, too. She was pretty incoherent, but Jackson's name came up... something about a playdate those two had last week.'

I sit up straighter now. 'What did she say?'

'Well, it wasn't so much what she said. It strikes me...' Steve hesitates. 'Look, it probably means nothing, but I've seen quite a bit of Digby this season, what with dropping him home every week after training...'

'What is it, Steve?'

He twirls the stem of the wineglass between his thumb and forefinger.

'Will's first wife died suddenly years ago and left him with Digby. He's had a few issues over the years, you know. Digby's turning thirteen this year. Miranda's his step-mum.'

I'm just not following.

'Miranda's raised Digby as her own alongside Rory, but not very happily. Ten years ago she was implicated, but never charged, in the death of a young girl by drowning at a local dam.'

My eyes widen.

'She almost got done for manslaughter, Jules. A child died. There wasn't enough evidence to put her away. It was just deemed an unfortunate accident.'

Steve bites into a square of chocolate, chewing it slowly.

'I've been worried about Digby's welfare at home, but I've never taken it any further. Jackson's spent a bit of time at their house lately, hasn't he?'

'Only... twice. What are you saying, Steve?'

Steve tips more wine into my glass. 'Did you ever ask Jackson what happened at Digby's, on the day he ran away from there?'

I frown. 'Yes, but he's not very verbal at the best of times.'

'Right,' says Steve. 'I just wonder if something might've happened... something involving Miranda and her alcohol problem.'

My heartbeat quickens. Did Jackson come to some sort of harm at Digby's?

'But if there was any truth in that, how could we find out?'

'It's sensitive territory.' Steve drains his glass. 'If the police interview me, I'll mention my concerns about Miranda.'

'But what if they *don't* interview you?'

'Well... Miranda asked me to pop over and play a bit of soccer with Digby tomorrow, to distract him from what's going on. I might see if I can find out anything from Digby directly.'

'Oh, could you? And could you do the same for Jackson?' I ask. 'I mean, he... respects you. Maybe he'd feel more comfortable talking with you, especially if he knows you've been chatting to Digby?'

'Mmm.' Steve rubs his forehead. 'I guess I could mention it when we're kicking the footy around. Just ask him if anything unusual happened at Digby's.'

'That would be amazing,' I gush. 'Thank you so much. I mean, I could try to talk to him but you might be...'

'No worries,' he says. 'I'll do my best.'

'Honestly, you're a lifesaver, Steve.'

He smiles and lays a hand across mine.

As I glance up at his face, I'm drawn to his eyes, the cleft in his chin, the curve of his lips. My stomach seems to fall away.

The doorbell rings.

Jolted off the stool, I peer down the hallway.

I'm surprised to see the silhouettes of Milla and Riley at the front door. They're home much earlier than planned.

'Did you forget something?' I call, moving down the hallway.

When I reach the door, I see that Milla is shaking. 'What's wrong?'

Milla bursts into tears.

'What's happened?' I open the door.

Riley puts a protective arm around Milla's shoulders.

'Someone's put... something gross in your little library, Mrs C. We checked out the waves and Milla told me about this surfing mag she'd seen in your library, so we came back to take a look and we found a... a...'

'A what?' I push past them, down the stairs and across the front yard.

When I open the Perspex door of the rainbow library, I smell it before I see it. Faeces – dog or human, I can't be sure – smeared across every exposed surface.

I gag and cover my mouth, then slam shut the door. 'I'll clean it up.'

'We only built it last week.' Tears are still streaming down Milla's face. 'Why would anyone do that?'

'I don't know, Millsy,' I lie.

'It's because of Jackson, isn't it?'

I consider how to answer.

'What did he do that's so bad, Mum?'

Steve materialises from within the house.

Riley looks up, surprised.

'This is Steve... Jackson's soccer coach,' I mumble.

'We've met before,' Riley reminds me.

Milla looks from Riley to Steve and back to me, her gaze settling on the wineglass in Steve's hand. 'When's Dad coming home?'

'Wednesday,' I tell her.

'What did... Jackson actually do?' Milla asks again. 'What would make someone... wreck our library like this?'

'That's what I wanted to talk to you about earlier.' I glance back at the stairs leading to Jackson's room. Lowering my voice, I say, 'We've been with the police all day. It's not clear what happened, but it could be very serious.'

'You two need to talk.' Riley tucks his skateboard under his arm. 'We can finish our walk tomorrow night, Milla.'

She looks disappointed.

Riley turns to me. 'Mrs C, where do you keep the bleach?

I'll need a garbage bag, a garden hose and a bunch of newspaper.'

'That's very kind of you, Riley, but I don't expect you to do that.'

'Too easy,' he says, ignoring me. 'It can dry overnight. Good as new tomorrow.'

Milla almost knocks him over with her hug.

Steve sets down his wineglass and moves to help too, but I shake my head. 'Please, Steve, you've done enough. Just... come back tomorrow and chat to Jackson?'

I nod meaningfully at him.

'Of course, I'll pop over in my lunchbreak.' He pats me on the shoulder. 'Get some sleep. Things will feel a little better tomorrow.'

With our little library vandalised on top of an already appalling day, I really don't see how. 'Thanks Steve.'

As Steve heads off, Riley turns to me. 'Where's the laundry room, Mrs C?'

'Are you sure you want to do this, Riley?'

'Yes, Mrs C.'

His persistence is impressive.

'Okay. Milla, go get some gloves from under the kitchen sink please, and some newspaper from the recycling bin. This way, Riley.'

We walk the length of the driveway to the laundry room at the rear of the house.

'You really don't have to do this, Riley...'

'I want to, Mrs C.'

My hands tremble as I take a bucket and fill it with several sponges, a garbage bag and a three-litre bottle of bleach.

'Thank you, Riley.' I can't conceal my shaking as I pass the materials to him. 'There's a tap for filling in the front yard near the gate.'

Riley starts back along the driveway, then turns. 'It's going to be okay, Mrs C. Nothing a whole lot of White Tiger won't fix.'

'You sound just like my mother, Riley.' I smile at him.

If only it were as easy as a bottle of bleach. If only Mum was here to help.

16

'Are you hungry?' Mum asks, for about the gazillionth time.

We're sitting at the dinner table on the day after the police interview. It's Taco Tuesday and Mum's got all my favourite things on the table, like refried beans and sour cream and cheesy salsa surprise. She's even used her new Thermowhizz for the guacamole. Even though I haven't eaten all day, I'm still not hungry.

When I don't answer, Mum just sighs. 'I don't feel like eating, either. I've made too much.'

I reckon Ruby will still want those tacos when she's finished watching *Catwalk Chickens*, and Milla and Riley might be hungry when they come back from their walk, and Dad might have some for dinner tomorrow night when he comes home from New York.

'We'll have to start eating again sometime,' says Mum. 'And we're going to have to start on your schoolwork, too. We don't want you to fall too far behind.'

'I've only missed two days of school.'

Schoolwork isn't something I'm worried about ever, but I

am pretty worried about not playing in my soccer team and never dancing with April Kennedy again or maybe even going to kid prison.

'Well, we don't have to figure it all out tonight.' Mum sighs again. She's been doing that all day. 'We'll have to plan things properly if I'm going to be teaching you for a while. It's called lesson planning, Jackson. It's a bit like menu planning.'

I'm about to ask her what food they have in kid prison, when suddenly there's a sharp knock on the front door and Mum's face turns pale.

'Stay here.' She tiptoes out to the lounge and peels back the edge of the curtain, trying to see who's outside.

A moment later, there's another loud knock.

'Who is it?' I whisper, moving closer to Mum.

'I don't know,' she whispers back. 'Hopefully not... that idiot who put poop in our little library last night.'

She creeps over to the door, then points at the sofa. It's a signal for me to hide behind it, so I drop to the floor and hold my breath, peeping around the edge.

Mum opens the door a fraction. On the doorstep is a smiley lady with rainbow hair, so Mum opens the door a little bit more.

'How can I help you?' Mum's voice sounds all proper, maybe because she's never met Miss Marion before.

'Actually, I thought that maybe *I* could help *you*.' Miss Marion beams. 'I'm Marion, Jackson's dance teacher at Queenscliff Public.'

'Oh.' Mum hesitates a moment, then opens the door wide. 'I'm Julia.'

'It's such a pleasure to meet you.' Miss Marion steps forward and pulls Mum into a hug as if it's a handshake.

'Well,' says Mum, and I can see she's a teensy bit embarrassed. 'Please, come in.'

Miss Marion strolls into our living room and they both sit down on the sofa opposite me. I can see their faces perfectly, even though they can't see me.

Miss Marion shifts around a bit, putting two cushions behind her to get comfortable, but Mum doesn't move.

After a while, Miss Marion breaks the silence.

'I was so... sorry to hear about the incident at school last week, Julia.'

'Yes, it's terrible.' Mum's voice sounds as cold as a corpse. 'I'm devastated for Sienna and her parents.'

I can tell that Mum's about to cry.

'I'm sure it's been distressing for everyone,' Miss Marion says. 'For Jackson, too. And for you and your family.'

Mum sort of coughs. 'You do know what the... allegation is, don't you?'

Miss Marion nods. 'There's talk of everything from bullying to... a lot worse. The police are still conducting their investigations, the last I heard. That doesn't make you criminals, Julia.'

Mum looks surprised. She just sits there, like a stuffed turkey on a Christmas platter while Miss Marion keeps talking.

Her words surprise me too, because she's telling Mum how *unusual* and *talented* and *special* I am, compared to all the other kids she's ever taught.

'And as a mother of a child who's been through the juvenile justice system,' she continues, 'I can really relate to how you must be feeling right now, Julia. I want to help, if I can.'

I didn't know Miss Marion had kids, but Mum doesn't seem too shocked. And maybe because someone shoved poop in our rainbow library yesterday, she starts to cry.

Mum drops her face into her hands, then her shoulders

start to shake. I never like seeing Mum cry, so I pull my head back behind the sofa and start hoping she'll stop.

Everything goes quiet in the lounge for a long while. I'm thinking that maybe Miss Marion has snuck out the back door, so I peek out from behind the sofa. She's still there, and she's giving Mum a super long hug. It's funny, even though Mum's face is still really sad, her eyes are telling me that she *really* likes Miss Marion.

Then Miss Marion starts telling Mum all about my special part at the Winter Eisteddfod and how I've learned aerial skills and how I'm *a natural.*

'It will be a travesty if Jackson doesn't dance his part in this routine, Julia. Not after all the hard work he's put in.'

Suddenly my throat feels scratchy and I think I'm going to cough and then I can't help myself, it just comes out like an explosion. A second later, Miss Marion pops her head over the top of the sofa.

'Well, hello, Jackson!' She's staring straight down at me. 'Come on out.'

So I crawl out from behind the sofa and across the rug and sit down next to her.

Miss Marion takes my hand in hers, but she doesn't say anything at all. Then she reaches for Mum's hand too and we just sit there, the three of us, holding hands. It's a bit weird, then I start to get used to it and somehow it actually feels *right.*

After a little while, Mum stands up and says, 'How about a cup of tea, Marion?'

'I thought you'd never ask.' Miss Marion winks at me.

It feels like she should be in our lounge *every* night.

Mum goes and makes us all a cup of tea and one for Ruby who's still watching *Catwalk Chickens* in the other room. I can hear her clucking along with them, almost the whole of Grade Three watches it.

When Mum comes back with the tea, Miss Marion says, 'We need to talk about Jackson dancing. Want to hear my plan?'

Mum's face tells me she's not sure if she does.

'Even though Jackson's been suspended from school, he can keep practising from home.' Miss Marion blows across her tea. 'There's absolutely no reason he can't take part in the Winter Eisteddfod.'

'Wrong,' says Mum, so snappily she's sure to hurt Miss Marion's feelings. 'He's not allowed to go anywhere near third-grade kids.'

'He won't.' Miss Marion doesn't seem offended or upset at all. 'Jackson won't be at school, Julia. He'll practise at home, then he'll only have contact with other students on the day of the performance at the town hall. All the other dancers are in Years Five and Six, not third grade. As an extra precaution, I can keep him tucked away in the green room beforehand. Afterwards, he can go straight home with you.'

Mum doesn't look convinced. 'Maybe the others won't want to dance with...' She stops short, but I know what she was going to say. It makes me feel like a festering pile of dog poop.

'I'm confident I can manage it,' says Miss Marion. 'Jackson's understudy, Lucy, will work with the girls during the practices. Then I'll just announce that Jackson's performing on the day.'

That sounds sneaky to me.

'What about Lucy?' I ask. 'Won't she be... sad not to dance at the town hall?'

The words take a long while to come out, but Miss Marion is super patient.

'That's kind of you, Jackson,' she smiles. 'The dance season goes until September, so Lucy will get her turn. April will be thrilled to have you back.'

My body goes fizzy just hearing April's name. I look down into my cup and start counting the tea leaves swirling around the bottom.

Miss Marion turns to Mum. 'Lucy's good, but Jackson's the star of the routine. It's just not the same without him. April and Jackson have a special chemistry on stage.'

Mr Thompson teaches us chemistry once a week, but I've never done any experiments with April.

'How can I rehearse without... proper silks, Miss Marion?' I ask.

'Well, lucky for you, I have friends in high places. Pardon the pun.'

Miss Marion cackles so loudly then, it makes me laugh too. Even Mum smiles.

Then Miss Marion explains how her friend Roberto can install some practice silks somewhere high in our house, just like he did at school.

'Shall we find where the best spot might be?'

Miss Marion doesn't wait, she hops up and starts checking all our rooms without asking, then she heads out the back door and into the yard. Mum turns on the spotlight and we cross the lawn to our big old garden barn; it holds heaps of junk but there's still lots of room.

As soon as Miss Marion sees its high ceilings and timber beams, she does a little dance on the spot. 'This is it!'

I get a shiver down my back because I'm excited or nervous maybe, it's hard to tell the difference sometimes.

Miss Marion looks super happy and pulls out her phone. She messages Roberto and then *ding!* she tells us that he can definitely install the silks tomorrow morning, so I won't have to miss a *single* practice session.

'I'm probably behaving a bit out of school policy,' says Miss Marion, as we walk back to the house and into the kitchen. 'I appreciate your flexibility, Julia. It's a small thing I can do at what must be a very difficult time.'

Mum's nose goes all sniffy again, so Miss Marion gives her an even bigger hug than she did on the couch. Mum leans into the hug this time.

When Mum lifts her face, she doesn't look like a zombie any more.

'Thank you, Marion,' she says in this super-calm voice.

'Someone should be looking after you,' says Miss Marion, still holding Mum's hand. 'Do you have much support, Julia?'

Mum doesn't say anything for a while.

'My husband's away at the moment, but he's... back tomorrow.' She glances at me. 'My parents passed away a few years ago. I don't have any siblings. I've got a few friends here and there, more on Facebook than the real thing now. I'm not exactly sure how that happened...'

Miss Marion harrumphs like a cranky camel.

'Oh, social media's the worst thing in the world. It's turning us all into addicts and robots, not to mention fake friends. Don't you feel like just doing something really *real* for a change?'

Mum nods.

I'm guessing Miss Marion would *hate* Alt-World.

'Why don't we go counter trend, Julia, and have some proper "facetime"? I can pop over this Friday afternoon after school for a cuppa again, if you'd like?'

Mum looks a bit surprised, but really pleased too. 'I'd like that.'

'Deal,' says Miss Marion.

I'm glad Mum said yes, because you can't stop Miss Marion when she sets her mind to something.

'Roberto's going to need some help installing the silks tomorrow in your shed,' says Miss Marion. 'Will Jackson's dad be available in the morning, by any chance?'

Mum shakes her head. 'He's flying in tomorrow night. But I'm pretty sure Jackson's soccer coach will help, if I ask him.'

'You mean Steve?' Miss Marion asks. 'Good thinking. He's a great guy.'

Miss Marion turns in my direction. 'Jackson, we'll be practising two mornings a week, starting this Thursday. I'll come over bright and early, if that's all right?'

'Any time after 5.17,' I say.

'Noted.' Miss Marion grins at me.

She steps closer, then pulls me into a big hug. After a while she sort of shimmies over to Mum and pulls her into the hug, too. I'm sandwiched in between them, which feels really nice.

'I know it's hard to believe right now,' says Miss Marion, 'but this too shall pass.'

Everything feels a whole lot better with Miss Marion here in our kitchen.

17

'Welcome back to day ten of home-school!'

Mum's acting super cheerful, like she's a real teacher or something. Maybe she's happy that Dad's back from New York, he's been home almost as long as we've been home-schooling. She pushes today's activity list across the kitchen bench at me. It's getting longer every day and it's actually pretty interesting.

On the first day of home-school, Mum made me Family Librarian, which means I have to keep our rainbow library stocked full of books. I've watched people taking books out of the library and putting them back in, so I've figured out that adults like reading about unsolved murders and gang wars and big complicated families, but kids prefer books about wizards and dragons and farts.

On day three of home-school, Mum made me Bathroom Magician, which means I get paid to clean the bathroom twice a week. I thought I'd hate it, but then it started to feel good cleaning the toothpaste off the basin and the skid marks out of the loo and the grubby smudges off the mirror. It felt like I was making things sparkly new again, like Dead Granny and Grandpa dry-cleaning people's clothes at Kaminski's.

'Any questions about today's activities?' Mum pours herself another cup of coffee from a glass jug called a French press. I don't know what's French about it, but Mum won't start home-school until after her second or third cup. So lessons always start much later than at Queenscliff Public, after Milla's caught the bus and Ruby's gone off to real school, even though she doesn't like going any more.

Ruby always used to be the first one waiting at the front door in the morning, she loved 3R and Mrs Reilly and her friend Tessa. Now she starts crying whenever it's time to leave. This morning she lay down on the driveway and screamed so loudly, Mum had to hold her under the armpits and sort of drag Ruby into the car. Mr Lovell stuck his head over the fence and watched the whole thing which made Mum really upset, and that made me cry too.

'Why can't Ruby join home-school with me?' I ask.

Mum looks up from her coffee. 'We think it's best for Ruby to keep some friends around her, for the time being.'

Thinking about Ruby makes my eyes start to twitch. Loads of kids keep asking about what happened in the toilets with me and Digby and Sienna Wilson-Brown. Dad tells Ruby to ignore them, but that's hard to do when kids are saying Sienna had her head bashed in and her face flushed down the loo and her pants pulled down.

I've told Ruby I didn't see any of that happen, but she still hates going to school. Mum keeps saying, 'We'll find a solution,' but not even clever Jeff the lawyer can find a way to stop the other third-graders from bugging Ruby.

Milla goes to high school at Pittwater North, so none of her friends have said anything to her about me. I'm worried that might change though, because Dad says, 'Bad news travels fast.' Milla said that happened on the Monday we visited the police office at Chatswood, when someone posted about me on the Year Five Queenscliff Facebook group. Even though it was deleted pretty quickly, it was bad enough for someone else to decide to throw poop into our rainbow library that same night.

I'm pretty sure Milla's worried about her friends finding out. She's not bawling her eyes out every day like Ruby, but she almost never comes out of her room. She just lies on her bed scrolling through Instagram and messaging Riley. At least she's got Riley, he's been really nice to all of us. Mum told me he even cleaned up the poop in the library that night.

Riley visits every day, carrying a bunch of daffodils or buttercups or snapdragons for Milla or Mum. He works in a surf store at Brookvale on weekends, so I'm guessing he spends almost all his wages on flowers. He doesn't seem cross about that, though, he just keeps on smiling and laughing and high fiving me. He's even promised to teach me surfing in the spring.

'We'll hang out in the green room as soon as winter's done,' he's told me. 'There's no stress in the green room.'

When Riley says 'the green room', he doesn't mean the place where dancers hang out before they go on stage. It's the words surfers use for the ocean. Riley talks about the green room so much, it makes me want to start learning to surf *tomorrow*. But Riley says winter's too cold for beginners, it's better to wait until September instead.

I wish I had a friend like Riley, or that Crazy Daisy would let me go back to school so I could see April Kennedy again. But Crazy Daisy told Mum on the phone that I can't go back 'until further notice', and Dad thinks that might mean forever. Maybe that's why Mum's so serious about home-school, and why she's giving me more work than Mr Thompson *ever* did.

I look at this morning's pile: at least fifteen maths and English worksheets. Mum makes me finish all my worksheets before lunchtime, except when Francesca from FACS is visiting. I've seen her three times already. She's small and serious and always asks me the same question – 'Has anyone in your family ever asked you to keep a secret, Jackson?' – and each time I say no. I haven't told Francesca about Digby's two secrets, because he's not part of my family. And Mum always says you should keep your promises, no matter what.

Other people interrupt home-school too. Coach Steve comes around every day to practise soccer drills with me. Yesterday Dr Louisa visited for the fourth time in two weeks. Some mornings I have to meet clever Jeff, who's really short but fills up the room with his big voice. I don't like the way he rushes about; he's got loads of other important work. He always asks me the same questions too, about what happened at school on Pyjama Day and at the police office in Chatswood.

Sometimes Jeff gets worked up because my answers don't come out fast enough, or because Mum has to kind of translate for me. Clever Jeff's still learning to be patient with that. We've all got to be patient, because no one knows how long the police will take with their investigations, or if they'll make me go to the Children's Court. Every time Jeff says those two words, Mum looks so frightened it makes me scared too.

I check the timetable to see what's happening this afternoon, because *that's* when home-school gets really fun. Afternoons are when Mum pulls out the guitar and we sit together on the sofa singing her hospice songs like 'Blackbird' and 'Leaving on a Jet Plane' and 'The Boxer'. Even though the Special Ps at Care Cottage are really missing Mum's songs, she can't go back and see them yet because she's too busy home-schooling me.

The timetable says that after lunch today we've got Kitchen Science, which isn't like a normal science class with Mr Thompson. Instead of being all cranky, Mum puts on these flashy gold glasses from Ruby's dress-up box, then she gets heaps of ingredients from the pantry and says, 'Let's blow up the kitchen, Jackson.' So far we've dissolved an eggshell with vinegar, built our own pH indicator using red cabbage, and started growing basil and chives in our kitchen garden.

Mum's made me Chief Botanist for our kitchen garden because she's got a black thumb, which means she murders plants without even trying. Last week we read about how playing classical music can help plants grow, so we've started playing Vivaldi's 'Four Seasons' to the herbs. We always start with 'Spring' but my favourite is 'Autumn', because that's when you can hear the wind whipping up inside the music.

There's a part of me that wants to stay at Mum's home-school forever, even though Nanna Pam is trying to get me an interview at Clontarf Grammar. Nanna says she's going to pay for all the school fees if I get in, and maybe even Ruby can go there too. I don't want to go to a new school though, because how will I keep up my dancing and see April Kennedy and Miss Marion?

Miss Marion comes over every Tuesday and Thursday morning at 6.30. She never knocks on the front door, she just walks down the driveway and meets me in the garden shed. I'm always waiting for her there, and she gives me a big hug and says, 'Get up there, Jackson!'

So I climb the silks and she puts on some warm-up music using a portable speaker. Miss Marion's instructions are much easier to follow than Mum's activity sheets, because aerial silks are like sleeping or breathing for me.

First we go through Anohni's 'Hope There's Someone' three times. After that, Miss Marion puts on her 'improvisation playlist' and we dance around the shed together. Her songs are really different to Mum's hospice music, with 'Mr Brightside' and 'Iris' and 'Youngblood' and so many others I like. Just after eight o'clock when Miss Marion has to go to school, she says goodbye and gives me another big hug.

'I can't wait for next time,' she always says.

This morning when Miss Marion was leaving, Mum ran down the driveway in her robe with some money in an envelope. She tried to stuff it into Miss Marion's pocket, but she wouldn't take it. Miss Marion just said, 'It's a privilege teaching Jackson, Julia.' That made Mum cry again and even Miss Marion got tears in her eyes, which I'd never seen before.

Coach Steve won't take any money either, even though Mum's tried to make him. He just keeps playing passing drills with me in the back yard whenever he visits, which is usually on his lunchbreak from the workshop. Coach Steve is a mechanical engineer, which makes him really good at fixing things. Some lunchtimes he even helps with broken stuff that Dad doesn't have time to fix, like the blinds in Mum's bedroom that I accidentally pulled down ages ago.

Dad was really surprised to find brand new blinds hanging there when he got back from New York. For some reason he's not sleeping in the bedroom with Mum any more, maybe he doesn't like the colour Mum chose. It's nice having Dad back though, even if he's still got to work long hours at the office.

'No morning appointments today, if that's what you're wondering,' says Mum, checking the timetable over my shoulder. She smiles at me. 'Which is a good thing, because today I'm giving you the biggest research challenge of your life.'

That sounds like a hard thing to do.

'Never fear, Jackson, it's all about... guinea pigs. You've got to prove to me that you're ready to look after one. If you show me you are, we'll buy one.'

I stare at her for a bit, then start to smile too. I've wanted a guinea pig *forever*.

'You've got to have it ready by lunchtime though,' she says. 'Your time starts now.'

She moves off to her bedroom, so maybe she's going for a lie down again. Mum's been lying down a bit more than usual, because the doctor gave her some medicine to help her sleep at night. Only problem is, it makes her sleepy in the mornings too. If I work super hard, maybe I can finish the project before Mum wakes up?

I start listing out everything I know about guinea pigs. I've got heaps of information in a massive animal encyclopaedia that Nanna Pam gave me for my ninth birthday. I've also got my memory download from the programme I watched on guinea pigs in the police waiting room.

I write about how guinea pigs are herd animals and in some countries like Switzerland, it's illegal to have just one guinea pig. You've got to have at least two, because they really like playing chasings and chattering to each other all day.

Then I list out all the things guinea pigs need to stay healthy, like crunchy vegetables and clean water and careful handling. Their insides are so fragile, you have to be careful not to squeeze when you cuddle them. I add a special section on friendships between guinea pigs and dogs, because I don't want Snickers getting grumpy with our guinea pig.

After about two hours, my research paper is fifteen pages

long. I staple all the pages together and sit outside Mum's bedroom, waiting for her to wake up.

Finally, she does.

Mum almost falls over me when she opens the door.

'Wow, good work, Jackson.' She crouches down on the carpet and reads the whole thing.

'Incredible!' she says, closing the final page. 'I've learned so much.'

She stands up and goes to her special stationery box in the dining room. She takes out a big fat strawberry sticker and slaps it on the front page of my project.

'Ten out of ten, Jackson. I think you're ready. Let's go to Pet Palace.'

'Now?' I can't believe she's even said it.

We pack some snacks and water because Pet Palace is a long way away, then we climb into the Red Rocket and drive to the other side of the city. It feels strange, like maybe we're going back to Kaminski's. My memory download is showing me that we definitely drove this way a long time ago.

After about an hour, we arrive at a massive purple warehouse that sells kittens and puppies and axolotls and ferrets and albino pythons and Japanese fighting fish and other pets I haven't even heard of. I wander down the aisles wishing we could buy all these amazing animals, until we get to the guinea pig cages.

As soon as I see them, I *know* they're coming home with us: two perfect Dalmatian guinea pigs. One of them has a weird black pattern like bat wings spread across his hairy white back. The other's got a dark stripe over his eyes that's a bit like a robber's mask.

'Batman and Robin,' I say.

Mum laughs out loud. 'Let's take them home to show Steve this afternoon.'

'And Milla and Ruby,' I add. 'And don't forget Dad.'

'Of course not,' she says.

But something about Mum's expression tells me that maybe she almost did.

18

'Do up your shoelace, Jackson,' whispers Pamela, buttoning her smart cream blazer. 'First impressions count.'

I glance at my watch, unreasonably nervous. Our meeting with the principal of Clontarf Grammar was due to commence ten minutes ago.

Jackson raises his left foot and hooks it over his right knee, inspecting the wayward lace. He's wearing the expensive navy trainers that Pamela generously purchased for the occasion, along with a crisp white collared shirt and corduroy trousers. The outfit was a thoughtful gesture, given the dilapidated condition of most of Jackson's wardrobe.

'It's undone on purpose, Nanna,' he objects. 'It's a network cable for my shoe-phone. I'm waiting for a call from Dead Granny. She hasn't called since...'

'I see,' says Pamela, exercising remarkable restraint. 'Could it possibly wait until after our meeting with Mrs Hemingsworth? We're lucky to be seeing her. She's a very busy woman.'

I'm indebted to Pamela for deploying all her diplomatic

influence, as well as citing her late husband's status as a Clontarf Grammar alumnus, to secure this interview. Without her advocacy, Jackson's application for a place may never have been accepted, let alone processed so quickly.

'Just tie the shoelace, Jackson.' My voice is clipped, reflecting how much I want this.

We've survived one month of home-schooling, but I'm uncertain I can sustain the momentum for much longer. All my best intentions have evaporated: I've thrown a book across the room once and wept twice. Jackson's cried three times, after I locked myself in the laundry room and refused to come out. I've stacked on at least four kilos, from all the comfort eating.

Necessity may be the mother of invention, but it's become abundantly clear that I'm a mother, *not* a teacher. I'm also a music therapist who's neglecting my patients, while making pitiful attempts to instruct my son. Curiously, Jackson still seems to be enjoying our home-schooling, but the empty wine bottles accumulating in the recycling bin every passing week attest to *my* enjoyment levels.

'Okay.' Jackson ties his shoelace, just as my phone rings. His look of excitement turns quickly to disappointment. 'Oh, that's your phone, Mum, not mine.'

I raise the mobile to my ear. 'Hi Steve.'

'How are you, Jules?'

The colour rises in my cheeks. I've stopped trying to deny the effect Steve has on me.

'We're waiting for our interview at Clontarf Grammar.'

'Oh, good luck. Let me know how you go. I've just finished visiting Digby.'

'Is he okay?' Under instruction from Jeff Goldstein, our barrister, I've had no contact with Miranda or Will since the police investigation commenced.

'Well, you know, he's coping. I don't think they're quite as committed to home-schooling as you are, Jules. You're doing a terrific job.'

It's a compliment I'd been hoping to receive from Andy, I realise, despite our endless bickering since he returned from overseas. The pressure on our relationship has always been considerable, with Jackson's unique set of needs. Now, under the duress of a police investigation, it's practically untenable.

'Listen Jules, I tried again to get Digby to open up about that playdate he had with Jackson. I didn't get anywhere. I've tried a few times and neither of them has said anything about it ... or about Miranda's problem drinking.'

'Oh.' Part of me, ludicrously, is disappointed. It would be a relief of sorts to have someone else to blame amid this slow-motion catastrophe.

'I'm afraid I threw you a bit of a red herring there. Sorry, Jules.'

'No matter.' I sigh. 'Thanks a lot for trying, anyway. It's been a sanity-saver just having you around. Jackson's loved kicking the ball with you.'

'Anytime, Jules.' Steve seems to hesitate. 'Is... Andy really heading overseas again next week?'

'Afraid so.' I try to maintain an even tone, but I'm as disappointed by this as Steve is surprised.

'That's tough on you.'

'We need the income,' I say, parroting Andy's words. 'The world doesn't just stop. Bills need to be paid.'

'But it's still tough on you.'

The door to the principal's office swings open and a tall, wiry woman appears behind it.

'Sorry, Steve, I have to go,' I whisper.

As I slide the phone back into my bag, Jackson slips his hand into mine. He's as nervous as me, it seems.

Pamela smiles her encouragement at us both.

We all know what's riding on this interview: an educational alternative not only for Jackson, but for Ruby too.

'Good morning.' The principal motions at three tall leather chairs facing a spacious polished desk. 'Please, take a seat.'

Jackson takes the chair closest to the door. I sit down next to him, with Pamela on the other side.

'Thank you for coming in on such a chilly morning.'

It's almost mid-winter, but no one should be wearing *that* much black. Against a dark woollen dress and cardigan, black stockings and patent leather heels, the woman's teeth resemble pointy white blades.

'I'm Ruth Hemingsworth. Welcome, Jackson. What are your hobbies?'

Jackson stares at her, his mouth working. He grunts a little, clearly trying to formulate some words.

'Go ahead, Jackson,' prompts Pamela.

His eyelids start twitching.

Not the blinking, not now.

The silence seems to stretch on forever.

After an excruciating minute, the principal arches an eyebrow.

She looks pointedly at me for an explanation.

'Dance,' I say. 'He likes dance. And chess. And soccer. Right, Jackson?'

Jackson nods vigorously.

'When you're in Year Five, Jackson, you need to be able to speak for yourself,' says the principal. 'Tell me, what sort of dancing do you do?'

Jackson purses his lips. I fear he may say nothing at all.

'Sky-dancing,' he blurts. 'I'm a boy angel swinging on midnight silks.'

I flinch. 'He means aerial silks. He's been learning for six months at school this year. His dance teacher says he's become very skilled in a short space of time.'

The woman seems to be waiting for more.

'Jackson has... a few issues that interfere with his capacity to communicate at times,' I explain.

The principal glares at Pamela.

'Do you mean to say... there's something else, in addition to Jackson's involvement in the incident at Queenscliff Public? Does he have a medical issue?'

'There's no definitive diagnosis. Here's the documentation from Jackson's treating doctors and allied health workers over the years.'

I pass her a sheaf of papers.

The principal shuffles through them. 'That's a comprehensive set of tests.'

'For a long time we searched for some kind of 'label'. Now we just focus on day to day management with the help of a paediatric psychologist, Dr Louisa Kelleher.'

'It can help to have a label.' The principal passes the papers back to me. 'Then you know what you're dealing with.'

'I'm not so sure,' I say, indignant now. 'Sometimes labels just put special kids in boxes. Sometimes they just give adults an excuse to stop thinking.'

The woman stares at me over her spectacles.

'Mrs Curtis, here at Clontarf Grammar we believe that no sin is too great that it cannot be brought before the risen Lord. Are you taking comfort in your church community at this difficult time?'

My mouth drifts open, but I find no words.

'Even the most abominable acts can be redeemed through the redemptive power of Jesus,' she continues, 'and despite the circumstances, I was prepared to consider Jackson's application for a place in Year Five. Based on what you've just shown me, however, I'm afraid our school is not set up for...'

I lurch forward in my seat.

'It's very Christian of you to consider our case,' I say quickly. 'You can't imagine how devastating the incident at Queenscliff Public has been, for everyone. We're not really regular church-goers, mostly Easter and Christmas, but I was hoping the school might be sympathetic to Jackson and his sister.'

My voice is quivering.

'As a Christian school, we welcome children who are... burdened.' The principal folds her hands on the desk. 'However, I'm afraid we are not adequately resourced to respond to Jackson's idiosyncrasies.'

'He won't be an imposition,' I insist. 'Jackson was doing just fine at Queenscliff Public. He was totally integrated with the other kids, up until...'

'Mrs Curtis.' The principal's expression sours. 'How long has Jackson been receiving specialist support?'

'Eight years.' As soon as I say it, I realise how this sounds. Jackson has been undergoing some form of psychological treatment for more than seventy per cent of his life.

'Clontarf Grammar simply does not have the resources for managing all the moving parts of this scenario.' The principal tugs at the cuffs of her cardigan. 'There are duty of care considerations, all kinds of associated risks. If Jackson's issues aren't well defined or understood, how can we gauge whether or not he might be inclined to... do the same again, in our school toilets?'

I blanch.

'With due respect, Mrs Hemingsworth, the police are still investigating. No formal charges have been laid. There was another boy involved, too. Believe me, we've done a lot of soul-searching about... the incident in the school toilets. But Jackson's getting the support he needs and, I can assure you, it won't ever happen again.'

'How *can* you be so sure?' The principal eyes Pamela with an *I'm sorry* expression, then reverts her attention to me. 'I understand this is difficult for you, Mrs Curtis, but our parents are our most important stakeholders. Their sympathies will lie with the victim.'

It's as if the woman has leapt over the desk and slugged me in the stomach.

'The victim, yes.' I'm breathing heavily now. 'Not a day goes by when I don't think about the victim, and how appalling this is for her and her family. I hope she's getting the help she needs. I hope she recovers and goes on to live a fulfilling, happy life, despite everything. I want that more than anything.'

My voice cracks.

'But Jackson's a victim, too, Mrs Hemingsworth. He's a victim of a unique genetic profile, delivering him a brain that operates differently to the rest of the world. And he's a victim of being misunderstood by almost everyone around him, including me, his own mother.'

A rogue tear slides down my cheek.

'What about walking in someone else's shoes? What about compassion? The truth is, every single one of us is just a step away from the abyss. It only takes one misunderstanding, one wrong move, for your whole life to change. "There but for the grace of God go I" – what about that?'

I turn to Pamela.

'I'm so sorry. I know you were trying to help and it's wonderful that you tried, but I think this interview is over.'

Pamela is sitting rigid in her chair.

'Yes,' she says, after a moment. 'I don't think we're welcome here. Come along, Jackson, let's go home.'

She stands up, straightens her blazer and links her arm through Jackson's. Together, they move towards the door.

Despite my fury, I feel a surge of gratitude.

Following Pamela's lead, I stand and hoist my handbag over my shoulder.

At the doorway, I turn to address the principal once more.

'We're about to go and pick up Jackson's younger sister from school, Mrs Hemingsworth. Ruby's a victim, too. She's a talented little girl with the wrong family right now. She's barely coping at Queenscliff Public, but no one gives a damn about her, either.'

The principal sits stony-faced as I close the door.

We file out of the administration building and into the carpark. Once in the van, my anger begins to settle into despondency.

I start the engine and steer the van back onto the road that will take us to Queenscliff Public.

Pamela is slumped in the front passenger seat, her eyes closed, pressing hard at the sides of her forehead.

Jackson sits in morose silence behind us.

In the rear-vision mirror, I can see his blinking worsening.

'I didn't... say... the right things.' Jackson's words are slower than ever.

'Nonsense, Jackson,' snaps Pamela. 'It was Mrs Hemingsworth who didn't say the right things.'

The road blurs in front of me as my eyes fill with tears.

'Thank you, Pamela,' I murmur.

We join the car queue in the Kiss-N-Go Zone outside Queenscliff Public School. As students stream out of the front gate, parents mingle at the fence line, like any ordinary school day.

'We're not a normal family, are we?' asks Jackson.

I say nothing for a moment, then let out a long sigh. 'We're a bit unusual, granted. Especially at the moment.'

'That's my fault.'

Pamela twists around in her seat to look directly at her grandson.

'It's no one's fault, Jackson, especially not yours. Everyone's unusual. Just you remember that. No one's bloody normal.'

Jackson's eyes widen with surprise. 'Yes, Nanna.'

In fifteen years, I've never once heard Pamela swear.

'I'm so sorry, Jackson,' she continues. 'I'm not sure how Clontarf Grammar claims to be a Christian school. I'll be writing to the School Council about it, and the Department of Education. We're just going to have to regroup and sort this mess out on our own.'

Right now I can't see how, but I'm comforted by Pamela's determination.

'Look!' Jackson jabs a finger in the direction of the school gate. 'There's Eddie from soccer!'

The Dragons' goalie is walking with his mother, Lola, a woman I considered my friend only a month ago. The last time I saw Lola was on the morning the school principal turned us around in the playground, and I haven't heard from her since.

I haven't heard from *any* parents since.

Eddie and Lola are strolling along the footpath just as we're inching forward in the car queue. It's impossible to miss our bright red van, so I arrange my face into a neutral smile, half-hoping and half-fearing that they'll stop to say hello.

But Lola keeps her eyes trained on her son, as if we're not in her direct line of sight. Passing within centimetres of our van, she puts a protective arm around Tommy's shoulder and turns her face away.

Jackson opens the window to call out to them.

'Don't!' I hiss. 'They don't want to talk to us, hon.'

As we edge forward again in the queue, Jackson unclicks his seatbelt with a flourish. I'm terrified he's going to climb out of the van and follow Eddie.

'Jackson, please...' I begin, then realise he's slid down onto the van's floor. 'What are you doing?'

'They don't want to talk to me,' he intones, staring up at the roof. 'They don't want to see me, Mum.'

We've reached the front of the queue now. The automatic door opens at the side of the van and Ruby hops in, almost falling over Jackson.

'What are you doing, Jack-Jack?'

'Put your seatbelt back on please, Jackson,' urges Pamela.

Reluctantly, Jackson slides back up onto his seat and clips himself in.

'We had an interview at Clontarf Grammar, Rubes,' I explain, accelerating away from the pick-up zone. 'It's not going to work out, unfortunately. Jackson's a bit upset about that.'

'Oh.' Ruby sounds disappointed too. 'So... where are we going to go to school?'

'I'm not sure,' I say, merging onto the main road now. 'We'll have to come up with a Plan B.'

'Was your day any better today, Ruby?' asks Pamela.

It's a rhetorical question of sorts, and Ruby doesn't answer.

We turn into our street and pull up in the driveway.

'I wish we could go back to Erskineville,' says Ruby glumly. 'Could we move back there, Mummy?'

I'm not sure how to respond.

'Let's have some afternoon tea,' I say. 'Why don't you two go and say hello to Batman and Robin?'

Ruby and Jackson climb out of the van and run down the driveway to the back yard.

'Thank God for those guinea pigs,' I say, glancing over at Pamela.

She's pressing her fingers to her forehead again. Only this time, silent tears are streaking down her face.

I lean across and put my arm around her shoulder.

I've never seen Pamela cry like that before.

19

I'm listening hard in the darkness for the top-knot pigeons, but all I can hear is the sound of Dad snoring on the sofa downstairs. He sleeps there most nights, maybe because his snoring disturbs Mum. It doesn't bother me though, it's nice tiptoeing downstairs and curling up with Dad. I've been doing that a lot lately, because my memory download keeps waking me up and replaying what happened in the school toilets.

I'm sick of seeing it over and over, so I've been putting it on mute and slow-mo, then I've started *editing* it. In the edited clip, I burst into the cubicle at just the right moment and grab Sienna's hand. We bolt out of the toilets, across the playground and into the school office, then we tell the nice lady behind the front desk that we're in trouble and we want it to stop because *we don't like it*. The lady just smiles and calls our mums, then both of us go home and stay friends forever.

It's the thirty-third day since that Monday morning in the school toilets. Maybe the top-knots have gone to wherever pigeons go for winter, because there's still no sound outside my bedroom window. Those birds are lucky; *I* haven't been allowed to go anywhere since the police told me to stay away from school and soccer and the third-grade kids. Apart from the pet warehouse, the only places I've visited are the supermarket and Clontarf Grammar and *they* weren't fun at all.

Two days ago in Woolies, we turned our shopping trolley into aisle seven and almost bumped into Sienna Wilson-Brown's mum. She had a box of breakfast cereal in one hand and a four-pack of toilet rolls in the other. Her hair was greasy, her eyes were puffy, and her cheeks looked like she needed to eat something really quickly.

Mum and Hannah just stood there, staring at each other.

After a while, Mum took a step forward.

'Hannah, I'm so sorry...' she started.

Sienna's mum backed away like Snickers in a thunderstorm.

'Please,' called Mum, but Hannah just dropped her cereal and toilet rolls right there and ran away from us down the aisle.

Mum got woozy then. She had to lean up against the shelves for a really long time.

'Are you okay, Mum?' I asked a few times, but she didn't answer.

Finally when she looked up, it was like I wasn't there. Part of me wished I *wasn't*, because I'm the one who ruined everything.

I check the clock on my bedside table now. The numbers and letters are swirling around like always, before plopping into place. It's 5.17 on Friday 8th June.

I sit bolt upright.

I'm like a rooster ready to crow its head off, because today's the day of the Winter Eisteddfod. Soon I'll be dancing with April Kennedy at the town hall, in front of my whole family and Coach Steve and heaps of VIPs and even a busload of Mum's Special Ps from Care Cottage.

Dad's coming too, he's leaving the agency early today. He's

already seen the aerial silks hanging in the shed, but I've tried to keep it a special surprise. Dad used to want me to play cricket, but lately he's been asking me loads of questions about aerial silks. I'm glad he'll see me dance before he flies to New York again.

I'm sad he has to leave.

Mum and Dad fought about that last night, it was one of their bad ones too. I'm pretty sure they didn't say sorry to each other either, they just walked away when they'd had enough of the yelling. They won't be fighting like that today though, because today's way too special.

I'm wondering if Mum's home-school will be cancelled today, so I hop out of bed to check the activity list. I'm *really* hoping there's nothing there at all, but there is; I've got to finish two sheets of long division before I leave for the town hall.

So I sit down at my desk and sharpen my pencil and do fifty sums in fifteen minutes. Long division is super easy for me, it's just the reverse of multiplication. I can do it in my mind really quickly with numbers up to a thousand, but my favourite is the number 192. Dr Louisa says it might be a special number power, but Mr Thompson in 5T never thought so, he just yelled at me for using a hidden calculator. Once I tried to tell him that my brain was the hidden calculator, but Mr Thompson didn't let me speak. I don't miss that about Queenscliff Public.

When I've finished my sums, I'm ready for dance. My costume is hanging up in my cupboard, Miss Marion dropped it in yesterday. I unzip the bag and stroke the white feathery armbands. My angel's wings are as soft as clouds and I can't wait to put them on and fly above April Kennedy again. Part of me is worried about what I'll say after not seeing her for so long, but mostly I'm excited.

The clock on my bedside table says it's 6.20, so there's still another three hours to wait. Miss Marion asked me to be at the town hall two hours before everyone else, we're meeting at the rear entrance where nobody will see us. Our dance group is performance number fifteen on the program, so I have to take loads of snacks and a pack of cards to keep me busy while I wait. Maybe I could call Dead Granny while I'm waiting, and maybe she could watch my performance through her shoe-phone?

I'm going to play Patience, too, which is an old-time game that Dead Granny taught me. It's mostly about luck and the way the pack is shuffled, but you do need some skill. Dead Granny always used to say, 'Patience is like life, Jackson. You can't control the cards you're dealt, but you can choose to use them wisely.'

Mum always calls my room 'a pig-sty', but I know exactly where everything is. I move the Pokémon figures off my bottle-top collection, shift my Lego and the library books out of the way, then find my Flying Kangaroo cards right under my marbles collection. Even with playing cards for Patience, it's still going to be hard to wait so long.

At least I know what's coming *after* the waiting, though: I'll be flying like an angel with April Kennedy. The worst thing about the waiting I've been doing since the police interview at Chatswood is that no one knows what's coming afterwards. Not even clever Jeff knows, so the last thirty-three days have felt like thirty-three years.

The clock on the bedside table says it's almost seven o'clock now, so Batman and Robin will be waiting for their breakfast. I pull on my robe, creep down the hall into the kitchen and take a big bunch of celery out of the vegetable crisper. Snickers starts scratching at the laundry door, so I slide a doggy treat underneath to keep him happy. Then I unlock the back door and walk across the yard to the guinea pig cage and post the celery through the feeder.

Batman and Robin start crunching on the celery straight away. I really love that sound and I'm pretty sure Batman and Robin love me too, because they're always chirping and making happy little *chk-chk-chk* noises whenever they see me. Sometimes after Mum takes Ruby to school, I pick them up out of their cage and bring them indoors and snuggle with them on the sofa. Snickers always growls because he thinks it's *his* sofa, but I tell him to *Remember his Manners* because Batman and Robin are family now.

After Batman and Robin have finished their celery, I take them out one at a time and stroke their silky fur. Then I lie down on the lawn with both of them, just staring up at the sky. Today doesn't feel as cold as winter should be and the sky is clear and blue like spring. Robin stretches out across my stomach and Batman curls up on my chest, he's the really snuggly one. They both feel a bit like hot water bottles, so I close my eyes and wait for time to pass.

* * *

'There you are, Jackson!'

My eyes fly open. Mum's voice is super snappy.

'I've been looking for you everywhere. It's almost nine o'clock!'

I scramble to my feet, my head fuzzy, and rush to put Batman and Robin back into their cage. Batman chirrups at me, and I think maybe he just said 'good luck' in guinea pig language. I can't be late for the Winter Eisteddfod.

I hurry inside, collect my costume and backpack, then run out to the Red Rocket. When we're in the van, the empty feeling in my tummy tells me I've missed breakfast and suddenly I remember I haven't brushed my teeth either.

'Do you have any mints?' I ask Mum, because I don't want foul breath when I'm dancing with April Kennedy.

Mum passes me a little tin of sugar-free mints that she always keeps in her handbag.

'How on earth did you fall asleep in the back yard? That's not like you, Jackson. Couldn't you sleep last night?'

If I tell her about my memory download playing the day after Mother's Day on loop, she might get worried and call Dr Louisa.

'Were you too excited about the performance?'

It's almost the truth, so I nod.

Mum beams at me in the rear-vision mirror. It's her real smile, I've missed that a lot lately. Dad's smile has faded as well.

'I can't wait to see you dance,' says Mum.

We pull into the parking lot at the back of the town hall. Miss Marion is standing at the stage door, looking much more serious than usual. Her socks are amazing, though; they're pure gold, pulled up right over her knees. It's really hard *not* to look at them

Mum parks the Red Rocket in a loading zone. Miss Marion opens the side door so I can climb out, then she walks around to Mum's side and gives her a big hug and a kiss. They start nattering like they always do, so I get my costume and backpack out of the boot and just stand there waiting for them to finish. They're always talking about stuff they both love, like red wine and dark chocolate and foreign films and singing.

'All right,' says Mum, after they've finished. 'I'll be back for the performance at two o'clock, with everyone else.'

I'm too excited to speak.

'Bye, Maz.' That's the special nickname Mum has for Miss Marion now. 'Break a leg, Jackson.'

Why do people even say that before a performance? Breaking a leg is never a good idea, especially when you're doing aerial silks.

Mum beeps the horn and drives off.

All of a sudden, I'm really nervous.

Before I get too worried though, Miss Marion puts an arm around my shoulders and guides me through the rear entrance, telling me exactly what's going to happen next. She shows me the green room where the other dancers are going to wait, then she points out the boys' change rooms and toilets.

Then she walks me to the special place I have to wait by myself, which is actually a storage room. It's pretty small and full of mops and brooms, but right in the middle is a big soft chair that Miss Marion's set up just for me.

I feel bad that she's got to keep me here, away from all the other kids. Miss Marion must feel bad too, because suddenly she takes my face in her hands.

'It's not about you, Jackson,' she says. 'It's about the parents.'

She pulls out a packet of Minties from her bag and says, 'Knock yourself out, Jackson.' Then she passes me an iPad with all her amazing music on it and a set of massive noise-cancelling headphones. Suddenly my beans go bouncy inside of me, and I do a happy-headstand.

Miss Marion drops into a headstand too, so that we're looking at each other upside down.

'Your Mum knows about the Minties,' she says. 'Save some for later, please?'

It's hard to nod in a headstand, so I just start laughing.

'The iPad's only got music and chess on it, there's no inter-net. So don't try to play games, okay?'

'Okay.' I giggle.

'Great headstand, Jackson,' she says. 'But maybe we should conserve your energy for the performance?'

We roll out of our headstands and I take a seat in the comfy chair instead.

Miss Marion tells me she'll be back at one o'clock to help me with my costume and makeup, then she waves goodbye and closes the door of the storage room.

It's cosy inside with the light on. Miss Marion's special headphones carry me into my own private disco. She's created this really cool playlist called 'Jackson's Jives', with all the songs we've ever danced to in our morning sessions in the garden shed. 'Today's the Day' is the very first song on the playlist. I close my eyes and suck on a Mintie, listening to the lyrics.

Maybe that song was written just for me. Or maybe Miss Marion put it first because she knows I've been waiting for this day my whole life.

20

Poor Jackson, I think to myself. *Stuck in a broom cupboard while the other dancers hang out in the green room.*

I line up the potatoes, carrots and green beans on the kitchen bench next to the chopping board. I understand why Maz has done it, of course, but I wish she didn't have to. How many times have I caught myself fantasising like this over the past month? *I wish... If only... Poor Jackson.*

Prepping for the evening meal is a simple thing I *can* do now, to slow down my busy mind. Liberating potatoes from their skins, drinking a sneaky glass of prosecco from a bottle delivered yesterday by Steve during his regular pop-in.

Steve. In the briefest of periods, he's morphed from soccer coach to friend to confidant to... *what* exactly? Amid outraged parents hurling abuse online or smearing excrement across our property, Steve has been a rare bright spot in the long, colour-less weeks since the day after Mother's Day.

I take another large gulp from my glass, relishing the slightly astringent sensation in my throat. Only a month ago, I was refusing champagne at my Mother's Day breakfast. Right now, I'm on my second glass before lunch.

Riley flashes past the kitchen window, his green skater jacket billowing behind him. He's carrying yet another bunch of flowers, yellow roses this time. He leaps off his skateboard with ease, leaning it against the shed in the back yard.

Knocking on the back door, he waves at me through the window.

'Hi Mrs C,' he says, stepping into the kitchen. 'Ready for Jackson's big day?'

'Sure am,' I say.

His gaze lingers on my wineglass for a moment. 'Is Milla home from school yet?'

'She's in the lounge with Ruby. We'll leave for the eisteddfod as soon as Andy gets home.'

As Riley moves into the lounge, I hear Milla gushing about the flowers.

He's certainly attentive, and he's been a lifeline for Milla. For all of us, really. A welcome diversion while we await the outcome of the police investigation and, in all likelihood, a summons to a hearing in the Children's Court. In his latest attempt to avert that, Jeff has asked us to supply evidence that Jackson has 'demonstrable special needs'. But how can we, without a formal diagnosis? That's been part of the problem for so many years: no one *wants* a diagnosis for their child, but without one, you're screwed.

I slice the potatoes and toss them into the slow cooker.

I've given Jeff – and the police investigation team – unfettered access to every medical and allied health record ever generated about Jackson. What other evidence can I provide? There's still no medical consensus about Jackson's special needs, nor any definitive proof that they might interfere with his ability to know right from wrong. Yet this is precisely the argument Jeff is mounting to defend us from a court hearing.

I'm not convinced by it myself. As his mother, I'm certain that Jackson *does* know the difference between right and wrong. So why is our lawyer pursuing an angle I don't subscribe to?

Blinking back tears, I begin dicing the beans. I've been reading about juvenile detention a lot lately, trying to prepare myself for the possibility.

I move to the refrigerator and seize the green bottle once more, upending it over my glass. I'm starting to understand Andy's reliance on beer at the end of a day; I *really* get it because I *really* want it, and much earlier than ever before.

The front door opens and I hear Andy's familiar footfall in the hall.

'Hi kids,' he says, passing by the lounge.

'Daddy's home!' Ruby squeals and intercepts him. She throws herself into his arms, giggling as he dangles her upside down. 'Want to play Monopoly?'

'I'll just see Mum first.'

He moves into the kitchen and pulls up a stool at the island bench.

'Have you just...?' He motions at the empty wine bottle standing on the sink.

'Yes, I have. It was already open.'

I rummage in the vegetable crisper for a butternut pumpkin. As I set about peeling it, Andy walks to the fridge and cracks open the top of a light beer.

'All right, I'll join you.' He tips the beer against my wineglass. 'Cheers.'

I drain the last of the glass.

'I saw Jackson practising his aerial stuff this morning,' he says. 'I had no idea he could do that. It was... impressive.'

I'm pleased to hear the pride in his voice.

'Did you tell Jackson that yourself? He'd probably love to hear it from you.'

The pumpkin is older and softer than it should be. I scoop up the peelings and toss them into the composter.

'Not yet, but I will.' Andy's chin quivers as he raises the beer to his lips. 'I've screwed up a lot of things lately. And not-so-lately.'

I stop slicing the pumpkin and look at him.

'I guess with everything that's happened, I've been forced to stop and think.'

Andy takes another long swig of his beer.

I wait for him to say more.

'Raising Jackson's been tough on us,' he says. 'For years I couldn't admit it. I was too caught up in trying to create some kind of... ideal family life, I guess. With you running it, me funding it. It put us both under pressure, but especially you.'

I'm taken aback by his insight.

'I've been A-type. You've told me that before. Way too focused on my work. There's not much I can do about all the travelling, but... I can see it's been much easier for me being away, than for you dealing with our homelife.'

I can barely digest this. 'It's good to hear you... actually say that, Andy.'

'You've done the lion's share.' He motions at the chopping board. 'I know I'm a bit late to the party, but is there anything I can do to help?'

'Well, yes,' I say, surprised again. 'There's a load of washing in the laundry. You could hang that out?'

'I meant... with dinner,' he says. 'Any veggies to chop or something?'

Frustration rises within me.

'Well, if you really want to help, Andy, you can start by giving me the help I need. Not the help you feel like giving me.'

He stares at me.

'Fair enough,' he says, after a moment. 'Do I do that a lot? Must be bloody irritating if I do. A bit like asking for a surf-board for Christmas and getting socks instead.'

I laugh out loud.

'Can you do me a favour, Jules?' Andy finishes his beer and tosses the bottle into the recycling bin. 'Ask me for the help you want. You've got to tell me what you need.'

The resentful part of me wonders why I should have to spell it out, but I can see that he's trying.

'Okay,' I say. 'I guess you can't be a mind-reader.'

Andy smiles. 'Hey, look at that. Maybe middle-aged dogs can learn new tricks? Change is possible.'

He takes a second beer from the fridge and clinks it against my empty wineglass.

'This is so bloody difficult,' he says. 'Any couple would struggle. It was already hard with Jackson, but now with the police investigation...'

My phone rings.

'It's her.' I recognise the number.

I'm fearful of talking to Detective Annabelle Johnson but, if I don't, it will only prolong the inevitable. It might be easier buoyed by the bubbly.

'Julia speaking.' I hope the detective won't notice the slur in my voice.

'It's Annabelle Johnson here. I called over this morning, but you weren't at home.'

'Oh?' I must have been dropping Jackson to the town hall, but I'm not about to tell her that.

'Is now a good time, Mrs Curtis?'

My stomach clenches. 'Go ahead.'

'The results on Jackson's DNA swab came back today.'

I sink onto a stool. Jeff has briefed us on this moment. Closing my eyes, I brace myself for a summons to a closed hearing in the Children's Court.

'The DNA detected in Sienna Wilson-Brown's samples doesn't match Jackson's results.'

My eyes fly open. Jeff never mentioned *this* possibility.

'Are... are you sure?' I stammer. 'Could there be a mistake?'

'The findings were further confirmed by interview with the victim this morning. There's no mistake, Mrs Curtis.'

'Wait,' I blurt. 'Andy's here too. I'm just going to put you on speaker.' I position the phone in the centre of the bench. 'Can you... please repeat that?'

The detective clears her throat.

'The DNA tissue found on Sienna Wilson-Brown belongs to someone else, not Jackson. As a result, we conducted another interview with Sienna earlier, which provided us with... additional clarity.'

'Hang on,' says Andy. 'What kind of evidence did you collect?'

'A pair of underpants were retrieved from beneath the victim's bed. The sample was intact and well-preserved.'

'And it's definitely not Jackson's DNA on them?' Andy presses.

'No, it's not,' the detective confirms. 'It's not uncommon for children who have experienced trauma to be unable to... articulate themselves properly, in the first few weeks.'

'Then whose DNA is it?' I ask.

'Our interview with Sienna this morning prompted us to collect a DNA sample from another person of interest. We've requested urgent processing of the results.'

The alcohol-induced fog inside my brain begins to clear. 'You mean, Digby?'

'I'm not at liberty to confirm that,' says the detective.

'He's the only other person of interest,' snaps Andy. 'He was the only other kid in the toilets.'

'But didn't Jackson... make an admission in his interview at Chatswood?' My hands are shaking so badly, I'm forced to grip the kitchen bench. 'He said he touched Sienna. I heard him say that to you.'

'The DNA samples don't match,' the detective repeats. 'Which means, Jackson's original interview is... inconsistent with the physical evidence.'

'But why?' I ask, incredulous. 'Why would Jackson... admit to something he didn't do?'

I couldn't care less if Annabelle can hear that I've been drinking. I'm intoxicated by something else entirely – a chance that my son *isn't* a perpetrator, after all.

'There are all kinds of possible explanations for false confessions, Mrs Curtis. Peer influence can be very powerful.'

Andy's jaw tightens as he leans closer to the phone.

'Or, how's this for an explanation? Jackson is a neurodiverse boy who should never have been subjected to that first interview you conducted with him. Not without proper support and legal advice, anyway.' His tone is steely, but tears prick his eyes. 'Is that one of your possible explanations, Detective?'

It's the first time I've heard Andy openly acknowledge Jackson's neurodiversity. For years he's dodged it, dismissed it, pretended it away.

'It wasn't... clear to me at the time whether Jackson's cognitive functioning was normal.' The detective sounds flustered. 'From the initial discussions we had, it didn't seem clear to

Julia, either. But it was evident that an assault had occurred and it was important to observe due process...'

'So you just kept pushing through, even though you didn't know if Jackson was capable of answering your questions?' Andy turns to me. 'This changes everything, Jules.'

No one speaks for a long while.

'But if Jackson was still... involved in the incident in some way,' I venture, 'can't he still be charged without DNA evidence?'

There is another long pause before the detective speaks.

'In the absence of any physical evidence implicating Jackson in the assault, there is no basis for a charge. Sienna's interview this morning suggests that Jackson wasn't... necessarily proximate when the assault occurred. He may not have been privy to it at all.'

'Oh, my God.' I collapse against the bench, half-gulping for air, half-weeping with relief. No charge means no court appearance, which means *no* juvenile justice.

Andy clears his throat. 'If Jackson wasn't 'privy' to the assault, then where was he?'

'We think he was... nearby, but not directly involved. We're going to have to re-interview Jackson as soon as possible, given the initial interview inadvertently led us in the wrong direction.'

'The wrong direction?' Andy barks. 'What a bloody euphemism. We'll have our lawyer present for the second interview, thank you very much.'

'As you wish.' The detective sounds chastened. 'I'm... sorry for the inconvenience. It's been a difficult investigation. I have a nine-year-old daughter at home myself.'

For a fleeting moment, I feel sorry for her.

'Oh yeah?' says Andy. 'We've got one of those too. And a

fourteen-year-old. All of us have suffered because of this...
"inconvenience" you've created, Detective Johnson. Heads will
roll.'

'I'll call you back on Monday to organise a time for Jackson's
next interview.' The detective sounds subdued. 'Goodbye.'

As the call ends, we stare at each other in shock.

Andy shakes his head. 'She'll bloody understand the defini-
tion of inconvenience when Jeff Goldstein hears about this.'

I begin to cry and cannot stop.

Andy moves around the bench and takes me in his arms.
Allowing him to hold me for the first time in weeks, I inhale his
familiar scent.

'Shhh. It's going to be okay.' He cradles my head against his
chest. 'Jackson's going to be okay.'

I look up at him. 'Jackson wasn't... even near Sienna
Wilson-Brown. Did you hear her say that, too?'

Andy nods.

'Mummy!' Ruby yells out from the lounge. 'It's past one
o'clock! We have to go to the performance!'

Andy brushes the tears from my face with his fingertips.

'We're all going to be okay,' he whispers. 'Let's go see
Jackson dance.'

21

Just after one o'clock, the door of the storage room swings open.

'It's showtime!' says Miss Marion. My stomach goes all zippy with nerves.

When she's finished covering my face in creamy foundation and black eyeliner and cherry red lipstick, she helps me slide the angel's wings over my arms.

'Right Jackson,' she says, in a way that makes me listen carefully. 'It's time to move backstage. I've just told the girls you'll be performing today. Can I suggest that you try not to touch anyone backstage?' Miss Marion looks uncomfortable. 'I'm sorry, Jackson, but it's just to be safe.'

She pushes open the door of the storage room to lead me outside. The bright lights make my eyelids start to twitch.

'Oh, darling.' Miss Marion closes the door again and steps back inside. She takes my hands in hers. 'Some things are just too hard, aren't they? But listen, I want you to dance your heart out today, Jackson. The world needs you dancing, Jackson.'

That makes me smile.

Miss Marion puts an arm around my shoulders. 'You've been so committed to your rehearsals at home. You know this routine better than anyone. You've got this, Jackson.'

She gives me a big hug.

'Ready, Jackson?' She asks. 'It's now or never.'

'It's now,' I say.

Miss Marion pushes open the door of the storage room again and I shield my eyes with my hand. The green room is noisy, packed with kids wearing flamingo costumes and white tutus and some in silver sequined overalls who look like glitzy garbage collectors.

There are a few mums in the green room too, helping with sequins and ribbons and hair spray, but I keep my head down. Miss Marion moves me through the gaps in the crowd. We walk into a concrete corridor leading to some stairs, then down into a dim room that's like a bunker. Along the way we pass a few adults who try to talk to Miss Marion, but she just says, 'Can't stop, sorry.'

On the other side of the bunker, we arrive in a carpeted room with a big video screen on the wall that shows exactly what's happening on stage. Three groups are waiting here, and one of them is Queenscliff Public.

My eyes find hers before hers find mine.

April Kennedy is even more perfect than I remember, so maybe I'm not a memory magnet after all.

As Miss Marion guides me through the group, I look at the carpet and try not to draw attention to myself. She plants me right next to April Kennedy, and somehow our kneecaps touch.

April looks up. I'm worried she won't want me anywhere near her.

'Are you all right, Jackson?' Her hand brushes mine. 'I've missed you.'

I grasp the ends of her fingers and look into her eyes. Even though I can't say the words, I'm pretty sure she can hear my heart talking.

'Three minutes,' Miss Marion announces. 'Stretching please, dancers.'

'I tried to find you,' whispers April. 'But I didn't know where you live. You're not on Facebook, or Instagram or...'

'We live in a cottage with a rainbow library in the front yard,' I tell her. 'Near Queenscliff beach.'

'A rainbow library?' April smiles at me.

'Stretches!' Miss Marion calls again.

April drops my hand. My palms are sweating so much, I can't focus on stretching at all.

Suddenly a man with a clipboard appears. He's wearing a swishy purple coat that makes him look important and mysterious. He nods at Miss Marion, then we all stand up and follow him out through a padded door.

On the other side of the door are black curtains floating at stage left. Behind them, I can see the stage itself. A group of dancers dressed in leopard skins are leaping and pouncing in the final minute of their routine. They're dancing to a Katy Perry song, so Ruby's probably jiggling in her seat right now.

I crane my neck to spot Ruby in the audience, or anyone else in my family, but I can't see a thing. The stage lights are too bright and everything else is pitch black.

'Come with me, Jackson,' says Miss Marion.

I follow her to a spiral staircase behind centre stage.

She gives me a quick hug and says, 'You know what to do.'

And I do. I climb the spiral like a cat burglar and walk out along the metal platform high above the stage. I reach for the silks in the centre, looping them around my body and feet in all the right places. It's exactly as I've practised a gazillion times before.

The music ends, the audience cheers and the leopards strut off the stage.

The lights dim for the changeover and a swarm of prop people move out of the shadows like ants, pushing the hospital bed onto centre stage. The dancers take their positions, with April Kennedy slipping out last. She lies on the bed below, looking up. Even in the darkness, I can see her white teeth smiling at me.

Pale blue light dawns across the stage as the first notes of Anohni's song echo around the hall. The acoustics in the town hall are much louder than anywhere we've practised. Goose bumps ripple over me as my body recognises the music again. I watch the other dancers moving below, check my double foot lock, then swing out into the darkness. The nothingness around me doesn't feel empty at all, it's as if an invisible force is holding me up.

The music starts rising and falling like ocean waves lapping against the shore. The dancers move with it, like swirling sea creatures floating on the tide. April Kennedy stays still, she's so frail she can only move one limp arm above her head. As the notes grow louder and more discordant, I feel them swelling up inside of me. The music's about to change and then *bang*, suddenly it does.

At exactly two minutes thirty, the piano goes all choppy and nothing harmonises any more. April starts tossing in her bed, then she's up on her knees begging for someone to help her, 'Please-please-please.'

And that's *my* cue to lower myself from the ceiling in the X position, so that Mum and Dad and everyone else out in the audience can see me.

The other dancers go wild as they circle the hospital bed, and April is beating her fists so hard against the mattress that my angel heart is filled with pity. I dangle forward in the figure-head position, my arm-wings outstretched, but she's still out of reach. Angels never give up though, so I move into the butterfly position and hang upside down.

April stops thrashing and looks up. Her eyes lock with mine and suddenly I realise this isn't an act at all. Suddenly I know that I was *born* to do this, and that it's my job to be a flying boy angel for *all* the people who are suffering on earth. I can actually feel the mercy flowing through me like a silver-blue electrical charge.

I cross the silks behind my back and wrap them tightly around my torso, then lock them between my legs like Houdini's chains. When I'm ready, I look down at April and smile. I've done this so many times before, I don't even have to think about it any more.

I start split-rolling and tear-dropping, slowly at first and then faster. April's pretend-pulling at her hair and the violin is arguing with the cello and the piano is going nuts and Anohni is singing in her spooky howling voice.

And then I hear something else. A strange, low sound.

'Mooo.'

Like a cow inside the town hall.

Miss Marion always says, 'The show must go on, even when you're distracted.' So I just keep twisting and turning above April, who's busy shaking her fists as the crescendo builds.

'Mooo.'

But where is it coming from?

April glances from left to right, looking out into the audience and then back up at me. I keep reaching down anyway, preparing for the finale.

I hear the sound again, only this time it's much nearer.

'Booo.' It's a man's voice, and he's standing up in the front row. 'Booo.'

His hands are cupped around his mouth and his face is purple-red. I think it might be Tommy's dad, but I can't see for sure. Whoever he is, he's trying to knock me off the silks with his voice.

'Scum!' I hear, just as I start the final descent. 'Boo!'

The silks begin unravelling before I check my final foot lock.

I'm spinning faster and faster and my hands are reaching for April, only this time it doesn't feel right. The silks are slipping across my thighs and stomach and up over my shoulders, unwinding and tightening in all the wrong places.

I *know* it's not right.

'Boo!'

The silks wrap around my neck, but I can't stop my body whirling.

An unstoppable angel, falling.

Something slams around my throat and pulls tight. I hear popping and tearing sounds from inside my body.

The stage lights turn brighter than the sun.

'Mum,' I call out, but I choke on the word.

22

'Call an ambulance,' shouts Riley, hurdling a row of seats and bolting down the centre aisle towards the stage.

Andy takes off after him, followed by Milla and Ruby.

My vision contracts to the head of a pin.

I fumble for my phone, but it's slippery in my hands.

There's confusion on the stage. Some of the girls are still dancing, some are standing frozen. I can't see anything of Jackson, except for the aerial silk pulled taut from the ceiling and disappearing behind the bed.

As the song ends, it's like the world has ended too.

A little girl starts bawling from the front rows.

The curtain drops.

I manage to dial the three digits. The emergency operator asks a barrage of questions that I'm unable to answer.

'Oh, God.' I thrust the phone into Pamela's hands. 'Speak to her, please.'

Pushing my way past strangers, I charge down the aisle towards the stage. Adrenaline courses through my body as I fight my way under the heavy black curtain.

I'm utterly unprepared for what lies beyond it.

Jackson is spreadeagled at centre stage, a red welt encircling his neck. His face is deathly pale bar the broken capillaries in his cheeks.

Riley is crouched over him, pumping at his chest. Marion stands weeping next to him.

I lurch forward, but Andy's arms restrain me.

'Jackson!' I struggle to reach our son.

'Riley's a lifesaver,' says Milla. 'Let him work.'

I sink to my knees, watching Riley push long breaths into Jackson's mouth, interspersed with the dreadful chest-pumping.

A woman in a high-visibility vest hurries onto the stage with a first aid kit. She crouches down and shines a torch in Jackson's eyes. His forehead is bleeding badly.

Ruby whimpers. 'Is Jackson... dead?'

A wail rises in my throat.

Andy turns to Milla. 'Take Ruby to Nanna Pam now.'

As Milla bundles Ruby off the stage, they clutch each other, sobbing.

Jackson's body rebounds like a mannequin beneath Riley's hands.

Andy's arms release mine. I scramble forward.

'Please, Jackson.' I seize his hand, pressing my cheek against it.

Marion crouches next to me, tears streaming down her face. 'I'm so sorry, Julia.'

Two men in blue uniforms stride onto the stage, carrying backpacks and a stretcher.

They shunt Riley and the first aid officer out of the way.

'We'll take it from here. Who's the patient?'

'Jackson,' I bleat. 'My son.'

'How old is he?'

'Eleven.'

'And what happened to Jackson?'

'He fell...' I can't say the words.

Riley takes over. 'He fell from a height with a silk wrapped around his neck. He wasn't breathing when I reached him. I got the silk off his neck, cleared the airway and started CPR.'

'His feet were on the floor when you found him?'

'Yes,' says Riley.

The ambulance officer places his hand against Jackson's neck, then lowers his face to watch Jackson's chest and feel for his breath. Grasping Jackson's hand, he yells, 'Jackson, squeeze my hand!'

No response.

'Breathing, but not responsive,' announces the first officer. 'Oximeter, please.'

'Keep breathing,' I whisper.

'ECG,' says the officer. The man attaches a probe to Jackson's index finger, then applies patches and leads to Jackson's chest, connecting him to a monitor. His colleague fits an oxygen mask over Jackson's face, then assembles an intravenous drip.

'Oxygen saturation low, blood pressure low,' reports the first officer. 'Cannula and IV, please.'

The second officer inserts a cannula into the fleshy inner crook of Jackson's elbow, starting the flow of fluids.

'Suspected fracture of the cervical spine. C-spine hard collar and pat-slide, please.'

I cover my mouth with my hands.

They apply a collar around Jackson's neck and slide a thin piece of board under him.

'Slider onto stretcher,' announces the first officer. 'Careful of the spine.'

They unfold the stretcher, lock the wheels into position, then shift Jackson onto it. Repacking their backpacks, they hoist the stretcher up between them.

We follow them off the stage, through a holding area, down a long corridor and out the rear stage door, where an ambulance is idling.

'Just one of you, please,' says the driver, motioning at a seat next to Jackson's stretcher.

'You go,' says Andy, tears running down his cheeks. 'He needs you more.'

* * *

In intensive care, I sit at Jackson's bedside, stroking his fringe. Watching a team of medical personnel monitor his vital signs and ferry him away for neck X-rays and brain scans. Weeping sporadically and gazing at Jackson's translucent eyelids, willing them to open.

If Jackson's airway is uncompromised and he's breathing normally, why *isn't* he waking up?

Andy is on his way, leaving Pamela with the girls at home. I've received two messages from April Kennedy's father, who must have obtained my number from Marion, asking about Jackson's welfare. I can't bring myself to reply.

My phone vibrates again and I check the message. From Jeff, the barrister.

Good news on the DNA win. Police re-interviewing Jackson next Wednesday @10.00am. I'll brief you beforehand. Assault charge dead in the water. Happy Friday!

It's good news come too late. A spark of fury ignites within me.

Had Jackson not been made a pariah among his peers, been forced into hiding, trialled by media and heckled publicly by a parent, might *this* have been avoided?

I stare at the v-shaped abrasion around Jackson's neck.

Another message pops into my inbox. From Marion, this time.

I feel totally responsible.

If anyone is responsible, it's *me*. For failing Jackson at the first police interview. For not fighting hard enough for him, not asking the right questions, not demanding legal advice early, not protecting him from incensed members of the school community. Marion merely tried to keep Jackson doing what he loves.

'Hello, Mrs Curtis.' A tall man in green scrubs materialises at the foot of Jackson's bed. 'I'm the trauma surgeon.'

It's a speciality I've never heard of. The doctor begins talking about possible complications of 'near-hanging', a condition I never knew existed.

'Hypoxic encephalopathy, infarction or abscess of the brain. Oedema of the lungs or larynx, pulmonary compromise, cerebral softening, aspiration pneumonia...'

Part of me refuses to believe it's *my son* we're discussing in such foreign terms.

'Due to incomplete encircling of the ligature and partial drop force, there was only limited suspension. With no necessity to intubate, Jackson's prognosis is better than most.'

My heart leaps at these words.

'I need to canvass the views of other specialists. Neurology, cardiology, ENT, vascular, psychiatry... When he wakes up, we'll need to do some neuropsychological testing too. We'll observe him closely.'

'When will Jackson wake up?'

'All his vital signs indicate it shouldn't be too long now.'

The surgeon disappears behind the privacy curtain.

My phone rings in my lap. I just want it to stop.

Reluctantly, I raise the phone to my ear. 'Hi, Steve.'

'Jules, are you all right?'

'No.'

'Of course not. Bloody stupid question.'

He says nothing for a while.

'Can I bring you some takeaway a little later? Beats hospital food.'

'I'm okay, thanks. Andy will be here.'

If I hadn't been so distracted by Steve in recent weeks, might I have been more focused on Jackson? More alert to this impending disaster?

'Of course. Can I drop in some dinner for both of you, then? I won't stay long.'

'Thanks, Steve.' Could the three of us be friends, when this nightmare is over?

'See you then,' he says.

I put my phone away and turn back to my son.

'Jackson,' I say, leaning closer.

Taking his hand in mine, I squeeze one of his fingernails hard, mimicking the medical staff.

I study his face for a pain response. Nothing.

I press his fingernail even harder. 'Jackson!'

This time, Jackson's eyelids flutter.

'Jackson, can you hear me?'

Slowly, his eyes open.

He blinks a few times, then smiles at me like it's Christmas morning.

I gasp and throw my arms around him.

'Oh, Jackson.' Tears leak out the corners of my eyes.

He coughs. 'Where's Dead Granny?'

'Shhh. It's all right.' I wipe my eyes with my sleeve.

'Where am I?' He moves his head, trying to look around the room. An oxygen prong pops out of his nose.

'Oh, darling.' I attempt to reinsert it. 'You're in hospital. I'm so sorry.'

He stares at me for a moment, before a look of recognition settles across his face.

'No, I'm sorry,' he rasps. 'I wrecked the eisteddfod.'

'You didn't wreck anything.' I try to sit up, but Jackson holds fast to me.

'I wrecked it for everyone,' he says. 'The man was yelling and I...'

'Shhh,' I soothe.

'They'll hate me,' he says. 'They won't want to be my friend.'

Sitting up now, I take his hand in mine. 'Not true, hon. Everyone is worried about you. Miss Marion, Nanna Pam, Steve, April's dad. You haven't lost April Kennedy as a friend.'

Jackson looks at me intently.

'You were amazing up there.' I shake my head at him. 'How did you learn so much, in such a short time?'

'Miss Marion's an amazing teacher.'

Suddenly Andy appears from behind the privacy curtain.

'Oh my God.' He falls to his knees beside Jackson's bed. 'Oh... my boy.'

'I'm okay, Dad.' Jackson's voice is stronger. 'Dead Granny looked after me.'

Goose bumps cascade down my arms. 'What do you mean?'

'When everything went black, Dead Granny was there. She smelled like Kaminski's and ginger tea. She told me it wasn't time for me to migrate to the Otherworld. She sent Saint Jhudiel to untie the silk and make me breathe again.'

'Riley did that,' says Andy, his eyes moist.

Jackson shakes his head. 'It was St Jhudiel. He looked exactly like the statue Dead Granny gave me when I was little. He's the mercy specialist.'

'That was Riley,' repeats Andy, and I wish he would stop.

It *was* miraculous that Riley was there, with the skills to keep Jackson alive before the paramedics arrived.

'St Jhudiel in human form, maybe?' I observe.

'Maybe.' Jackson looks thoughtful. 'What did Riley do?'

'He helped you breathe when you were unconscious. The fact your feet were on the floor... probably saved your life. You were lucky.'

I'm feeling faint retelling it.

'We're lucky Riley likes Milla so much,' says Jackson, 'or he mightn't have come to watch me dance.'

'We're lucky with a lot of things, buddy,' says Andy.

An intensive care nurse moves inside the curtain and switches off a monitor. 'I see you're awake now?'

Jackson grins at her. 'I'm back.'

The nurse peers into Jackson's eyes, inspecting his pupils.

'I have a little test for you,' she says. 'Can you tell me your name and date of birth, please?'

Jackson takes a few moments before answering. 'My name is Jackson Curtis and I was born on blessed Saint Jhudiel's day.'

'Is that so?' the nurse replies. 'And can you tell me what day today is?'

'It's thirty-four days after Mother's Day,' answers Jackson.

'Interesting.' The nurse cocks her head. 'Okay, here's a tricky one. Who's the President of America?'

Jackson shrugs. 'He rhymes with chump.'

The nurse laughs. 'Well, that's quite a special set of answers for my special little test. You've passed... I think. I'll ask the doctor to come and see you shortly.'

She bustles away.

'You're a special boy, Jackson,' I whisper.

'Always have been, always will be,' says Andy. 'I'm sorry we forgot that for a while.'

Jackson smiles at both of us, and it feels like the rising sun.

23

'I'm tired,' complains Jackson. 'When can we go home, Mum?'

He glances around the bland, grey-walled ward that's been our home since Jackson moved out of intensive care two days ago.

'Maybe tomorrow,' I say. 'The doctors want to keep you here a little longer, but hopefully there won't be any more tests.'

Jackson groans. 'Dr Cahill's tests were super hard. What sort of doctor is she?'

'A neurologist,' I reply.

'And the other one?'

'Dr Lloyd? She's a neuropsychologist.'

'How are they different?'

'Er...' I smile sheepishly. 'Why don't you ask them that?'

For hours yesterday, Dr Cahill and Dr Lloyd ran Jackson through a barrage of tests: cognitive screening and physical tests of his nerves, eyes, balance and reflexes; then a raft of assessments on memory, lateralisation, executive function, language, calculations, IQ, visuospatial and visual-motor function, attention and psychomotor speed.

All of this was followed by interrogating Jackson about specific dates and events in his life, before cross-checking his answers with me.

'Detective Annabelle wants to interview you again, Jackson.'

'She does?' Jackson perks up at this news. 'Why?'

I try to maintain a neutral expression.

'Well, she says you didn't touch Sienna Wilson-Brown in the school toilets, after all.'

Jackson frowns.

'The DNA test results came back. Detective Annabelle rang last Friday before the eisteddfod. There's no evidence that you touched Sienna anywhere that... might worry the police.'

Jackson's eyelids begin to flicker.

'So either the results are wrong,' I observe, 'or you confessed to something you didn't do.'

He's blinking rapidly now.

'I did touch her.' Colour rushes into Jackson's cheeks. 'Her slipper was in a puddle so I reached under the door to fix it up and... I accidentally touched her leg.'

'Her leg,' I repeat. 'Did you touch her anywhere else?'

He shakes his head.

Jackson has always been so literal and linear in his thinking; I shouldn't be surprised.

'Did... Digby touch Sienna, too?'

Jackson grabs a fistful of bedsheet and pulls it up under his chin. With his other hand, he covers his eyes to slow his blinking.

I resign myself to waiting.

'I thought Digby was... tickling Sienna,' he mutters. 'I couldn't see for sure. Afterwards, he told me not to tell anyone, so maybe it wasn't a nice tickling.'

'Why didn't you tell Detective Annabelle that?'

'She didn't ask.' Jackson's shoulders slump. 'And Digby made me promise not to dob. I had to *Be Polite*, Mum. It's our first family rule. And you've always told me to keep my promises.'

More literal interpretations.

'Some promises shouldn't be kept, Jackson,' I say quietly. 'We've talked about that before, too.'

'But Digby's my only friend at Queenscliff, apart from April Kennedy.' Jackson looks conflicted. 'No one else talks to me. When he told me not to tell anyone about Alt-World or Sienna, I kept my promise.'

'What's Alt-World?' I ask, feeling a cold weight in my stomach.

Jackson flushes a deeper shade of red.

'It's just... a game. Digby showed me it on his laptop. We put on these black goggles that took us into another world where there were real people. Other players.'

He looks more awkward than I've ever seen him.

'Tell me more.'

'There was this... lady with no trousers. She was being chased around by a pig-man who did stuff to her.'

'A pig-man?' My mind is reeling. 'Was it... some sort of pornographic clip?'

'It was a real place, Mum. We used HAIR tech. I could smell the tunnel. I could see the lady crying. I hated it.'

I'm aware of HAIR tech and what it's used for. Even if we could afford it, I wouldn't allow it in our home. 'When exactly did this happen?'

Jackson shrugs. 'The first time I went to Digby's house, after soccer training.'

I try to restrain my alarm.

'So you went into... Alt-World at Digby's that Sunday afternoon after soccer training and the two of you watched a lady being hurt by a man?'

Jackson nods. 'Digby watches a lot of stuff like that in Alt-World. His parents let him.' He looks worried. 'I didn't like it though, Mum, I really didn't.'

'I believe you,' I say. 'I'm just trying to piece it all together. Tell me, you went into Alt-World with Digby on that Sunday afternoon... and the next day in the school toilets, Digby hurt Sienna?'

Jackson nods miserably.

'This is something Detective Annabelle needs to know about, Jackson. We have to tell Jeff Goldstein, too.'

I reach for my phone and start composing a message to the defence lawyer.

'But I don't like Jeff,' protests Jackson.

'Neither do I really, but he's very good at his job. You're going to have to tell them both about Alt-World in your interview tomorrow.'

'Will Annabelle send me to prison?' Jackson's face is fearful.

'No, hon. We just need to tell her all the facts. I know you were trying to do the right thing by Digby in your first interview but... you can't keep secrets from the police. Or from me. Promise?'

'Promise.' Jackson looks contrite. 'No secrets, Mum.'

'Good.' I fish around in my handbag for a chocolate bar. 'Snickers wanted you to have this, to help keep your energy up. He's a bad influence. Those guinea pigs of yours aren't much better. They sent these.'

I toss a packet of lollies into his lap, breaching all my usual rules about sugar.

Jackson grins. As he tears at the chocolate wrapper, Milla appears at the door.

'Knock, knock,' she calls, then enters the room carrying a huge bouquet of flowers. Riley follows her inside.

'Hi, you two.' I glance at my watch. The passing of time seems interminable in hospital, yet now I see it's past three o'clock.

'Hey Mrs C,' says Riley. 'Hi, buddy!'

He high-fives Jackson, then sits down on the edge of the bed.

'How are you feeling?' asks Milla, bending down to hug her brother. 'I thought these might brighten things up a bit.'

Milla passes him the flowers.

'And I brought you these.' Riley passes Jackson a large paper bag stuffed with surfing magazines. 'Study up, bro, because spring's coming!'

'Oh, and we've got some good news to share.' Milla glances at me.

'Does Riley want to marry you?' asks Jackson.

Riley guffaws.

'Er, no.' Milla looks embarrassed.

Riley's face is alight. 'Go on, tell them.'

'You know that poetry competition I entered, Mum? Well, my poem was... Highly Commended. One of the top five entries.'

'Congratulations!' I exclaim. 'Judged by real poets, too.'

Milla beams, clearly chuffed.

'Which poem?' asks Jackson.

'It's called "Rainbows" and it's dedicated to you, Jackson.' Milla reaches into her schoolbag and passes Jackson the poem. 'It's about how great the world is when people can be different, and that's okay.'

Milla bends down and hugs her brother again.

My eyes fill with tears.

Riley nudges Milla. 'You're squeezing him to death.'

Milla laughs and sits back.

Two women carrying clipboards appear in the doorway. I recognise them as the doctors who conducted Jackson's assessments yesterday.

'Sorry to disturb. We have Jackson's results,' announces Dr Cahill.

'Time to head,' says Riley, standing up. He points at the magazines. 'I'm taking Milla surfing right now, bud. But I'm coming for *you* next.'

Jackson giggles.

'Thanks for visiting,' I say. 'Come again tomorrow, if you'd like?'

'We will,' says Milla, moving to the door.

As I wave them off, Dr Cahill pulls up a chair next to Jackson's bed.

'Now for the results. It's quite a complicated picture.'

I ready myself for the usual observations about *atypical* this and *nonconforming* that.

The doctor scans her notes. 'We've not seen it before, but... the results point to hyperthymesia. Also known as Highly Superior Autobiographical Memory. It's extremely rare, but those who have it can remember an abnormally large number of their life experiences in vivid detail.'

I look from one doctor to the other. 'Are you... sure?' Despite a myriad of tests over the past decade, this condition has never been raised.

'Well, it's a qualified diagnosis, which means hyperthymesia can't explain all of Jackson's issues. But it certainly explains some of them. Does Jackson spend a lot of time thinking about his past?'

'All the time,' Jackson pipes up. 'I talk to Granny on my

shoe-phone about my memory download. It's got stuff in it from when I was really small.'

Dr Lloyd nods. 'Our brains are constantly making little recordings of what's happening to us. People with hyperthymesia seem to be able to access a lot more of those recordings from the past.'

'It's not hard for me to remember,' says Jackson. 'I'm a memory magnet.'

'I thought he was just... making it up,' I say, feeling terribly guilty now.

'Well, that's understandable. It's an extremely rare condition.' Dr Lloyd smiles at Jackson. 'It's almost like a superpower.'

'Why is it considered a 'condition', then?'

'Sometimes, but not always, there are detrimental cognitive impacts,' explains Dr Cahill. 'The constant stream of memories can cause disruption to everyday life. Hyperthymestic children aren't being deliberately naughty, they're often just... distracted by cascading memories.'

The words resonate. 'That sounds a lot like Jackson.'

'Ten years ago, hyperthymesia wasn't even recognised by the medical profession,' she continues. 'It would have been considered 'personality'. It usually goes undiagnosed for a long time. Parents know something unusual is going on, but it's hard to pinpoint. Kids often get misdiagnosed or misunderstood or both.'

She passes me a sheaf of paper.

'Here's some recent research. It's still not clear if hyperthymesia is an all-or-none condition, or whether some people have it in degrees. For Jackson, it seems to be a matter of degrees, hence the qualified diagnosis.'

I scan the title of the article: 'Polymaths or put-ons? Brain-scan and psychometric testing results of hyperthymestic patients with fifteen age-matched controls.'

'How did I catch it?' asks Jackson.

Dr Cahill smiles. 'We don't really know how it develops, Jackson, because so few people have it in the world. Your brain scan was normal, but for other people with hyperthymesia, there are abnormalities in their prefrontal cortex and hippocampus.'

'Their hippopotamus?' Jackson cackles.

Dr Lloyd laughs too. 'It's a part of the brain.'

Dr Cahill turns back to me. 'There's some research linking it to obsessive-compulsive disorder. People with hyperthymesia tend to fantasise and get deeply absorbed in things.'

I consider Jackson's fixations and fantastical imaginings, branded by Dr Kelleher as *intruder-thoughts.*

'Is there... any treatment?'

Dr Cahill shakes her head. 'Just a good dose of compassion. Hyperthymesia is not only about remembering things that other people can't, it's about not being able to forget. That can be quite a burden for a child. For anyone, really. It can be a very lonely place.'

'Some of the kids at school call me an outsider,' says Jackson.

'Is that so?' Dr Cahill turns to him. 'Well, the truth is, you're what scientists call an outlier. You're experiencing something that most humans never do, Jackson. Statistically, you're very special.'

'An outlier?' Jackson squints. 'I want to tell Dead Granny about that, but I can't find my shoe-phone. A nurse took it away.'

'They do that when you least expect it.' Dr Lloyd smiles.

'Is there anything we can be... doing to help Jackson?' I ask.

'There aren't any specific treatments for hyperthymesia, but we'll advise your family therapist of the findings,' she says. 'Supporting Jackson to understand and accept why his mind works the way it does should be the focus.'

I make a mental note to call Dr Kelleher as soon as possible.

'And it's worth reminding yourself that there are elements to Jackson's experience that elude diagnosis altogether,' adds Dr Cahill. 'Hyperthymesia is only part of Jackson's story. Labels aren't everything, as you probably know already.'

'They certainly aren't,' I say, recalling the interview at Clontarf Grammar.

Dr Cahill turns back to Jackson. 'Is it okay if we come back tomorrow, before you're discharged? And maybe stay in touch to check on how you're doing?'

Jackson nods.

'Great, well, we'll see you tomorrow then. Thank you both.'

The two doctors take their leave.

Jackson and I sit for a few moments, staring at each other.

'Are you surprised, Mum?'

'A bit,' I say. 'But those doctors have... answered lots of my questions, too.'

Jackson nods. 'Like why I can't get my words out, because my brain's too full of memories. Maybe that's why I feel better hanging upside down?'

'Maybe.' I smile at him.

We don't have to keep trying to *make sense* of any of it any more, I realise. Jackson's issues are unique, complex and treatable by empathy alone.

Reaching for the panel behind Jackson's bed, I press the call button.

'What are you doing, Mum? That calls a nurse.'

'We need to track down your shoe-phone,' I say. 'So you can call Granny and tell her you're an outlier, not an outsider.'

Jackson grins.

'And when you've finished talking to Granny, I'll borrow it to call Dad.'

'You're a weirdo, Mum.' Jackson laughs. 'You've got your own phone for that.'

24

There's a tentative tap at the door. I glance over at Jackson, who's still seated cross-legged on the hospital bed, talking to his dead grandmother. He's been yabbering on for the best part of an hour but, now that I better understand what his 'shoe-phone' is about, all my feelings of irritation have vanished.

The visitor taps again.

'Come in,' I call.

Detective Annabelle Johnson enters the room, her demeanour radically altered. 'Hello, Mrs Curtis.'

I nod at her coolly.

'Hi Jackson.' She pulls up a chair near Jackson's bed.

Jackson slams down his shoe-phone, obviously thrilled to see her. 'How's Jack Russell?'

'Jack Russ...? Oh, yes.' She glances at me uneasily. 'Fine, thanks. How is...?' She can't recall the name of our dog.

'Snickers.' Jackson prompts. 'He's made friends with Batman and Robin, my guinea pigs.'

'That's nice.' Annabelle looks uncomfortable.

'Jeff and Andy will be here soon,' I tell her. 'You might be interested in reading this, while you wait.'

I pass her a copy of the clinical summary.

'Jeff says you'll need to read up on hyperthymesia as you proceed with your investigation.'

Annabelle handles the document as if it's a grenade.

'Do you mind if...' I gesture at my phone. 'I've got a few things to organise on the home front.'

Despite the upheaval of the past five weeks, my responsibility for most of the domestics – the hamster-wheel of meal planning, after-school activities and household chores – remains remarkably intact.

'Go ahead,' says Annabelle, seemingly reluctant to make small talk with me. 'I'll set up for the interview.'

Several minutes later, the door flies open and Jeff strides into the room, exuding daunting levels of arrogance. Andy trots after him, struggling to keep up.

'Julia. Jackson.' The lawyer turns and eyes the detective. 'Jeff Goldstein, defence counsel.'

'Detective Annabelle Johnson.' She stands to shake his hand. 'We've met before.'

'Have we?' He touches her fingers limply. 'I don't recall.'

Jeff shepherds Andy into the seat next to me.

'Today's interview will be recorded and is admissible as evidence, yes?'

The detective nods, gesturing at a Camcorder she's positioned on Jackson's tray table.

'Good. I'll be monitoring the questions posed,' says Jeff. 'The same rules apply as the first interview. This one won't be as lengthy because – not to put too fine a point on it – the first interview was ballsed up, good and proper.'

Colour rises in Annabelle's cheeks.

'The DNA results returned last week negated the initial conclusions drawn during the first interview with Jackson,' Jeff continues. 'I've been studying that transcript with renewed interest, Detective.'

Annabelle bows her head, ostensibly referring to her notes. 'Who is going to be Jackson's designated support person for this interview?'

'Can I have both Mum and Dad, please?' asks Jackson.

'Certainly.' The detective reaches for the Camcorder, orients the lens at Jackson, then presses record.

'Recording now,' she intones. 'Jackson, we've spoken before about what happened in the school toilets at Queenscliff Public on Monday 9th May. Is there anything else you've remembered since we first talked, that you'd like to tell me about now?'

'Yes,' says Jackson. 'But... I never forgot it, Annabelle. You just didn't ask me about it the first time.'

Jeff snorts.

'Okay,' says Annabelle, ignoring him. 'Please, go ahead, Jackson.'

'Well... there were some secrets.' Jackson looks a little shaky. 'Digby made me promise not to tell anyone about what happened in the toilets and what happened in Alt-World.'

'You also made a promise not to lie when we spoke at the first interview, remember?' asks Annabelle.

Jackson nods, looking embarrassed.

'And in that interview, Jackson, you told me that Digby was following *you* on that Monday in the toilets.'

'No, I didn't.' Jackson looks hurt. 'You said that first, Annabelle. I just agreed with you.'

'This isn't a cross-examination of my client,' Jeff interjects. 'Where are you taking this, Detective?'

Annabelle looks entirely thrown for a moment.

'Right. Now that you don't have to keep any secrets for Digby, can I please ask you... what you saw with your own eyes, Jackson, in the toilets on that Monday morning?'

Jackson's lips tremble.

'I didn't see anything... because Digby was behind the toilet door with Sienna. He told me he was playing a trick on her. He made me guard the door. I didn't realise that maybe he was... hurting Sienna, the way the pig-man hurt the lady in Alt-World.'

Annabelle scribbles down some notes. 'And can you tell us a little more about this... Alt-World? Was it a game you played with Digby?'

Jackson nods. 'It's a place where lots of people play together. It's HAIR tech, so it's realer than real.'

'When and where did you play Alt-World with Digby, for the first time?'

'Straight after soccer training. Coach took us home to Digby's house because Digby's parents were working. Coach does that every week. Digby's dad was there, but he had to go do some work in his office.'

'When exactly was this, Jackson? Before the incident in the school toilets?'

'Yes,' he says. 'The day before.'

'Go on,' says Annabelle.

Jackson's cheeks turn a shade of scarlet.

'We were in the kitchen and Digby showed me his laptop. He gave me these big goggles to wear. When we put them on, we sort of... went somewhere else. It was underground, so it was pretty dark. There was this lady with no trousers being chased around by a man in a pig mask. He pushed her hard against a wall and...'

Jackson eyes fill with tears. 'Maybe in the toilets the next day, Digby.... I don't know, I didn't see it.'

Annabelle remains unflummoxed. 'Did Digby's dad or mum set up Alt-World for you, or were they close by when you played?'

Suddenly I recall Steve's concerns about Miranda and possible alcohol-related harm occurring in Digby's home.

Jackson shakes his head. 'Digby set it up by himself. He's allowed to do anything online. My mum only lets me play chess.'

He sneaks a look in my direction.

Annabelle pauses. 'Did anything else happen when you played Alt-World together?'

Jackson looks mortified.

'You can think about that for as long as you need to, Jackson,' adds the detective. 'There's no hurry.'

'I don't want to...' he begins, then glances at me. 'Okay, no more secrets.'

I nod my encouragement, even as my stomach clenches with fear.

Jackson stares at the tray table. 'Well, not much else happened in Alt-World, except my... thing went a bit stiff in my soccer shorts. It does that sometimes.'

He looks pained.

'I got embarrassed, but Digby just laughed and pointed at the dragon picture on my shorts. He said, "Your dragon's getting bigger and stronger, you'll have to tell Coach about that. He likes big strong dragons".'

The detective nods. 'Those were Digby's exact words?'

'Yes,' says Jackson. 'If you don't believe me, just ask Dr Cahill. I never forget anything. Except for boring stuff, like the right word for diurnal motion.'

The detective glances at the diagnostic summary.

'And your soccer coach, Jackson. What's his name?'

'Steve.'

'Have you spent much time with him?'

'He's pretty good friends with Mum now.'

Andy shoots me a quizzical glance.

'Coach comes and plays soccer with me most lunchtimes. He helps Mum, too. Once Mum had to go out to the shops and...'

I blanch at the expression on Jackson's face.

'What happened when Mum went out?'

'Coach just sat next to me on the couch and watched television.'

Jackson's eyes are blinking again.

'Is there anything about your soccer coach that worries you, Jackson?'

'No.' Jackson's tone is unequivocal. 'But... he did ask me to keep a secret once. Does that matter?'

'What secret?'

'It was the day after the interview at Chatswood. Coach came over and asked me lots of questions. He wanted to know what the police had asked me about Digby and Alt-World and Coach's car and what happened at Digby's place.'

Jackson must be confused.

'Can you remember your Coach's exact words, when he came over on that Tuesday after we met at Chatswood, Jackson?' Annabelle asks, still taking notes.

Jackson thinks about this for a while.

'Well, he said it would be better for everyone if we kept what we did in Alt-World a secret, because he didn't want Digby and me to get into even more trouble.'

I'm struggling to imagine Steve saying any such thing.

'Did your coach say anything else?'

'No.' Jackson shrugs. 'Except that most adults wouldn't understand his friendship with Digby.'

Annabelle stops note-taking and looks up.

An icy numbness floods my chest.

'And... are you sure that Coach never touched you anywhere on your body, Jackson?' She presses. 'Not even for just a moment?'

Jackson frowns.

'He touched me once, on the knee, when Mum went to the shops and we were watching television at home. I don't even think he meant to; it wasn't for very long.' Jackson's eyes are brimming. 'Am I in more trouble now?'

The air leaks out of my lungs.

'You're not in trouble,' Annabelle reassures Jackson. 'Thank you for telling the truth.'

'Does that mean that Steve...?' Andy's eyes pivot around the room. 'I'll kill him. I'll bloody wait outside his house and...'

Jeff grimaces. 'Andy, let's discuss the implications in a moment.'

Annabelle turns off the recorder and closes her notebook. 'That's enough for today, Jackson. We'll need to speak to you again, once you're out of hospital.'

Jackson nods agreeably.

'Well done, Detective Johnson.' A sneer spreads across Jeff's face. 'For uncovering what you should have at the first interview.'

The detective doesn't acknowledge him, she just gathers up her things.

'Thank you, Jackson,' she says, walking to the door. 'Mr and Mrs Curtis, we'll be making more enquiries. I'll keep you informed.'

'Any further questions for the Curtis family are best

directed through me,' says Jeff. 'I'm already picturing the media exposé on police incompetence. Not to mention the possibility of formal redress for my clients.'

The detective closes the door behind her.

'See you, Annabelle!' Jackson calls hopefully. Almost immediately, he picks up his shoe. 'There's a lot to tell Dead Granny.'

He swings his feet off the bed and begins dialling the Otherworld.

Dazed, I await the defence lawyer's verdict.

Andy sits glowering at me.

'Well, there's definitely no case against Jackson,' says Jeff triumphantly. 'More concerning is that soccer coach. Sounds like he's been drip-feeding boys online porn and getting active in games himself.'

'How can you be sure?' I ask, horrified.

'It goes on at an alarming rate,' says Jeff. 'Digby may have come to considerable harm. He was grooming Jackson, too, by the sound of it. Seems he used the school incident to get closer to you, Mrs Curtis.'

I'm so ashamed of myself, I can't even look at him.

'Jesus Christ,' says Andy. 'I'll go over there and rip his...'

'Andy,' says Jeff sternly. 'Let justice take its course. The police now have a new person of interest. It would have happened earlier, if that detective had asked the right questions in the first interview.'

Jeff rolls his eyes.

'She's a bungler, that one. Desperate to prove herself with a career-launching investigation, but this mess she's created will be career-limiting. Given Jackson's neuropsychological vulnerability, it's professional misconduct.'

The barrister stacks his files into a large black box. 'We may have grounds to pursue formal redress from the police. And that's a sterling way to finish off my Tuesday, frankly.'

Jeff smiles, but I don't feel nearly as jubilant. A man I considered a friend – a man I'd developed *feelings* for – betrayed my trust.

How will I face Andy?

'I'll call you tomorrow,' says Jeff, letting himself out.

Jackson is standing in the corner, whispering into his shoe.

'Now I've got some questions for *you*,' says Andy. 'Let's do that outside.'

He guides me by the elbow into the empty hospital corridor, then wheels around.

'How much time did that bastard spend alone with Jackson?'

I tell him everything I can remember.

Bantering with Steve on the soccer sidelines, calling for his help on the day Jackson went missing from Digby's, sharing wine with him on the verandah.

Andy looks hurt.

'After the first police interview, Steve rang me. I know I divulged way too much, but it all felt very... natural at the time.'

'I bet it did,' Andy growls.

I can see it all so plainly, with the benefit of hindsight. How that exchange led to more wine, cups of tea, daily messages and visits under the guise of soccer drills and friendship. Small, incremental moments of intimacy that ultimately led me to leaving Jackson in Steve's company, alone.

'When did that happen?' Andy shakes his head in disgust.

'The day before you came home from New York. I ducked out to the supermarket for fifteen minutes.'

'And that makes it better?'

I shake my head.

'I'm sorry, Andy, I've been so stupid. I'll never be able to trust my judgement again.'

'Too bloody right you won't,' he snarls. 'You let it happen so easily.'

Bitterness rises in my chest and bubbles out of my mouth.

'While you were watching cabaret in New York, as I recall.'

'Look, I've apologised for being absent, Julia,' Andy spits. 'I did that before the eisteddfod, remember? At least I owned my flaws.'

'Sure, you said some nice words in the kitchen that day. Then you just kept going, business as usual. Planning your next overseas trip while I... I stopped work with the investigation. Someone had to home-school Jackson and support our girls. I was picking up the pieces and it was *lonely*, Andy. Steve was *nice* to me.'

Andy snorts. 'I've been lonely too, Julia. Why did you turn to him, when you could have turned to me?'

He looks at me reproachfully.

'*How* could I have turned to you, when things weren't right between us? They're still not right, Andy. We both know it.'

Tears well up in my eyes.

If only we'd stayed in Erskineville, in the home we'd shared and loved for so many years. If only we'd resisted the fantasy of a bigger, brighter, shinier us in Queenscliff. If only Jackson had never met Digby, *none* of this would have happened.

If only.

I walk to the door of Jackson's hospital room.

Beyond the window, Jackson is laughing into his shoe-phone.

After a while, Andy joins me. We stand together in silence, watching our son.

We *never* could have anticipated the challenges and joys of parenting a child as glorious and unusual as Jackson.

Andy turns to me. 'I'm sorry, Jules. I've been too harsh. We're in the eye of the storm and this kind of bickering won't help.' He exhales. 'Maybe all we can do is... survive this, for now.'

We look into each other's wan faces.

'Let's just get through this, until Jackson's out of hospital,' he continues. 'When we come out the other side, we can talk more about... us.'

It's a logical suggestion, reminiscent of my parents' lifelong refrain: 'Just keep turning up, Julia. It's the migrant mentality.'

Persisting through uncertainty, finding beauty amid the brokenness.

'Okay,' I agree. 'Let's call a truce and stay focused on Jackson.'

I'm clinging to the hope that, somehow, we'll emerge unscathed.

25

It's the first day of spring so the top-knot pigeons are every-where, back from their winter holidays. Nanna Pam is picking up Ruby after school, so it's just Mum and me in the Red Rocket driving back from Dr Louisa's office. I wish I could talk to Dad, but he's stuck in New York. He didn't want to go, but an important client got so cranky with him, he had no choice.

If Dad was here, I'd tell him how much Dr Louisa already knows about *hyperthymesia*. She's been doing heaps of research and has some good ideas about taming my brain beans. Next week, we're going to start practising them.

'Some of the research suggests hyperthymesia isn't an illness,' she told Mum. 'It's more of a processing issue that, one day, might be considered a strength.'

Mum was really happy to hear that. So was I, especially after all the other news we got at the CAS office this morning.

Mum and I had to go to a special meeting with the police in Chatswood at 9.00, but Annabelle wasn't there any more. We met a new detective called Danny instead. He had a big bristly beard and bright blue eyes, and he was super friendly. He said it was his job to tell us what happened in the school toilets on the day after Mother's Day. We'd been waiting 114 days to find out.

It made me really sad to hear how Digby pushed Sienna against the wall and pulled down her pants and made her so frightened that her family has to move away from Queenscliff. At first I was worried she'd never be okay, but Detective Danny explained that because I banged on the cubicle door, Digby didn't hurt Sienna in the worst way possible. She's got a 'much stronger chance of recovery', he said.

Detective Danny also told us that even though Digby did a terrible thing, the judge at the Children's Court decided not to send him to kid prison, because Digby got hurt too. His step-mum is drink-sick and his dad let him see a whole lot of bad stuff online, so now Digby needs some help from special doctors to *unsee* it. For now, the judge has taken away Will's computers and made Miranda go to a place for drink-sick people. Digby's been sent to a school for kids who break the law, he can't live with his parents until they all pass a test that shows the police they're ready to be a family again.

When Detective Danny told us that Digby got hurt by Coach Steve too, that made me even sadder. The police are still investigating, but Coach Steve definitely can't be a soccer coach any more because he bullied kids in really nasty ways. Detective Danny explained that Coach invited Digby and other kids into Alt-World, then he wore masks and frightened them and sometimes he hurt them, too.

So it was Coach who wore the pig mask inside Alt-World on the day that Digby and I played it. That gave me a big shock, then it made me sad. Why would Coach chase a lady like that and make her cry? Detective Danny said it was all part of something called 'grooming', which is different to what happens to

Snickers at Pooch Parlour, and Coach will probably have to stay in prison for a very long time.

We talked a bit about prison and Detective Danny answered all my questions. Miss Marion doesn't have to go there, he said, but she's still in a lot of trouble with the school. I cried a bit when I heard that. Crazy Daisy was so upset with Miss Marion for teaching me dance without permission, she's forced Miss Marion to take 'extended leave without pay' until next year. That's a long holiday with no money, so I hope she gets another job really soon.

When I asked Detective Danny about Annabelle, he told me she's in trouble, too. She made some mistakes interviewing me the first time, so the Big Police Boss made her stop work while he 'conducts a review of interview protocols for neurodiverse children'. I'm sorry that Annabelle's in trouble, because she was only trying to be nice to me.

'You all right, Jackson?' asks Mum. Her voice makes me jump. I was so busy watching my memory download from this morning's meeting with Detective Danny, I stopped seeing everything else around me. Dr Louisa says that's 'totally normal' for people with hyperthymesia.

'I'm okay,' I reply.

Mum steers the van into our street. 'That was a big session today at the CAS office with Danny, then with Dr Louisa. Are you as tired as I am, Jackson?'

'It's totally normal,' I say.

Mum smiles. 'Fair enough.'

As we park the Red Rocket in the driveway, I see that Milla and Riley are already home from school and they're standing in the back yard, looking down at Batman and Robin in their cage. They're still in their school uniforms, but Riley's got his green skater jacket on, just like St Jhudiel.

Riley waves and points at a whole bunch of surfboards lined up along the side fence. There are heaps of wetsuits hanging there too, so I'm guessing Tom and Tracey Lovell next door won't like that.

'What's this?' asks Mum, climbing out of the Red Rocket.

We walk down the driveway and join them near the guinea pig cage. I squat down to pet Batman and Robin, they're always so excited to see me.

'Mrs C,' says Riley, putting an arm around Milla. 'It's the first day of spring, so...'

Is he going to ask Milla to marry him now?

'We're going surfing! The green room is waiting.'

Mum laughs as Riley passes her a wetsuit.

Suddenly an engine roars behind us and we all turn to see Miss Marion parking her vintage car behind the Red Rocket. It's painted in rainbow colours, just like her hair.

'You and your car match our library, Miss Marion!' I yell.

She grins as she walks towards us. 'So I do, darling. There's definitely a rainbow theme happening.'

'Not today,' says Riley. 'Today, we're doing green.'

I wrap my arms around Miss Marion's waist and look up at her. 'We're going surfing in the green room.'

'Oooh, fabulous.' Miss Marion smiles. 'Any room for one more?'

'The more the merrier,' says Riley. He starts pulling wetsuits off the fence and holding them up under our chins.

'Where on earth did you get so many wetsuits, Riley?' asks Mum.

'We've got heaps at home.'

'Riley's Dad was a pro-surfer when he was young,' I tell Mum. 'I've told you that already, remember?'

Mum looks at me blankly.

Riley seems a bit embarrassed. 'Yeah, I'm from a... surfing family.'

'Surfing royalty, more like it,' adds Milla.

'Well, that's exactly what we need to teach a newbie like me,' says Miss Marion, unzipping her wetsuit. 'But I'm warning you, Riley. I'm a dancer, not a surfer.'

'They're almost the same thing.' Riley grins.

He holds a wetsuit against me, then tosses it back onto the fence.

Suddenly Mr Lovell's head pops up on the other side.

'I hope these won't be a permanent fixture.' He glares at the wetsuits.

'Hi, there.' Riley reaches over the fence to shake Mr Lovell's hand. 'I'm Riley. We're just warming the wetsuits in the sun. Want to join us for a surf?'

Mr Lovell's mouth opens, but nothing comes out.

He spots Mum in the back yard. 'Julia, these palm berries are appalling. It's been four months since we spoke about them. I'll have to ring the Council.'

Riley scales the fence to check out what Mr Lovell means.

'Those yellow berries on the grass?' asks Riley. 'No problem. We'll get rid of them. Won't take long.'

'When, exactly?' Mr Lovell looks like he's choking on a chicken bone. 'I don't just have time on my hands, young man...'

'Yes, you do,' I remind him. 'Mum said you did. Remember, Mum?'

Mr Lovell stares at me, then at Mum, but it looks like she can't remember it either.

'You've got loads of time on your hands. Those brown patches on the back of your hands means you've been carrying time around your whole life.'

Mr Lovell's mouth half-opens, then he stares at the back of his hands.

'And what that means,' adds Miss Marion, slinging an arm around my shoulder, 'is that we're going to get these wetsuits off your fence, then we're going to come over a bit later for a palm berry clean-up party. Is that okay by you?'

Mr Lovell squints, then disappears behind the fence.

A moment later, we hear his back door slam.

Miss Marion and Mum collapse into laughter, but I'm wondering if maybe he's just gone to get his swimmers?

Riley keeps handing out the wet suits, then we all go inside to get changed.

In my room, it's hard for me to get my legs through the rubbery tightness. Is it *this* difficult for Spiderman to change into his superhero suit? When it doesn't get any easier, I go downstairs and ask Riley for help. He puts my feet in plastic bags to help push my legs in, then he's reefing up the wetsuit around my bum. We both start laughing because the rubber's making funny squeaking sounds.

When I'm all sealed up like a sausage, we move out into the back yard where everyone's waiting for us. Miss Marion looks amazing with her rainbow hair poking out the top of her wetsuit, and Mum looks about a million years younger. I can tell Riley thinks Milla looks nice in her wetsuit too, even though he doesn't say it.

'Ready?' asks Riley, passing out the boards.

'Race you down, big fella.' He grins at me.

Suddenly I'm sprinting down the driveway after Riley, holding my board under my arm like a pro-surfer. My arms and legs are pumping like pistons, carrying me under the carport and out the gate and down the street, faster than ever before. I can't hear anything except the sound of my breath walloping out of me. It's like I've got fireworks in my heart, I've wanted to do this forever.

When we reach the beach, the sun is warm on my face and the sand is glittering like soft yellow diamonds. It looks like the beach Dr Louisa always asks me to imagine 'to stop thinking about blinking', only it's for real this time.

'Let's go!' shouts Riley, racing me into the sea.

The water is so green and clean and cold, it sucks the breath right out of me. At Kaminski's a long time ago, I remember Dead Granny telling me 'saltwater is nature's cleaner'. I lie on my back just looking up at the sky, letting the salt water clean me up.

'Let's paddle out,' says Riley.

I try to copy him, but I can't touch the bottom any more and I'm swimming next to the board. Riley shows me how to climb onto it and sit up, bobbing on top of the water. I'm super keen to stand, but it's not time yet.

'We're just tea-bagging at the moment, mate.' Riley smiles at me. 'It's good for the soul.'

I smile back at Riley, because everything feels so right. The waves are right too; they're not too big, not too small, just nice and even.

I turn my board around and watch Mum and Miss Marion and Milla running into the shallow water. I wish Ruby and Nanna Pam were here too, but maybe they're too young and too old for surfing? Dad would be just about right, though. I'm missing him like crazy.

Milla is squealing at the cold and Mum and Miss Marion are laughing and slapping each other on the bum which is pretty funny. I haven't seen Mum have this much fun in a long time.

'Watch this,' says Riley, pushing his board down and

leaping to his feet, before sitting back down again. He shows me a few more times, explaining how to paddle onto a wave and stand up.

'Ready to try, buddy?' asks Riley. 'Here comes a good wave.'

My brain's gone super quiet. I turn my board onto the wave and feel the water pulling me back. I start paddling like crazy and jump up onto my feet. My board's wobbling a bit as the wave draws up behind me. I crouch down in the curve and point at the shore with one finger, how Riley taught me.

Suddenly there's water all around me, and nothing else. I'm definitely in the green room now and it's dead-set beautiful.

As the wave breaks and I'm still balancing in the white-water, I hear everyone clapping. They're all watching me with these amazed looks on their faces.

'Awesome, Jackson!' I hear Riley call, just as I fall off the board.

When I pop up for air a wave knocks me under again, pressing me down to the sandy bottom. I open my eyes under-water, blinking a bit. It's as peaceful as a mermaid's cave down here.

I feel Riley's arms around my waist, pulling me back to the surface.

'Wow!' He says, grinning at me. 'Not bad for a first-timer.'

'Are you all right Jackson?' Mum looks a bit worried as she wades over.

I flick my wet fringe out of my eyes. 'Saltwater's the best, Mum.'

She smiles. 'Granny used to say that.'

We stay there for the rest of the afternoon, until I can't move my arms because of all the paddling. I love surfing so much, I never want to leave.

'The green room's got you in its grip,' says Riley, as we dry off on the beach.

A big yawn takes over my face and I'm shivering like a maniac.

'Your lips are turning blue, Jackson.' Mum looks concerned. She turns to Riley. 'The doctors told me not to let him over-exert himself. We shouldn't have stayed in the water so long...'

'Okay, come here, buddy.' Riley wraps me in his big green skater jacket and scoops me up in his arms. 'Let's get you into a hot bath.'

I giggle and pretend to struggle, but it feels good to be carried like a baby again.

Riley knows exactly what to do. He carries me all the way along Seaview Street, up the veranda stairs and inside. Then he takes me into the bathroom and runs me a bath, tipping in heaps of Ruby's bubble-bath. I'm glad she's not here to notice.

It's hard getting out of my wetsuit, and Riley helps me again. I'm a bit embarrassed when I climb into the bath, because Riley's fifteen and I don't want him looking at my private parts. But he doesn't, he just sits on the tiles and talks about how amazing our summer of surfing's going to be, and how every-thing's going to be 'totally all good'.

After a while, my teeth stop chattering and my eyelids stop flickering. My memory download fires up again, but it's like the salt water's turned the bad memories rusty and polished up the good ones so they shine like new.

'Thanks for taking me surfing today, Riley,' I say. 'I loved it.'

Riley grins and gives me a thumbs-up sign, then I notice that *his* teeth are chattering too.

Mum taps on the door and pokes her head around it.

Riley stands to go. 'I'll leave you both to it. See ya, matey.'

'That was an amazing afternoon, Riley.' Mum catches his hand as he passes. 'Thank you so much for taking us.'

'My pleasure, Mrs C. I'd better go rake up those palm berries for your next door neighbour.'

'Tom Lovell? Oh, don't worry about him. He's what you might call an Old Fart.'

Riley guffaws. 'Cool, Mrs C. I'll leave him alone for now.' He closes the door of the bathroom behind him.

Mum sits down on the tiles next to me.

She's holding the new trainers that Nanna Pam bought me for my interview at Clontarf Grammar a few months ago.

'Do you think I can use your shoe-phone, Jackson, to call Granny?'

I sit up in the bath and take one of the shoes from her.

'Maybe,' I say, checking the sole and the secret connection button that only cats and dogs know about. 'Can we let Snickers into the bathroom, Mum?'

She nods, then she whistles for Snickers really loudly, a bit like a farmer.

Snickers' toenails click-clack across the floorboards as he scampers down the hallway. He pokes his nose around the door and his chunky salami body follows. He's been breaking into the pantry to eat breakfast cereal lately.

'Hi Snickers,' I say, dangling one hand over the edge of the bath and rubbing his ears the way he likes it. With the other I press the shoe-phone against my ear and when I hear the connection click, I hold it out to Mum.

'It's ringing now. Granny must be home.'

Mum takes the trainer and puts it to her ear. After a moment she says, 'Hello?'

She just sits there listening to Dead Granny talking.

In a little while, Mum starts speaking. 'Well, the people in

Queenscliff aren't being... very kind. I'm out of ideas for schools. Do you have any?'

Mum leans back against the wall with her eyes closed, listening again.

Dead Granny must be saying a lot, because it's a long time before Mum opens them again.

When she does, she looks even calmer.

She smiles and puts the shoe-phone down on the bathroom floor.

'Jackson, I have our Plan B,' she announces.

'Granny's the best at fixing messes,' I reply.

26

It's *not* 5.17. It can't be.

Gentle sunlight filters through linen drapes floating against floor-to-ceiling windows. Feather-down cocoons me and warm air wafts across my face from an invisible, silent source. I feel certain I've woken up in an interior design magazine.

Staying overnight in Pamela's house is pure indulgence. What's more, she's hosting the four of us for the next few nights, until Andy returns from New York. It was an offer I initially resisted, for fear of imposing – until Pamela insisted.

'Please let me help, Julia,' she urged. 'I want to make things easier for you.'

I tried to be as gracious in accepting as she was in the offering.

Stretching out across a king-size expanse, I luxuriate in the firm mattress, wool underlay and Egyptian cotton sheets. Glancing at my wristwatch, I can scarcely believe my eyes: 7.43.

No wonder I feel so rested.

We're due in Ingleside at 9 o'clock, so I propel myself out of bed. Donning my robe, I tiptoe down the hallway and pause outside Jackson's room, listening for his habitual morning sounds.

Nothing.

Gently, I open the door and pad across the plush carpet. Standing at Jackson's bedside, I can't bear to wake him. Instead, I slide into the bed next to him and curl myself around his warmth.

Leaning up onto one elbow, I watch my son sleeping. His face is serene, although his twitching eyelids suggest he's dreaming. More than three months after the Winter Eisteddfod, the scar around his neck is still visible. Even if it fades completely, I doubt I'll *ever* be able to erase the mental image of Jackson plunging to the stage entangled in an aerial silk.

'Mum?' Jackson's eyelids flutter open. 'I smelled you before I saw you.'

I feign disgust. 'In that case, I need a shower.'

Jackson smiles. 'No, your robe smells nice, like flowers from Riley.'

'Were you having a dream just now?' I ask. Every day, I try to learn more about Jackson's superior autobiographical memory.

He nods. 'Someone was touching my face. It was...' Jackson looks self-conscious. 'I was in the green room.'

'Surfing?'

'Not *that* green room. I'd just done aerial silks. It was after the show and I was sharing rice crackers with... well, it was a nice dream.'

I'm relieved Jackson doesn't appear as traumatised as I am by aerial silks.

'We're going to take a look at another school this morning, Jackson.'

Jackson sits up in bed. 'Don't you have to sing to the Special Ps at Care Cottage?'

'Sunday is my first day back at work.' I nudge him with my elbow. 'I thought you had Superior Memory Power.'

Jackson nudges me back. 'That's *your* work, Mum, your life. I only remember everything that happens to *me*.'

'Oh.' I laugh. 'I'll try to remember that.'

'Which school are we looking at?' he asks.

'Ingleside Community School. It just popped into my head when... I was talking to Granny on your shoe-phone.'

'After our surf?' Jackson smiles. 'Did Dead Granny tell you about it?'

'I think she might have.'

'But it's Friday, Mum.' He looks concerned. 'Francesca won't like me missing any more home-school.'

'Francesca? Oh... right.'

We haven't had a visit from the Family and Community Services officer recently, but she's obviously made quite an impression on Jackson.

'Francesca doesn't need to know,' I say. 'But we can talk to Dr Louisa about it, if you're worried. I bet she'll be amazed to hear how you slept in until 7.45 this morning...'

I stroke Jackson's forehead. He appears to relax a little.

'I think maybe... my brain beans sleep better at Nanna Pam's place,' he says. 'Did you have to take your sleeping medicine last night, Mum?'

I can't recall ever discussing the sleeping tablets I was prescribed during the early weeks of the police investigation. But then, there's so much I've tried to forget about the whole harrowing experience.

'I've stopped taking that medicine,' I say. 'And I've stopped drinking wine. They both made my head too fuzzy in the mornings.'

'I don't like the smell of wine.' Jackson wrinkles up his nose. 'Coach liked it, though.'

Instantly I'm awash with self-loathing. How *did* I let a predator get so close to my vulnerable son? So close to *me*? With Dr Kelleher's encouragement, I'm trying to be less harsh on myself, but self-compassion doesn't come easily.

'I thought I could smell Dad here last night.' Jackson smiles again. 'Did he ever sleep in this bed at Nanna Pam's?'

I raise an eyebrow. 'A long time ago. Have you got extraordinary smelling powers, too? Let's ask Dr Kelleher about that later.'

'Is Dad going to come and live with us at Nanna Pam's when he gets back from New York?'

'Well, we can't stay here for too long,' I say, evading his question. 'This is Nanna Pam's place.'

'But I don't want to go back to Queenscliff.'

Neither do I, if I'm honest.

Jackson rolls over onto his stomach. 'Dad's... definitely going to come home to us, isn't he Mum?'

'Of course,' I reassure him. 'Dad and I are just... figuring things out for the future. Whatever happens, Dad and I love you more than anything.'

Jackson looks uncertain. 'What do you mean, "whatever happens"?'

I summon as much honesty as I can.

'Sometimes things don't turn out like in... movies or books, Jackson. Sometimes people have to make changes. Dad and I are keen to try something new, but we're still talking about what that looks like.'

Neither of us want to separate but, after everything Andy

and I have been through, we're not certain how we can stay together, either.

'I wish Dad was here now.'

'I know.' My voice wavers. 'But he can't just... fly back in an instant. We'll see him again next week.'

I rally my brightest smile.

'What would you like for breakfast, Jackson? Porridge?'

'A cup of tea,' he replies, climbing out of bed.

Jackson acquired a taste for sugary tea served by cheerful canteen ladies during his hospital stay. On discharge, I tried to replace the generous spoonfuls of sugar with stevia, a herbal alternative, but Jackson branded this *repugnant* – a word he'd learned from Pamela, apparently.

'Okay, let's make a pot of tea. No stevia, though.'

Jackson grins.

We walk along the hallway towards the kitchen. In the first room on the left, Ruby is curled up in a double bed, playing a game on her iPad.

'Breakfast soon,' I call softly. 'Finish it up, please, Rubes.'

'But Kirby's is educational, Mum.' Her smile implores me for more time. 'I'm learning everything about prime numbers. Just one more game?'

As usual, it's impossible to resist Ruby. 'Only one, okay?'

She gives me the thumbs-up, then returns to her screen.

'I never get another game,' complains Jackson.

'That's because Dr Louisa won't allow it,' I remind him.

In the next room, Milla is still asleep, tendrils of blonde hair spread across her pink silk pillowcase. Jackson peers around the door.

'She looks like a Disney princess.'

Repeated exposure from Ruby means he's familiar with them all.

'Which one?' I ask. 'Elsa? Sleeping Beauty?'

Jackson looks thoughtful.

'Pocahontas,' he announces, after a moment. 'She's the cleverest Disney princess. Pocahontas sings about colours of the wind, and Milla writes about rainbows inside people. They both care about important stuff.'

I shake my head in wonder.

'Are you grumpy, Mum?'

'No, hon. I think you're pretty amazing. But Milla's going to be grumpy if we wake her up. Teenagers need loads of sleep.'

We retreat, closing Milla's door. Jackson opens another, this time leading into the library. The walls are lined to the ceiling with bookshelves. A wooden ladder on rails hangs near the door, for reaching the highest titles.

'Whoa. That's way better than our rainbow library,' says Jackson. Running his hand along a shelf, he removes a random title.

'Is this good?' he asks, turning to show me *The Getting of Wisdom* by Henry Handel Richardson.

'One of the best,' I say. 'But that's not the author's real name. Henry was actually Ethel.'

Jackson nods, tucking the book under his arm. 'Like Antony, who was really Anohni? Lots of people are different on the outside to who they are on the inside.'

We move into the kitchen together. 'How about we cook some scrambled eggs?' I suggest. 'I'm hungry.'

'You haven't been hungry in a while, Mum.'

Another astute observation.

In the butler's pantry, a space the size of our kitchen in Queenscliff, we collect everything we need.

Jackson starts cracking the eggs over a large silver bowl,

then measures out the milk and butter. He's deeply absorbed and evidently enjoying himself.

'Can I be a chef when I grow up, Mum?' he asks, placing a frying pan over the hotplate.

'Boys can do anything, Jackson.'

He smiles, stirring the mixture in the pan. 'Can I cook pavlova and soufflé and egg dumplings?'

'You're taking after Granny,' I laugh. 'She cooked the best dumplings in the world.'

When the scramble is ready, Jackson begins dishing it out.

'I think I just heard Nanna upstairs,' I say. 'Let's save some for her?'

Jackson takes an extra bowl from the pantry.

'Breakfast is served, girls!' I call down the hallway. 'Outside in the garden!'

I hear Milla groan.

A minute later, Ruby runs out into the kitchen wearing a colourful silk kaftan, hitched and knotted at the waist.

'That's special,' I say. 'Did Nanna Pam lend it to you?'

'She *gave* it to me,' says Ruby. 'Its name is Camilla.'

'Do all Nanna's clothes have names?' asks Jackson, pushing a bowl towards Ruby.

'Thank you, Jackson!' she enthuses, choosing a different bowl altogether.

Jackson follows Ruby out into the yard, balancing the rest of the bowls on a tray. His expression of intense concentration reminds me of Milla's, some six months ago, carrying my Mother's Day breakfast into a bedroom devoid of Andy.

He's still not here, yet somehow I don't feel quite as isolated now.

The three of us sit down at a huge timber table under an old quince tree in the centre of Pamela's manicured garden.

'Good morning!' Pamela calls, crossing the green expanse. She looks as immaculate as ever, in a crisp lemon-yellow blouse today.

'Jackson made scrambled eggs,' says Ruby. 'He's a really good cook, Nanna.'

'Wonderful!' She pulls out a chair. 'I'm so glad you're using the kitchen. I've been rattling around this old house by myself for too many years.'

Milla shuffles outside, clearly disgruntled.

'It's cold,' she complains, slumping down at the table.

'It's not,' says Ruby. 'It's spring!'

'This isn't normal.' Milla grumbles. 'Why are we even eating outside?'

'Normal doesn't exist, darling,' says Pamela. 'It's just a cycle on the washing machine.'

Jackson laughs so hard that egg sprays out of his mouth. I'm certain Pamela will disapprove, but she merely smiles and passes him a serviette.

'You're like Mum, Nanna!' says Jackson, scooping up more scramble. 'She says everyone's atypical.'

'Your mother's right.' Pamela smiles at me. 'So, how are the next few days looking? A bit atypical?'

I laugh. 'Well, tomorrow's an ordinary Saturday morning for the girls with gymnastics. But on Sunday, I'm starting back at work. It's just an experimental first shift, easing my way back into things...'

'Glad to hear it,' says Pamela. 'I retired way too early.' She leans forward and whispers to Ruby. 'Only because they forced me to.'

'Why?' asks Ruby, wide-eyed. 'What did you do, Nanna? Were you a spy?'

'Oh, that's classified.' Pamela smirks. 'I'll tell you when

you're older. On the plus side, early retirement means I've got loads of time for my grandchildren.'

She turns back to me. 'Would you like me to take Milla and Ruby to school this morning?'

'That's a lovely offer,' I say, 'but I don't think Milla would miss the bus for anything.' I glance at Milla, who studiously ignores me. 'Ruby and Jackson are coming with me to... look at another school. I've explained our... circumstances to them, but they're happy to consider an application. Would you like to come along?'

'Not after what happened at Clontarf Grammar.' Pamela shakes her head. 'I've never been so disappointed in an institution in my life. Edward would be furious, if he knew.'

'I'm still so grateful that you tried, Pamela.'

We smile at each other.

It occurs to me that, for the first time in fifteen years, Pamela and I might just be becoming *friends*.

'I don't want to go to a new school,' objects Milla.

'You won't have to,' I assure her. 'It's just an option for Jackson and Ruby. I know you love Peninsula Secondary, and Riley's practically part of the family now.'

'Okay.' Milla sounds rather bored by this, but I can tell she's secretly thrilled.

'If things go well at the new school today though, we might have to reconsider our living arrangements. Maybe we could get a temporary rental somewhere...'

'Dad won't like it,' says Milla. 'The coastal cottage is his dream house.'

No one says anything for a moment.

Pamela arranges the cutlery on her empty plate. 'Well, Andy might come around to the idea, if there's an inexpensive alternative.'

I'm not sure what she's driving at.

'You're welcome to have this place, rent free, for as long as you need it.' Pamela motions at the house behind us. 'Then you'll have plenty of space to... work through your decisions about the future, without the pressure of having to make them too quickly. The past few months have been... appalling, for all of you.'

I'm gobsmacked. 'Oh, Pamela, that's an incredible offer, but...'

'Nonsense.' She waves a hand at me, still at her imperious best. 'It's only a temporary measure, just while you and Andy... sort things out. It has the right number of rooms for a family of five, and I can live quite happily alone at Queenscliff for a while. We can "house swap", isn't that what they call it? I'd like a stint in a cottage by the sea, actually.'

She sniffs.

'But God help anyone who puts a nasty surprise in that library of yours. I'll hit them with my handbag and call the bloody police.'

Ruby laughs out loud.

'Thank you, Pamela,' I say. 'I think I've... misunderstood you, in the past. I'm really sorry about that.'

She nods. 'I'm sure there have been misunderstandings on both sides, Julia.'

Jackson puts down his spoon. 'Dr Louisa says misunderstandings usually happen when people don't walk in other people's shoes.'

Ruby wrinkles her nose. 'I never want to walk in anyone else's shoes. My shoes are the nicest.'

'It's called getting perspective, Rubes,' says Milla.

'But what if... Andy doesn't think living here for a while is a good idea?' I ask.

Pamela shrugs. 'Well, he may find it difficult dissenting from both his wife and his mother.'

I stare at her in wonder.

'You'd best get going,' she says. 'I'll clear the breakfast dishes.'

I glance at my watch. 'It's almost eight-thirty! Come on kids! Get some clothes on, brush your teeth, we've got to...'

I stop myself mid-sentence, determined to do things differently.

'You know what to do,' I say calmly, standing up from the table. 'We've done this about 3,000 times before. See you in the van in ten minutes.'

I reach over and squeeze Pamela's hand. 'Thank you again.'

Jackson stands up and throws his arms around his grand-mother. 'I think you're awesome, Nanna Pam.'

She smiles. 'And I think I've waited my whole life for someone to tell me that, Jackson.'

27

It's two days since we found our new school but still three days until Dad's due home from New York. It's also Mum's first day back at work and because it's a Sunday and we've got nothing else to do, we're tagging along with Mum to Care Cottage. The Big Boss Lady at the hospice said it was okay, maybe because they've all really missed Mum, so Miss Marion and Riley are joining us too.

It's fun driving the Red Rocket when it's so full, we've even squeezed in Snickers. We've packed our boards and wetsuits too, because Riley's figured out that Care Cottage is really close to a 'sick break' which actually means super-good in surfer language. After Mum's finished her music therapy this morning, we're all going to have another surfing lesson with Riley. I can't wait to get into the green room again. Riley's told me that some people can even do a *headstand* on a surfboard, so I really want to learn how.

We're driving and singing some of Mum's old Beach Boys tunes as a warm-up. It's been months since Mum sang at Care Cottage and she's worried about being 'a bit rusty'. Miss

Marion says she'll be 'amazing as ever' and Riley's told her she's 'so pro', I just hope Mum starts believing them soon.

We've just finished 'Surfin' Safari' and we're pulling into the Care Cottage carpark, when I notice a man standing near the front office.

'Dad!' I scramble out of the van before Mum's turned off the engine. 'You're back already!'

I run over and give him a massive bear hug, breathing in the spicy Dad smell I've missed so much.

He laughs, then waves at Mum, who lowers her window.

'Surprise, Jules.' Dad grins at Mum. He looks a bit like Snickers when he's caught a tennis ball in his mouth, all perky and proud.

Everyone piles out of the Red Rocket now, except for Mum. She stays in the driver's seat, looking a bit shaky.

Miss Marion turns to Riley. 'How about we wait inside for a bit?'

'Awesome idea,' says Riley. They disappear into the front office.

The three of us try to hug Dad, but he's got a rolled-up piece of cardboard in one hand and a really big bunch of yellow roses in the other.

'Hang on, kids.' Dad walks over to the Red Rocket, pulls a schmaltzy pose and holds out the flowers to Mum.

'I've been watching Riley all winter,' he says. 'I'm sorry I'm such a slow learner.'

Mum takes the flowers through the open window and buries her nose in the petals.

'They won't make everything better,' says Dad. 'Or normal.'

'They help,' says Mum, smiling a little.

Mum and Dad talk a bit more, their voices hushed. Even

though I can't hear what they're saying, I can tell they're not fighting.

'Is... everything okay?' asks Milla, when the three of us can't wait any longer.

Dad turns and smiles. 'To be honest, Millsy, we don't know.'

I wish he'd just say that everything *is* okay, especially between him and Mum.

'But one thing's for sure; Mum and I love each other. And we're never, ever going to stop loving you kids.'

It's exactly what Mum said too.

Dad opens the car door for Mum.

'I've got something to show everyone.' He unrolls the cardboard he's carrying. 'New family rules. The old ones weren't working. I'm sure we've all got something to contribute. I've changed the first one already, see?'

He smiles at me. 'Especially for you, Jackson.'

On the cardboard, Dad's scratched out the first family rule, *Be Polite*, and changed it to *Be Honest*.

As I say the new rule out loud, he pulls me into a hug so tight, I can barely breathe.

'You need to know, Jackson, that I'll never be angry at you again for telling the truth.' He bends down to look into my eyes. 'The truth as *you* see it, mate. Even when I don't understand it, or maybe I don't like it. I'm sorry I stopped hearing you.'

He's got sad-glad tears in his eyes.

'Thanks, Dad,' I say.

He ruffles my hair with his hand, then points to the second family rule on the cardboard: *Be Considerate*.

'What should it really be?' He looks around at the four of us.

'Be Compassionate,' Mum blurts. 'I think we all need more compassion for each other, and for ourselves.'

I remember how Mum asked about compassion at Clontarf Grammar, but she didn't find any there.

'I like it.' Dad pulls out a black permanent marker from his pocket, draws a line through 'considerate' and replaces it with 'compassionate'.

Milla grabs the marker out of his hand. 'May I?'

'Be my guest.' Dad passes her the family rules.

Milla changes the third rule from *Gentle Voices* to *Gentle Hearts*.

'That's beautiful, Millsy,' says Mum.

'Riley has a gentle heart,' explains Milla, looking a bit shy. 'And it's what's inside your heart that's more important than what comes out of your mouth' – she glances at me – 'especially if it doesn't always come out right.'

Mum gives Milla a big hug.

Ruby stands staring at the last two rules. After a minute, she yells, 'I've got it!' She points at family rule number four – *Remember Your Manners* – then does a little ballerina leap. 'Our new rule is – Remember You're Magical.'

Dad laughs and changes the rule. 'Fantastic, Rubes. We're all unicorns.'

Ruby looks at me. 'There's only one rule left, Jackson. It's your turn to change it.'

It's *Think First*, rule number five.

I'm thinking hard, so I close my eyes.

I'm remembering how Mum screamed that at me when I fell out of the tree in Erskineville, then we all sat around the kitchen table with coloured markers and a big piece of butcher's paper to create the *old* family rules.

When I open my eyes, Mum smiles at me. It's one of her best beam-of-light smiles, which usually only happen when she's doing something she loves. Like singing or chatting with Miss Marion or learning to surf with Riley.

Suddenly I know what our fifth family rule has to be.

'Surf First,' I say. 'It gets all your beans out.'

Dad looks a bit surprised. 'Great, Jackson.' Before he can say anything else, Ruby launches herself into his arms.

'I'm so glad you're back, Daddy!'

Suddenly we're all jumping up and down and hugging in a big tangle-mangle of arms and legs.

'It's a Festival of Hugs!' Ruby yells.

After a while, Dad turns to Mum. 'I suppose everyone's waiting inside for you?'

Mum nods.

'Jackson, can you please get my guitar and amp out of the boot?' she asks, rummaging in her bag for her sheet music folder.

I walk around to the back of the van and open the boot.

'I'll help you, mate,' says Dad, reaching for the amp. With his other hand, he presses something into my fingers.

'I found this in the letterbox when I got home from the airport,' Dad whispers. 'I figured it might be private.'

I look down at a yellow envelope with the words 'For JC from AK' printed in the neatest handwriting I've ever seen. Right away my heart feels like it's been roasted on a Bunsen burner, but in a totally good way.

'Come on, boys,' calls Mum.

I pick up Mum's guitar case and follow her into Care Cottage, even though I'm not really in today-time any more, I've been teleported to a spacetime dimension of April Kennedy.

'What's happened to you, bro?' asks Riley, as I walk into the front office.

I grin at him.

Miss Marion takes Mum's guitar from me and carries it inside. They're such good friends now that Nanna Pam even invited Miss Marion to come and stay with us at Balgowlah if she needs to, until she starts her new job next year. Mum and Miss Marion were a bit surprised by that, but Nanna Pam just said, 'What's a big old house good for, if you don't fill it with friends?'

The music therapy room at Care Cottage is like an enormous lounge with lots of soft cushions and comfy sofas and about a dozen Special Ps lying or sitting on them. Some of the people are really old or crumpled or in wheelchairs, but a few are more like Mum's age. One of them is really young, maybe about eleven like me. She's got no hair and a really nice smile and she's sitting on a sofa.

She waves at me and I wave back.

Barry's sitting in a wheelchair, parked next to the girl on the sofa. I know his name because he's wearing a t-shirt with the word 'Barry' on it, in big gold letters. He's playing cards on a tray table, and it looks like he's a pro at Patience. Everyone must get really good at Patience here, while they're waiting for the Otherworld.

Mum plugs her guitar into the amp and sets up her music on the stand.

'I'm sorry I'm late,' she says, looking around the room and smiling. 'But my husband just surprised me with a very sweet gesture in the carpark.'

'Did he now?' Barry crows. He's got a gold tooth that matches the gold letters of his t-shirt. 'It's hard to be romantic after forty-seven years of marriage, I tell you.'

'True. Sometimes all we can do is keep turning up, Barry.' Mum glances at Dad like they're sharing a secret. 'Any special requests this morning?'

I pull a cushion over my lap and unfold the note, so no one else can see it. There's not much writing, but I can hear April's voice saying it inside my head:

Hi Jackson,

I can't believe what happened at the eisteddfod. You were so brave. I was really sad when I heard you're not coming back to Queenscliff Public.

My Insta handle is missaprilviolin, but I don't think you're on social yet?

Dad says I'm going to Killarney Performing Arts College in Year 7. It's co-ed and they do dance and drama. Can you apply too?

If I see you on the first day of Year 7, it'll be a dream come true.

Until then I'm...

Yours,

April x

A dream come true. My heart's beating super fast and I'm smiling like a goof. Barry stares at me suspiciously but I don't care because April's just told me she's *mine*.

'All righty then.' Mum pulls a tambourine out of her guitar case and passes it to me. 'This is a song Jackson knows well. We've been playing it a lot at home lately. It's a tune from 1967 and it *always* makes us want to dance.'

Suddenly she's channelling Van Morrison and her voice has warm sweet layers inside it, like a freshly baked pudding. I just can't help jumping to my feet and banging the tambourine against my hip. I'm grinning because *I've* got a 'Brown Eyed Girl', and her name is April Kennedy.

When Mum gets to the part about 'slow Tuesday', Barry

suddenly throws his Patience into the air. The cards scatter everywhere, but he just laughs with this big deep voice like one of those tenors in tuxedos. He stands up out of his wheelchair then, and I'm thinking that maybe it's a miracle of St Jhudiel, but Barry's not that weak after all. He grabs Milla's hands and dances with her until Riley walks over and says, 'May I cut in?'

Miss Marion starts spinning around the room, doing some of her best 'modern interpretative dance' that we usually do in the back shed together.

'Join me!' She calls to everyone. 'It's good for you!'

So Dad jumps up too, but he's not as professional as Miss Marion. He walks over to this shrivelled old lady who looks like she's about to break into a million pieces.

'Would you like to dance?' Dad asks.

I'm pretty surprised because I've never, *ever* seen Dad dance. And I'm even more surprised when the lady smiles like she's just won the lottery and says, 'Yes, please.' Dad scoops her off the sofa and sets her feet on the floor, then he puts his big strong arms around her and jiggles her tiny body across the room.

Ruby gets excited watching all of this. She starts twirling around, doing arabesques and sautés and grand jétés.

I walk up to the bald girl with the nice smile and slide my arm through hers. Suddenly we're the King and Queen of the tambourine, bouncing our hips together.

Some of the hospice staff are milling about in the doorway. One of them is the Big Boss Lady, she looks important and a bit stern. She's got her arms folded across her chest and it makes me worried that maybe she's going to shut down our concert.

But she doesn't.

As I groove past her with my new friend and the

tambourine, she leans towards a nurse and shouts over the music, 'This is all a bit unusual!'

Mum's fingers are flying over the guitar strings. Her voice is making everyone smile, it's like we're all floating inside an invisible bubble of joy. When she gets to the 'sha-la-la' part of the song, even the staff can't help themselves. They're all shimmying and waving their hands in the air and the Big Boss Lady starts tapping her foot in time.

Suddenly Riley's next to me and he steals the tambourine right out of my hand. He runs off with it, shaking it above his head and laughing like a lunatic, but I don't mind one bit.

Right now, dancing with people I love and singing with strangers waiting for the Otherworld, I'm happier than even I can remember.

I'm making new memories now, and they're glowing in technicolour.

If this is all a bit unusual, then I'm okay with that.

JACKSON'S JIVES: THE PLAYLIST

Hope There's Someone (Anohni)
Today's the Day (Pink)
Issues (Julia Michael)
I Love It (Icona Pop, feat. Charlie XCX)
Dress (Taylor Swift)
Mr Brightside (The Killers)
Iris (The Goo Goo Dolls)
Drops of Jupiter (Train)
We Are Young (Fun)
Never Be Like You (Flume, feat. Kai)
Best Day of My Life (American Authors)
Happy (C2C)
Price Tag (Jessie J)
Green Light (Lorde)
Faded (Alan Walker)
Youngblood (Five SOS)
What You Waiting For? (Gwen Stefani)
Surfin' Safari (Beach Boys)

Brown Eyed Girl (Van Morrison)
Things Can Only Get Better (D:Ream)

ACKNOWLEDGMENTS

I'd like to thank Boldwood Books, led by the visionary Amanda Ridout, for their commitment to bringing my unusual boy into the world. I am especially grateful to Publishing Director Sarah Ritherdon for her editorial intuition, attention to detail, and for loving Jackson almost as much as I do. Thanks to Nia Beynon for her marketing prowess, and to all the team involved in the making of this book.

I am blessed to be a member of the best mothers' group in the southern hemisphere, if not the world. Thanks to legendary ladies Kim Healey, Sarah Bramwell, Michelle Taylor, Gaile Timperley and Natasha Brain for reading early (and somewhat painful) drafts, as well as to Amanda Thomas and Sarah Barrett for their ongoing support.

Subject matter experts to whom I'm indebted for providing medical, sporting, legal, policing, neuropsychological and child protection advice for this novel include: Sarah Bramwell; Gareth Banks; Dr Kylie Ladd; He Who Must Not Be Named (you know who you are); Megan Donnell; Briana Blackett; Dr Connie Diakos and Danny Russell (whose knowledge of his subject matter is only exceeded by his knowledge of where to seek answers). I'm deeply appreciative of all of you, not only for your sector-specific smarts, but for your friendship.

Thank you to Virginia Lloyd for believing in this novel from the beginning and for walking with me along the tough road of early evolution and beyond. I am grateful to the insightful Ewa Wojkowska, the diligent and thoughtful Alex Lagalée-Kean, and to my writing bestie, Kylie Ladd, for feedback on specific iterations of this work.

For the delightful combination of friendship paired with peculiar talent, my thanks are due to Ellen Fanning, Peter Dredge, Jovy Gill, Sarah Alderson, Duncan Trevor-Wilson, Alice Chen and John Fairfax. I am grateful to Luisa Brimble, photographer extraordinaire, Kurt Daniels and Michelle Taylor of Divine Marketing, and to Jenny Lalor for her legal support.

Deep and heartfelt appreciation to Anohni, for her generous granting of permission to reproduce lyrics from her extraordinary song 'Hope There's Someone'.

To those who have offered reassuring noises and practical support, thank you. Honourable mentions include: the Attias (all six of them), Amanda Collins, Tim Haydon, Lesley Collins, Beverley and Richard Higgins, Margie and Andrew Bale, Cate and Peter Campbell, Suzanne Kent, Bertoes, Ibu Professor Doctor Jan Lingard, Johanna Featherstone, Jane Kenny, Genevieve Freeman, Debbaku, Tegan Molony, John Kelleher, Alice and Roly O'Connell, Emma Hodgson, Libby Fairfax, David Frost, Tim Elliot, Andrew and Becky Edwards, Jodie Thomson, Peter Kerr, Honie Farrington, Jane Porter, Greg Purcell, Amanda Preston, Tanja Schweifert, Veronica Abolins, Rikki Andrews, Nathan and Kate Fabian, Mark Clancy, Timur Nugroho, Sandra Baltar, Judith and Des Huxley, Dorothy McRae-McMahon and Don Norris.

Thanks to the entire team at Australian Philanthropic Services for putting up with an author in the office. Special thanks to Natasha O'Connor for her second-to-none services in knee-jerk insight, and to the exceptional Cat Feeney for her marketing and communications expertise.

Finally, to my own little family, all my thanks and love. Stuart, you're sensational. Oliver, you're thrashing it at thirteen. Skye, you're epic at eleven. And Lukey, you're the ultimate nine-year-old ninja warrior.

Yes, we're all crazy, but it's not a competition.

BOOK CLUB QUESTIONS

1. In what ways, if any, could you relate to Julia's experience of her 'unusual' boy?
2. How did you find yourself responding to the character of Jackson and his unique perspectives on the world? Did your responses change over the course of the book?
3. The author describes An Unusual Boy as 'a hymn to human diversity'. What do you think she was hoping to achieve by writing this novel?
4. Has Fiona Higgins written a love letter or lament to parenting?
5. What did you make of the portrayal of the authorities in An Unusual Boy?
6. What did you make of Julia's relationship with her husband and how it fared throughout the novel? What do you imagine lies ahead for them?
7. What did An Unusual Boy tell you about

motherhood, both through Julia's character and also
Pamela's?

8. Many experts in Australia wish to raise the age of
criminal responsibility - the age at which children
can be convicted of a criminal offence – from 10 to
14, to bring it in line with other jurisdictions around
the world. How old do you think children should be
to understand the difference between right and
wrong? In the novel, was Digby a perpetrator or a
victim?

9. What did secondary characters such as Miss Marion
and April Kennedy and Riley bring to the novel,
along with their artforms of dance, aerial silks and
surfing?

10. 'The real culprit in this novel is unfettered internet
access for children'. Discuss.

MORE FROM FIONA HIGGINS

We hope you enjoyed reading *An Unusual Boy*. If you did, please leave a review.

If you'd like to gift a copy, this book is also available as an ebook, digital audio download and audiobook CD.

Sign up to Fiona Higgins's mailing list for news, competitions and updates on future books.

http://bit.ly/FionaHigginsNewsletter

ABOUT THE AUTHOR

Fiona Higgins is the author of three previous novels - *Fearless, Wife on the Run* and *The Mothers' Group* - and a memoir, *Love in the Age of Drought*. Her novels have been translated internationally in the Netherlands, France, Germany, Spain and Estonia.

Outside of writing Fiona has had a longstanding career in the Australian not-for-profit sector and has worked with organisations specializing in international development, youth at risk, rural and regional issues and youth mental health.

She is a founding director of Australian Philanthropic Services (APS) and is a volunteer Crisis Support Worker on Australia's national crisis and suicide hotline, Lifeline.

She lives in Sydney with her three children.

Visit Fiona's website: https://www.fionahiggins.com.au/

Follow Fiona on social media:

 twitter.com/fionahiggins101

instagram.com/fionahigginsauthor

facebook.com/fionahigginsauthor

 bookbub.com/authors/fiona-higgins

ABOUT BOLDWOOD BOOKS

Boldwood Books is a fiction publishing company seeking out the best stories from around the world.

Find out more at www.boldwoodbooks.com

Sign up to the Book and Tonic newsletter for news, offers and competitions from Boldwood Books!

http://www.bit.ly/bookandtonic

We'd love to hear from you, follow us on social media:

 facebook.com/BookandTonic

 twitter.com/BoldwoodBooks

 instagram.com/BookandTonic

Made in the USA
Monee, IL
02 May 2021

67512613R00177